A GOOD CHANCE

The surrendering gang members were getting to be a real pain in the butt. Ben walked over to the ragged line of punks, all standing with their hands tied behind them. Ben pointed to one man, and gave an order: "Cut him loose."

The man rubbed his wrists for a few seconds, then asked, "You gonna hang me now, general?"

"No. I'm going to talk with you. Come on."

Ben sat down on what remained of a windowsill, dug in his pack and came up with the Rebels' version of the old MRE—Meals Ready to Eat—and tossed the package to the man.

"I thought a condemned man got his choice of food for his last meal," the man said.

"Be glad you're getting that," Ben said, then went on, "You're old enough to remember what it was like before the Great War. So tell me why you chose a life of crime."

The man glared at him. "The whole damn world falls apart, Raines," he said bitterly, "and you go out and build yourself a friggin' nation. No big deal for you. You just do it. Well, let me give you a news flash. There are some people, Raines, who just can't, or won't, live under your rules and laws."

"Millions of them," Ben agreed. "But while they choose not to be a part of the Tri-States philosophy, they do live under a basic set of rules and laws. You and your kind won't even do that much."

"Maybe not, Raines. But you can't kill us all."

Ben chuckled. "You want to bet?"

SLAUGHTER
IN THE
ASHES

WILLIAM W. JOHNSTONE

PINNACLE BOOKS
Kensington Publishing Corp.
http://www.kensingtonbooks.com

PINNACLE BOOKS are published by

Kensington Publishing Corp.
119 West 40th Street
New York, NY 10018

All Kensington Titles, Imprints, and Distributed Lines are available at special quantity discounts for bulk purchases for sales promotions, premiums, fund-raising, and educational or institutional use. Special book excerpts or customized printings can also be created to fit specific needs. For details, write or phone the office of the Kensington special sales manager: Kensington Publishing Corp., 119 West 40th Street, New York, NY 10018, attn: Special Sales Department, Phone: 1-800-221-2647.

Pinnacle and the P logo Reg. U.S. Pat. & TM Off.

ISBN-13: 978-0-7860-2081-2
ISBN-10: 0-7860-2081-4

First Printing: April 1997

10 9 8 7 6 5 4

Printed in the United States of America

I don't like you, Sabidius, I can't say why; But I can say this: I don't like you, Sabidius.

—*Martial*

Prologue

In the waning days of the last four years of the administration of the most liberal president in the history of the union, the once greatest nation in the world collapsed. The United States could have shrugged off and emerged stronger after the limited nuclear and germ warfare that very briefly engulfed Planet Earth; could have, but didn't.

America just fell apart. As the clouds of smoke began drifting away, a large percentage of its citizens looked around them and cried, "But where is the government? Why doesn't the government send people in to help us? We need food. We need clothing. Above all, we need someone to tell us what to do. We just don't know what to do. Big Brother promised to care of us. What are we going to do now?"

Around the battered nation that was once called America, certain men and women who had refused to bow down and kiss the socialistic ass of the liberal Democrats in Congress viewed it all with dark humor.

These men and women didn't fall down in a hanky-stomping snit after the collapse. They just dug up the guns they'd been forced to bury—rather than turn them in—during the frenzied gun grab. For a dozen years, these much maligned groups of men and women had been forced to endure the barbs and blather of half-truths and sometimes outright lies from the liberal-controlled press, left-wing extremists in elected and appointed positions of government power, and hanky-waving, blubbering, snot-slinging stiffs who wouldn't recognize reality, or know how to cope with it if it reared up and bit them on the ass. (One must remember that these are the people who believed that if you left the keys in your car and a thief stole it, it wasn't the fault of the thief, it was *your* fault for leaving the keys in the ignition). No one with a modicum of common sense could ever find any logic in that statement.

Left-wing extremists openly belittled and ridiculed those who practiced the art of surviving in any type of emergency. The government sent infiltrators in to spy on the survivalists and the militias that sprang up during the final years before the collapse. Many in the news media were openly scornful of those who quietly stockpiled weapons and ammunition and food and water and emergency gear, calling them conspiracy freaks.

"Gun nuts!" others ridiculed.

"Right-wing kooks!" still others jeered at them.

But when the end came, those who had taken the time to prepare and had endured the hostility of the biased press, the spying and snooping from government agents, and the derision of often well-intentioned but badly misinformed liberal groups, fared the best. They were able to fend off the rampaging hordes of punks and thugs and human vermin that always seem to lurk on the fringes of society, waiting for some type of disaster to befall the law-abiding public before they slither in to rape and assault and loot.

One of those who believed in speaking his mind (most of the time very bluntly) and being prepared as much as possible was a man called Ben Raines.

For years, Ben Raines had spoken out against the growing socialistic movement of big government in America. And, as so many thousands of other heretofore law-abiding Americans had done when Congress finally pushed through the infamous gun-grab bill, Ben hid his few guns rather than turn them in.

But in the end, the disarming of American citizens came to naught, for anarchy became the king of America. And as has been predicted by many, when the United States falls, so goes the world. Within days, there was not one single stable government anywhere on earth.

After months of roaming around the battered nation, and seeing no real effort being made toward rebuilding, Ben and a few others linked up and started talking about a dream they shared: the formation of a government that would be based truly by the people and for the people.

The Tri-States philosophy of government was born, and since it was based on a commonsense form of rule and law, the liberals could not understand it. When it comes to common sense, defined simply as sound practical judgment, liberals as a rule, are left out in the hinterlands, wondering what in the hell is going on.

A commonsense form of government, with its laws and rules, is really quite simple to understand: it means that each citizen is responsible for his or her own actions, deeds, and destiny.

Liberals will usually respond to that with an expression of utter confusion and by saying, "Huh?"

Attempting to explain common sense to a liberal is much

like trying to teach a pig to fly. It is a waste of time for all concerned and is quite annoying to the pig.

Liberals believe that big government should be involved in every aspect of a citizen's life. Tri-Staters believe that the primary responsibility of government is to protect our shores, make sure trains and planes and buses leave and arrive on time, and deliver the mail. That is, of course, an over-simplification, but not by much. Tri-Staters must be a special breed of person. They must respect the rights of others, regardless of race, religion, or creed. They must accept full responsibility for their own actions and deeds and by doing so understand that honor and truth must play a large part in day-to-day living. Con artists, slick-talking flim-flam operators, and people who misrepresent the truth in any type of business dealing don't last long in any Tri-State society. Bullies and people with abrasive and argumentative personalities quickly learn to back off and temper their emotions. In any community embracing the Tri-States philosophy, citizens have the right to protect their lives, the lives of their loved ones, and their personal property without fear of arrest, prosecution, and/or civil lawsuit.

Right and wrong and morality is taught in public schools, and if parents don't like that, they can take their children and leave. And don't come back. Right and wrong is not up for debate.

Living in any Tri-States society is not a right, it is a privilege. And for many people it proves to be not just difficult, but impossible. Ben Raines correctly calculated that only three out of every ten people could live in such an open society. It took a special person to live where they controlled their own destiny.

Nearly everything in the Tri-States is low-key. High-pressure salespeople and boiler-room operators quickly learn that the Tri-States is not for them. In the Tri-States, no means no, not maybe.

Eventually, the United States government outside the Tri-States staggered to its feet and began whipping its citizens into line. Then it threw all its might against the Tri-States and those who had chosen to live as free people.

After days of fierce fighting, the Tri-States was overwhelmed and the government of the United States (once again in the pretty little hands of left-wing liberals) declared victory against Ben Raines and his followers.

That declaration was a tad premature, for while the president was patting himself on the back and proclaiming victory, Ben Raines was busy putting together a guerrilla army. Within weeks he declared war on the government of the United States.

It did not take long for those in power to offer the olive branch of peace to Ben and his Rebels. For a full-scale, all-out guerrilla war had never really been fought on American soil . . . at least not in anyone's memory, and certainly not against forces who fought as savagely as Ben Raines's Rebels.

After a handshake and a promise of cooperation between the two nations within a nation, and as the Tri-States was rebuilding and hopefully settling down into a peaceful period, the government of the United States once more collapsed and the world again followed suit.

Brush wars spread like wildfire and governments that were attempting to stabilize disintegrated into bloody civil war. The United States was no different.

That collapse could have been expected, especially in what had once been called the United States. For in what had once been called the United States, millions of people had been conditioned to expect the government to do everything for them: house them, clothe them, feed them, provide them with free medical care, and give them money for doing nothing except laying up on their lazy asses.

These types joined with other malcontents and went on a rioting, looting, burning, killing rampage.

When the smoke cleared, punks and other more or less human street shit controlled the cities, self-proclaimed warlords and their gangs of worthless human vermin prowled the countryside, preying on the innocent, and only one man and his small army stood between order and anarchy: Ben Raines and the Rebels.

One

How many times are we going to have to do this? Ben questioned silently. *How many times must we fight others' battles for them? When do I call a halt to it?*

His eyes were on the passing landscape but his mind was pondering many issues as the long convoy began their pull-out of West Virginia. For the most part, the state was clear of large bands of thugs and outlaws. Ben knew a few small bands remained, as they did in every state the Rebels had cleared outside of the SUSA—the Southern United States of America. But in the SUSA, any band of thugs remaining there would not last long, for Raines's Rebels and Rebel supporters had a very short tolerance for law-breakers of any kind.

After the Rebels had pulled out of Europe, returning to North America to once more clean it out of thugs, punks, warlords, outlaws, creepies, and other bits of more or less human crap, Ben had found the nation cut in half. Simon Border, a self-proclaimed religious leader and his

Army of the Democratic Front, with the help of several left-wing senators and representatives representing the New Left Party, had staged a coup against President Blanton, and the result was the nation was once more leaderless and in chaos. When Ben and the Rebels returned from Europe, Simon and his people beat it across the Mississippi River. Simon now claimed much of the Western United States: 16 states, with the exception of Texas, which was a part of the SUSA. The new capital of the United States, Charleston, West Virginia, has been destroyed by looters and other lowlifes, and was nothing but a shambles. Simon Border, whose face bore a striking resemblance to a cottonmouth snake, wanted to be king of America.

On the eastern side of the Mississippi, America would, again, have to be rebuilt from the ground up, once the Rebels cleaned out the nests of outlaws. And it was solely up to the Rebels to do it. Again.

Ben began by clearing out the SUSA and starting his factories running 24 hours, seven days a week, pumping out medicines, munitions and field rations and all other necessities needed for a protracted war.

After his Rebels once more reclaimed their old Base Camp One, Ben got in touch with President Homer Blanton—who was now out of a job—and offered him the position of Secretary of State of the SUSA, a position that Blanton quickly accepted. Then, after the Rebels began their push to once more clean out America, Senator Paul Altman, at Ben's urgings, was sworn in as President of the NUSA—the Northern United States of America. Many of the states that would make up the NUSA had yet to be cleared. With a smile, Ben assured Altman that they *would* be cleaned up . . . be patient.

"Do I have a choice?" Altman asked.

"Not really," Ben replied. "Where would you like your new capital to be?"

Altman sighed. Ben Raines moved very quickly. "As a matter of fact, I've given that some thought. How about Indianapolis?"

"Fine with me. Consider it done."

Ben did not believe in wasting time.

As often as it takes, I suppose. Ben answered his own question, as he pulled his eyes from the passing landscape and brought his mind back to the present.

"Word must have spread fast," Jersey spoke from the second seat of the big wagon. "I can't believe all the punks have left the state."

Word had indeed spread fast about the Rebels. They had encountered no resistance as the long convoy snaked its way through West Virginia. They had received some very hostile looks from a certain type of person as they moved northward, but no shots had been fired at them.

Cooper moaned in dismay as the wagon lurched over a particularly bad spot in the cracked old highway.

Highways all over the nation were in rough shape, having received no maintenance for years. Only in areas controlled by the Rebels were roads in good shape. There, any new people who had applied for resident status and were not yet qualified to do anything else, and were physically capable of hard work, Ben put to work assisting road crews during the day. Then they went to school for several hours at night and all day on Saturday to learn a trade. If they objected to that schedule, they were escorted to the nearest border and kicked out and told not to come back.

In the SUSA, for years called the Tri-States, everybody capable of doing so worked at something. Nobody laid up on their asses and did nothing. There was just too much to do to put up with shirkers.

"They haven't all run away, Jersey," Ben said, unfolding

a map. "A lot of them are hiding in the timber and the hills and hollows. They'll surface as soon as we clear the state. But they're going to be in for a very rude surprise when they do surface with stealing and raping and killing on their miserable little minds."

Now, when the Rebels left an area that had agreed to align with them, they left behind them local men and women who had sworn to uphold the Tri-States philosophy of law and order. That meant that the life expectancy of criminals was about 20 minutes, max. Under the Tri-States form of government, law-abiding citizens have the right to protect and preserve life, loved ones, and personal property by any means at hand, including deadly force, without fear of arrest, prosecution, or civil lawsuit. Citizens were certainly not required to use extreme measures in protecting what was theirs, but they were encouraged to do so.

"We keep chasing these assholes and pushing them back and back," Corrie said. "And when we get them into the northeast part of the country, they'll cut up into Canada and scatter. Seems like we've done this before."

"Yes, we have," Ben said with a sigh. "This is certainly covered ground. Most of it anyway. We've been fighting to restore order in this beat-up nation for years. We clear one area, and I'll be damned if the citizens don't allow the thugs and punks to move right back in with near impunity. Tell you the truth, I'm getting weary of it."

There was a finality in Ben's voice that his team had not heard before. The boss was getting tired of fighting other peoples' battles for them. As Ben was found of saying: Enough is enough and too much is an amplitude of sufficiency.

"When this push is over," Jersey asked, "are we going to stand down?"

Ben smiled. "Now, I didn't say that, Jersey. As long as I

have the stamina to stay in the field, the field is where I'll be. But the next time we're asked to trace old footsteps . . . well, hell, I don't know what decision I'll reach."

Ben's team relaxed. With the exception of Anna, the blonde, pale-eyed young lady Ben had brought back from Europe and adopted as his own, the rest of the team—Corrie, Beth, Jersey, and Cooper—had known nothing but the field for years. All of them had joined Ben while still in their teen years. Corrie, the communications expert. Cooper, the driver. Beth, the statistician. Jersey, Ben's personal bodyguard.

"Don't scare us like that, boss," the usually quiet Beth spoke from the rear seat of the big wagon, where she had her nose stuck in a book, as usual. She was reading a novel written by Robert Vaughan. "You'll make us think you're sick, or something."

Ben smiled. "I never felt better in my life," he informed them. And that was the truth. Ben always felt like a million bucks when a push began. He loved the field, even though he was middle-aged and knew he was approaching the time when he should think of getting out of the field . . . or at the very least, slowing down some.

But he wouldn't seriously entertain that thought. For years he had known, somehow, perhaps as a premonition, that when his time came to face the Almighty, he would die in the field, in combat. That was his destiny, and Ben realized it.

Corrie broke into his thoughts. "Receiving from Scouts, boss," she announced. "What is left of Pittsburgh is filled with creeps. And fly-bys confirm that the punks have broken up into small groups and have taken to the country-side."

Ben nodded his head. "Just like we figured. What about the citizens?"

"Militia and survivalist groups are holding in spots around the state. But they need to be re-supplied ASAP."

"I bet they do." Intelligence had informed him that a few of the militia and survivalist groups were racist—some even aligned with notorious anti-Semitic and anti-black organizations—but not the majority. However, right now, Ben and his Rebels needed all the help they could get. He would sort it all out later. Besides, it sure as hell wouldn't be the first time he'd shaken hands with the devil in order to complete a mission, nor, he was sure, would it be the last time. "All right, Corrie. Find out what they need and arrange for airdrops. I want to know the exact location of each militia group and I want to meet with the leaders head-to-head later on."

"Right," Corrie responded. A moment later: "Bivouac area one hour ahead. We'll be right on the Ohio line. Approximately 50 miles from Pittsburgh."

The long column pulled off the interstate just outside of what was left of a small town on the West Virginia side of the state line. Before the Great War, the town had boasted a population of about 700. Now there was nothing except looted, trashed, picked-over homes, and a few burned-out hulks of what once were businesses.

Scouts had inspected the ghost town and declared it free of hostiles.

"Hell," Cooper remarked. "It's free of *everything*. Place is spooky."

"Be sure and look in your sleeping bag before you crawl in there tonight, Coop." Jersey stuck the needle to him. "There might be a creepie in there just waiting to give you a great big sloppy goodnight kiss."

Cooper flipped her the bird and otherwise ignored her. Then he shuddered and said, "Yuck!" at just the thought of the Night People. He walked away.

Some years back, after the dust had settled from the first

collapse of civilization and the Rebels were just getting organized, bands of what the Rebels would eventually refer to as "creepies" began surfacing. They were the most disgusting people the Rebels had ever encountered, and the Rebels hated them with a passion that was unequaled, for the Night People were cannibals. The adults either could not or would not allow themselves to be rehabilitated, and the children simply could not be rehabilitated. Ben's scientists were still trying to determine why the creeps lived as they did. But so far, no luck.

The Rebels learned about the offspring of the Night People the hard way. After several Rebels had been killed and more than a dozen maimed by vicious attacks, the Rebels were forced to cease their attempts to rehab the kids they captured. Since none among them wanted to shoot a child, the Rebels, if they could possibly do it, just let the kids escape, knowing full well they would someday have to face them in combat as adults. Ben just didn't know what else to do with them.

And now the Rebels knew for sure that within the ruins of Pittsburgh the creepies were waiting for a fight to the finish, for the creeps never surrendered. Retreated yes, surrendered no.

As dusk began spreading over the land, Ben sat outside the large motor home he had begun using as his CP. His team sat away from him, knowing without being told that he did not wish to be disturbed.

Just give it up, Ben, a quiet voice spoke inside his head. *You and the Rebels don't owe these people anything. They're adults, they can fight their own battles. Just stand everybody down and go on back to the SUSA and let everybody else fight their own battles.*

You can't do that, another voice said. *You can't let one area of the country tear itself apart with anarchy while another section prospers.*

Give me one good reason why not? the first voice demanded.

Because if you allow the creeps and the punks and the gangs and the human vermin to flourish, it will only be a matter of time before they'll be strong enough to attack the SUSA and those areas aligned with the Rebel philosophy.

They might be strong enough to attack, but they won't be strong enough to defeat the Rebels.

Perhaps not the first time, or the second time, or even the third time. But how long can the SUSA stand alone and hold out?

The second voice was silent, having no reply to that. Ben angrily shook his head, momentarily clearing it of the arguing voices only he could hear. He stood up and walked around the motor home several times, taking long strides, his big hands balled into fists.

His team watched in silence for a time, then Cooper said, "The boss is pissed about something."

"I don't think so," Beth said. "I think he's waging some sort of inner conflict."

Cooper cut his eyes. "What do you mean by that?"

"For once, I agree with Coop," Jersey said. She looked at him. "Don't let that go to your head, Coop. What do you mean, Beth?"

"I'd guess the boss is trying to make up his mind whether to go forward or stand us down and head on back home. I think."

"Now I am confused," Cooper said.

"Your normal state," Jersey told him. She looked at Beth. "He's maybe wondering if going on is worth it?"

"That would be my guess."

"Fight the creeps and the punks and the assholes now, or fight them later," Corrie spoke up. "Either way, we're going to take losses. But this way it isn't little Rebel kids who will be dying. If the boss pulls back and we bunker in, sooner or later we'll be attacked and Rebel kids and elderly will suffer."

Those who subscribed to the Tri-States philosophy never thought of themselves as anything other than Rebels.

"I have never known anything but fighting," Anna said. "I would think it would be very strange to live in peace."

"Tell the truth," Jersey replied, "I been scrapin' for survival ever since I was a little girl. I remember very little else. If we weren't fightin', what the hell would we do?"

"You could always come live with me and we could have lots of little Apaches," Cooper said hopefully. He was ready to leap up and head for parts unknown should Jersey make a move toward him.

But the diminutive Jersey only smiled. "Coop, what do you figure the odds are of any of us living long enough to settle down and have a family?"

Coop's returning smile was sad in the quickly gathering night. "Not too damn high, Jersey."

"Then we won't bring up the subject of family again, Coop," Jersey spoke softly. "It's just damn depressing."

"Yes," Beth said. "I never think about that."

"Me either," Corrie said. "Anna?"

The teenager cut her wise and young-old eyes to Corrie. "I have never thought about anything like that. In my country, it was a day-to-day struggle just to stay alive. Nobody really planned for the future."

Ben had paused in the shadows by a corner of the motor home, listening to the exchange.

"You believe in destiny, Jersey?" Cooper asked.

"Heavy subject, Coop. But, yeah. I've thought about it. I guess I do. Why?"

"Is this our destiny? I mean, what we're doing?"

"Do you think it is, Coop?" Corrie asked.

"Yeah, I think so," Cooper replied softly. "We're still together after all this time, aren't we? I mean, we could have transferred out, but we didn't. We may fuss and argue and get on each others' nerves every now and then, but when the shit hits the fan, we hang tough—right?''

Jersey started to tell him that was what being a team was all about, but she held her tongue. Besides, if Cooper wanted to think that was destiny, fine. Hell, maybe it was.

The team fell silent and Ben slipped back, deeper into the night, and walked over to the mess tent. There, he pulled a mug of coffee and wandered around until he found the tailgate of a pick-up truck open and sat down.

Destiny? *Well,* Ben thought, *I've often pondered the same question.* Maybe it was their destiny to wander about like warrior gypsies from fight to fight, making the land safe for decent people—and it made no difference whether or not those people subscribed to the Rebel philosophy. Ben smiled in the night: Robin and his 25,000 Hoods.

Maybe someday, when conditions around the nation reached some level of normalcy, somebody would make a movie about the Rebels. Then Ben shook his head. But Hollywood was gone, reduced to rubble. He chuckled softly as another thought popped into his head: Maybe that was just as well, for the left-leaning producers and writers and directors who had controlled the scripts and purse-strings of Hollywood would surely have portrayed Ben and the Rebels as the bad guys, waging war against the poor misunderstood criminals, who surely must have been spanked as children and that, of course, was the cause and therefore the excuse for their violent, anti-social behavior.

Ben laughed softly and slid off the tailgate and stretched. He really didn't give a big rat's ass how history painted him. If he had ever worried about that, he'd stopped years back. He doubted that historians would show that he and the Rebels had brought dignity back to all law-abiding citizens who lived in Rebel-controlled territory, as well as returning a high degree of honor and truth to government and to the business community and their relationship with the consumer. He rather doubted that historians would show that not just violent crime was practically nonexistent in any Rebel-controlled area, but *all* types of crime, and if they did mention that fact, it would be that it was accomplished at the point of a gun.

So what? would be Ben's reaction to that. The point is, it was accomplished.

Ben sipped his coffee and stared into the night. He sighed as he realized the Rebels just couldn't pull back in their quest to purge America of those who preyed on the weak, the old, the helpless. Even though all mixed in among those who truly needed the Rebels' help were strong, capable, able-bodied men and women who simply refused to pick up a gun and take care of the problem themselves.

It was difficult for Ben to hide his contempt for those types of people, and he usually didn't even make the effort.

Ben walked back to the motor home and opened the door, then turned and looked at his team, sitting within conversation distance from him. "Get a good night's sleep, gang. We'll start clearing the ruins of Pittsburgh tomorrow."

Ben stepped inside and closed the door.

Two

Just a few miles after the Rebels moved across the state line, the first thing they noticed as they rolled along the old interstate was no smoke from heating or cooking fires, no evidence of human habitation.

They all knew what that meant: the creepies had ranged out from the ruins of the city in search of food. They would be holding human snacks in basements and tunnels all over the city, fattening them up for the slaughter.

Jersey broke the silence of a few miles. "I hate these goddamn people. Sometimes you can rehab a punk and make something decent and useful out of them. But not these ... *cannibals!*" She spat out the last word as she shuddered in revulsion.

Jersey knew, as did every Rebel, that when fighting the Night People, laying back out of harm's way and letting artillery do most of the work just wouldn't cut it with the creeps. In the cities, they were nearly always bunkered in, deep underground, and when the big guns ceased their rain of death, the creeps crawled out of their stinking holes and waited to mix it up hand-to-hand. The Night People were a disgusting and despicable bunch, but no one who had ever faced them could short them on courage and fighting ability.

And they never surrendered. When confronting the creeps, the Rebels knew they could count on a fight to the death.

"Reports coming in." Corrie spoke from the second seat of the big wagon. "The creeps are waiting for us. Scouts report what appears to be a heavy concentration in the ruins."

Nobody had to ask how the scouts could tell when the creeps were all underground and approximately where and how many of them: the smell.

Creeps worldwide seemed to share an aversion to bathing, and their body odor was enough to put a polecat to shame.

"Battalions directly north and south of our position not yet in line with us," Corrie continued. "They're both at least half a day behind us due to the roads."

Georgi Striganov's 5 Batt, Rebet's 6 Batt, and Jackie Malone's 12 Batt were north of Ben, slogging through the spring rains and traveling on bad roads, hitting the larger towns and clearing them of punks and creeps. They had encountered only a few gangs of punks and they gave it up without much of a fight. Ike's 2 Batt and Greenwalt's 11 Batt were just south of Ben. The other battalions—with a couple of exceptions—were standing by, waiting for the big push to get underway, or helping small communities get back on their feet. Two other battalions were waiting for Ben's orders to move. Ben planned very carefully. But first there was a little game to be played between Ben and Corrie.

"What about this little town just ahead?" Ben asked innocently.

"That's where the scouts first reported from," Corrie said over a smile of her own. "It's a little bigger than a town, boss. It was a city of just over a quarter of a million before the Great War."

"Oh. Very well. We'll bivouac just west of the outskirts. Maybe we'll get lucky tonight," he added with a very thin smile.

The team grinned and exchanged glances. Ben knew that without Corrie telling him; it was a game they played. They knew what Ben was up to: he would have his people appear to be bivouacking for the night, but in reality the Rebels would be setting up ambush sites, hoping to sucker the enemy in under cover of darkness; night was the creeps' favorite time to fight. With luck, the Rebels would draw hundreds of creeps from the larger ruins to the east.

"Scouts report the main body of creeps have moved back into the rubble of the city," Corrie said.

"Pull the scouts back and tell them to pick a spot," Ben ordered. There was no need for him to tell the forward people to stay alert. That would have been a superfluous order. Nor did he have to tell them in code what he had planned for the night. They knew and would be eyeballing the best locations to lay out anti-personnel mines, stringing black wire ankle-high, and rigging other nasty little surprises the Rebels were famous for. Or infamous.

When it came to warfare, Ben Raines and his Rebels were not nice people.

"Order Buddy, Dan, and Buck to gear up and move in a bit closer," Ben ordered.

Ben's son, Buddy, who commanded 8 Batt, designated the special operations battalion, and Dan Gray, the former British SAS officer who commanded 3 Batt, and Buck Taylor, who commanded 15 Batt, had moved into position.

A few miles south, artillery units had moved into place, waiting for Ben's orders, and the souped-up P-51Es were waiting to go in at Ben's command.

As the Rebels were setting up their "bivouac" area, Ben said, "Hot coffee only, Corrie. We eat cold rations tonight. Everybody stay heads-up all the time."

The Rebels noticed that Ben was carrying his old Thompson SMG and his magazine pouch was filled with spares. He walked the area, stopping to chat innocuously enough for a moment with platoon leaders and COs. "Everybody stay in body armor. As soon as the creeps start rushing us, and they will just after dark . . ." The wind had shifted, coming out of the east, bringing with it a strong odor of unwashed bodies. ". . . The artillery will open up just behind them and keep up the barrage. That will prevent the creeps from retreating. We'll keep illumination flares up for the duration. Fly-bys have shown the creeps are concentrating on the this side of the city . . . facing us in a defensive posture and not paying attention behind them as they should. I don't think they realize they've been put in a box. If we have any kind of luck, we can get a lot of our work done tonight. I want everyone with two full canteens of water, enough ammo for a sustained fight. Plenty of grenades. Once they realize they're trapped, the creeps will come at us in their usual banzai attack." Ben smiled thinly. "This night is going to be very interesting."

As dusk drew nearer, the Rebels got into position, behaving as if it were the close of a typical day in the field. The mess tents were up, with the cooks moving back and forth as if everything was normal. But their weapons were within easy reach and when the first shot was fired, they knew exactly where to jump.

"Buddy and Dan in position," Corrie reported to Ben. "Artillery ready to go."

Ben nodded his understanding and looked around him. "Everybody in position?"

"Yes, sir. The tanks were the last to shift around. Everything is setting on 'go'."

"Full dark in about 15 minutes. Let's get the team into position."

To an observer, the camp looked normal. It was anything but normal. The Rebels were on high alert.

If Ben's plan worked, and indications were it was working to perfection, the creeps in the ruins of Pittsburgh had already shifted many of their people out and west, to beef up the creeps in what used to be the small city of Washington, hoping to catch the Rebels by surprise.

The surprise was going to be on the creeps.

Corrie was standing very close to Ben, behind what was left of a concrete block wall. "Scouts report a large wave of creeps coming dead at them, boss," she said in a low voice. "They are approaching what we have designated as the FFZ." No man's land, a free fire zone for the Rebels. Soon the slaughter would begin and the night would be sparked with muzzle blasts, the roar of heavy artillery, and the screams of those caught in the open.

"Tell our forward people to fall back."

"Yes, sir."

"The creeps never learn," Ben muttered. "Luckily for us."

None of his team replied, knowing no reply was expected.

Ben started to say that this time, on this sweep, they would get rid of the creeps once and for all. But he curbed his tongue, recalling that he'd said the same thing on the previous sweeps and the damn Night People just kept coming back. He frowned and shook his head. Scientists down at Base Camp One were now saying the cannibalism might be caused by an illness due to chemicals in their water.

"Years of drinking bad water?" Ben had asked, struggling to keep sarcasm out of his tone.

"Yes," they replied.

"The goddamn creepies are all over North America, Mexico, Central America, South America, and Europe. Every place in this world we have gone, we have run into creepies. And you want me to believe it was caused by bad water?"

"Well . . ." The scientists said in unison.

"Why didn't any of *us* go cannibalistic before we formed Tri-States and got water purification systems up and running, back when we were drinking whatever water we could find?" Ben asked.

The scientists had no reply to that question.

"Keep trying," Ben told them.

Ben smiled as he remembered that scene. His scientists were the finest in the world (he got them from all over the world) but they sometimes had a tendency to keep their heads in the ozone. Somebody had to bring them down and plant their feet firmly on the ground.

"Creeps approaching the point of no return," Corrie whispered. "Sixty seconds."

"Ready the IFs," Ben said softly.

"IFs ready, boss. Thirty seconds."

"Drop them in," Ben ordered.

The illumination flares were dropped down the tubes and the night was shattered, a harsh white light ripping the darkness. What appeared to be hundreds of robed men and women were caught in the glare just as 120mm and 155mm rounds began dropping in from miles away. Fifty-caliber machine guns opened up from the Rebel side, and those creeps who weren't torn apart by the heavy incoming artillery were cut down by machine-gun fire. It was bloody carnage, and that was exactly what Ben had planned.

As those creeps who had managed to survive the surprise ambush in the huge clearing came into range—and there were plenty of creeps to go around—Ben's people in the bivouac area opened fire. Rounds of .223s and 7.62s cut the night air and more dead and savagely wounded were added to the bodies already littering the ground in the free fire zone. Bodies and shattered pieces of bodies lay in grotesque and bloodied positions under the hard light of the illumination flares, which kept the night as bright as day.

Not a single creepie made it through the defensive line of the Rebels. A few of the stinking, robed and hooded men and women came close, but they were cut down by a hail of bullets from the Rebels, some no more than a few meters from the first line of defense.

"Cease fire, Corrie," Ben ordered, his voice hollow-sounding and dim to his ears after the sustained roar of battle. "Get me a casualty report from all units, please."

"Coming in now, boss."

Ben waited. He coughed several times, clearing his throat of the acrid taste of gunsmoke. He took a sip of water from one of his canteens. It tasted flat to his tongue.

"No dead, boss," Corrie reported. "Only a few slightly wounded. Nothing serious."

"We lucked out again," Ben said. "How many creeps are estimated to have made it back to the city?"

"Thirty-five to 40 percent."

"We'll have our work cut out for us tomorrow, then. Beginning tomorrow, that is," he added.

"Snipers in position and ready to go," Corrie said.

"Keep the flares up until they signal they're through."

"Yes, sir."

Rebel snipers would spend the next 20 minutes or so

putting lead into anything that moved out in the free fire zone. The Rebels did not take creepie prisoners. There was no point.

"I want bulldozers up here at first light," Ben ordered.

"Yes, sir. Contacting the combat engineers now."

The combat engineers would scoop out a huge hole and the creeps would be buried in a mass grave. Sometimes, when earth-moving equipment was not available, the Rebels burned creepie bodies. None among them liked that job, for the stench was horrible and the smell difficult to get out of one's clothing.

"I think I'll get some coffee," Ben said. "Have platoon leaders tell their people to stagger sleep shifts this night. The creeps just might decide to try it again. Although I doubt it. We kicked their ass pretty hard."

Ben ambled over to a darkened mess tent, carrying his old Thompson casually. As so often occurred when he used the old Chicago Piano—which was seldom now—the younger Rebels, and many of the older ones, shied away from him. The old Thompson, which had been reworked so many times there was not one original part left in it, was viewed by many (although never to Ben's face) as something almost godlike. Most Rebels refused to touch it. Ben knew all this, and knew too that the Rebels considered him almost godlike.

Ben Raines was legend, and not just among his own people. He had been wounded so many times he had lost count. He had been taken prisoner several times, escaped, and had singlehandedly waged deadly war against his captors. He had been caught in artillery barrages and survived. He had been shot and fallen off a mountain out west, and survived with only a few broken bones.

He could have almost any woman he wanted, yet the one woman he had loved with all his heart had constantly spurned him. Jerre had been killed in the Northwest a few years back, buried in a lonely, lovely spot that Ben had chosen. He had never stopped loving Jerre, and Ben knew he probably would take his love for her to the grave.

Ben pulled a mug of coffee and sat down on a bench in the darkened tent. He was left alone, and knew he would be as long as he sat in the tent, unless one of his own team came in to join him. Jersey, of course, had followed him to the tent; she never let him out of her sight. If anyone wanted to kill Ben Raines, they would first have to go through Jersey. He knew the rest of his team was close by, but they would leave him alone unless something came up.

Lonely at the top, Ben thought, sipping the strong coffee.

He remembered when the Rebels were first formed; he knew the names of every member of the small band, of Constitutionalists—the proper name for the Rebels—who had set out to form their own government, based on the constitution of the United States and the writings of the men who signed the Declaration of Independence. But of that original bunch, only a small handful remained. Most were dead. And those that remained, like Ben, were middle-aged.

Ben smiled in the gloom of the tent, remembering the women he'd known over the years. He had several children, but of them all, only Buddy Raines, his oldest son, showed any interest in command leadership. The others were fine kids, bright and good-looking and outgoing, but not interested in assuming any leadership role . . . at least not yet.

Ben doubted they ever would, for their mothers kept them as far away from Ben as possible. Ben seldom saw his kids, and doubted he would know them if they walked into the mess tent.

But if that was the way their mothers wanted it, that was fine with Ben.

He had wars to fight and a country to resettle.

He looked up as Anna strolled into the tent, his Husky, Smoot, on a leash. The adopted Anna was closer to him than any of his blood children, with the exception of Buddy.

Ben thought of his first Husky, Juno, whom he had found (or the Husky had found him, rather) down south, just after the Great War, and who had lived to be an old dog. Juno had died fighting government soldiers who had invaded the original Tri-States, up in the Northwest.

"Good fight, hey, General Ben?" Anna asked, sitting down beside him.

"Have you ever been in a bad fight, Anna?" Ben questioned.

"Only the ones when I was on the losing side back in the old country."

"I suppose that would spoil your day," Ben muttered. Anna lived to fight. Ben suspected strongly that in a couple of years, she would be requesting permission to move over to Buddy's special operations battalion. She had already been through jump training, and even Dan Gray, the former British SAS officer, admitted there was little he could teach the young woman about guerrilla warfare and the art of silent killing. Anna was a natural soldier.

"So we move into the big city tomorrow, hey?" Anna asked.

"What's left of it."

"Good," she replied, flashing a smile. "That means we get to kill creeps close up. See you, General Ben! I'll take Smoot back to the motor home." She was gone into the night.

Ben toyed with his coffee mug for a moment. He had never seen anyone who hated the Night People any more than Anna did. He supposed she had good reason to do so. Back in Europe, the creeps had chased Anna and her small band of young fighters for years, toward the end even offering a reward for her head.

Ben sat for a time, finishing his coffee, thinking, *Anna has no business being here. She needs to be back at Base Camp One, attending college, having fun and seeing boys her own age.* But whenever he brought that up, she fixed him with those cold pale eyes and shook her head.

"More coffee, general?" one of the cooks quietly asked, standing by the long table with a coffee pot.

Ben looked up and smiled in the gloom. "No thanks. I've had plenty." He stood up. "I'll see you in a few hours."

Ben walked slowly back to his motor home. The flares were still popping, filling the night with light. The crack of the sniper rifles was less frequent now. In another 30 minutes or so, the mortar crews would stand down and the night would quiet.

Shifting through the rubble of Pittsburgh would not take long, for if the creeps ran true to form, they would be exiting the ruins now, the women and children moving out first, the adult male survivors the last ones to leave. Only a few volunteers would remain behind, to harass the Rebels. When the Rebels pulled out of the rubble, they would leave behind them a dead city.

Ben slowed his step and cut his eyes. His team was a dozen or so yards behind; never far away. They would not rest until he was secure.

In his motor home, Ben cleaned the old Thompson and put it away. "Maybe it's time to put it away for good," he muttered. "Bring an end to an era."

But he knew he wouldn't do that. Not yet.

He took his cut-down M-16 out of a closet and cleaned the CAR, then filled an ammo pouch with full .223 magazines. In the distance, the artillery barrage against the city that lay to the east raged. It would continue all night. At dawn, Buddy's special ops battalion would seize the airport and make it ready to receive planes.

Ben showered and hit the sack. Smoot jumped up on the bed and curled up at Ben's side. Within minutes Ben was asleep. As usual, he dreamed of Jerre.

Three

Ben started hammering at the ruins of Pittsburgh from the west, north, and south. He deliberately left the east side open for a time, in hopes the women would take the small kids and bug out. The sight of dead babies was not something any Rebel enjoyed viewing.

The P-51Es would come in after the artillery stood down for a time, and drop napalm. Soon the ruins were blazing, sending black smoke spiraling high into the blue sky, while the main body of the Rebels stood back a few miles and watched and waited for their turn. Their turn would come the next morning, and that's when it would get down and dirty—grunt work, digging the nasties out of the stinking lairs, sometimes sealing the tunnels and basements closed, sometimes pumping tear or pepper gas into the openings, driving them out, then shooting them when they surfaced.

Within an hour after entering the rubble, the Rebels' clothing would be filthy with soot and ash and stinking from the odor of dead creeps. And although none of them ever expressed their feelings to Ben, it had gotten back to him on more than one occasion that many of the Rebels putting their lives on the line day after day wondered if the civilian population around the country really appreciated what they were doing.

"About half of them," Ben muttered. "Maybe."

The Rebels moved into the still-smoking rubble just as dawn split the eastern sky. This time they found only a few hard-core creeps waiting for them, but that did not lessen the hard and dirty and dangerous job of digging them out. Joined by other battalions, it took a full week to declare the ruins of Pittsburgh a dead area.

Five Batt moved north, up into New York state, 6 Batt stayed just north of Ben, in Pennsylvania, and Ben took his 1 Batt straight east, toward Altoona and College Station, while battalions 2 and 11 worked south of Ben, but always moving east. Buddy's 8 Batt stayed loose, ready to move in any direction.

Ben saw no signs of life until they were about fifty miles east of the smoking ruins of the city. In a small town on Highway 22, the Rebels encountered their first militia group since entering the state.

Ben relaxed when he saw that the group was racially mixed. Just before the Great War, some militia groups had aligned themselves with hate groups, and Ben wanted nothing to do with those hard-liners. But this group had members of all races within its ranks. Ben unassed himself from the big wagon and stood for a moment, gazing at the men and women who were staring back in him.

"Are you really Ben Raines?" A woman finally broke the silence.

"I am."

"My God, general. Are we glad to see you. We're just about out of everything—holding on with our teeth."

"Are you the commander of this group?"

She laughed easily and openly and Ben liked her immediately. "No, sir. That would be Sonny Kauffman. He's east of here checking out a report of a gang of thugs working the area. He'll be back later on this afternoon. I'm Sally Markham. Tell the truth, we can't offer you folks much, but we've had the water system working for some time and it's cold and as pure as it was before the Great War."

"Sounds good," Ben said, stepping forward and extending his hand. "When's the last time you folks had a doctor check you out?"

"Several years, general."

Ben turned to Corrie. She was already on the horn, telling the MASH unit behind them to set up and the medics to get ready to go to work.

"Nearest airport of any size, Sally?"

"Johnstown, sir. But that town is filled with punks and other assorted assholes. They moved in about six months ago. Maybe . . . three or four hundred of them. They control what is left of the town."

Ben smiled. "They won't for long." He turned to Corrie. "Six and 12 Batts stay here and assist these people. Let's go kick some punk ass."

Ben had ordered Ike and Greenwalt's 2 and 11 Batts to come up from the south, with Ike swinging around and blocking any escape to the west. Ben took his 1 Batt and drove down from the north.

Before the Great War, Johnstown had a population of about 50,000 and had been a pleasant little city. It was anything but pleasant now.

Just for kicks, Ben ordered several squadrons of P-51Es to do fly-bys over the town, flying very close to the deck.

When the souped up P-51Es came screaming in, the pilots laughingly reported punks running in all directions.

Ben, Ike, and Greenwalt were in position by late that afternoon, with several hours of daylight left.

"Communications says they're using CBs, boss," Corrie told Ben. "Channel 19."

"Naturally," Ben said. "All right." He held out a hand and Beth put a CB walkie talkie in it, set to 19. Ben keyed the mic. "You assholes in the town, are you receiving me?"

After a few seconds, a voice popped out of the speaker. "Who you callin' an asshole, you asshole?"

Ben smiled. "This is going to get old in a hurry, but what the hell? Let's have some fun."

Beth rolled her eyes.

"I'm calling you an asshole, you asshole."

"Who are you?"

Ben chuckled. "I know who I am. Who are you?"

Corrie bit her lip to keep from laughing.

"Huh?"

"I said, who are you, asshole?"

"Big John Parkens, that's who."

"I never heard of you. Are you sure that's who you are?"

Jersey sighed.

"Huh?"

"Boss," Cooper said. "That ain't no mental giant you're talking with."

"He was probably spanked as a child and that traumatized him deeply."

"I'm sure that was it," Cooper replied.

"John Prickins. Are you listening?"

"Parkens, goddamnit. Parkens!"

"That's what I said, Barkens. This is Ben Raines."

There was a very long silence from Big John. "So what?" he finally asked. But there was a definite note of worry in his voice.

"You and your scummy crew have been terrorizing the few good people left in that town, Fartkins. Take your gang and clear out."

"And if we don't?"

"We come in and clear you out. Take a good look around you, big mouth. You have Rebel battalions just waiting to come in and kick your ass."

After about three minutes of silence, the gang leader said, "There ain't no troops to the east."

"How observant of you. That is correct. Does that give you a clue, Barfins?"

"Parkens, goddamnit. Parkens!"

"Whatever."

"Ah . . . I guess maybe you want me and the boys to pull in that direction?"

"By George, I think he's got it," Ben said to his team. "Yes. Or if you choose, you can remain in town and we'll kill you. The choice is yours to make."

"You'll . . . *kill* us?"

"That's what I said."

"Who the hellfire do you think you are, Raines?"

"I know who I am, Arkins. The commanding general of the largest army known to exist on the face of the earth. You really want to tangle with us?"

"Not really, general."

"Then start moving out toward the east and keep going. When you reach a very large body of water, that will be the Atlantic Ocean. Once there, you either change your ways and become a law-abiding citizen, or you can make a stand and fight us. If you choose the former, you have a good chance of living a long life. If you choose the latter, we'll bury you. Do you understand all that?"

"I understand."

"Move! Now!"

"Yes, sir. Big John out."

"Scouts have him pinpointed, boss," Corrie said. "He's standing with some people on the roof of a tall building. Snipers say it's an easy shot if you want them to take it."

"Negative. If he'll leave peacefully, so much the better. That will give them all ample time to see what they're up against and quite possibly change their ways."

Big John Parkens had taken a long look through binoculars he had stolen and had paled at the sight of some sixty main battle tanks, the muzzles of their main guns pointed directly at the town, and hundreds of Rebels waiting to move in and kick ass. *His* ass. Within minutes, cars, trucks, and motorcycles began pulling out of the small city, most of them trailing blue smoke from engines badly in need of an overhaul.

"Either I'm getting soft-hearted in my old age," Ben muttered, "or the punks are wising up."

Anna looked up at him and grinned mischievously.

"And I don't expect a reply to the former," Ben added. She winked at him.

"Big John and his bunch were no better or worse than the other gangs who have come in here and thrown their weight around," the citizen told Ben. "For the most part, we left them alone and they left us alone."

"Uh-huh," Ben said drily. The man had the look of defeat stamped all over him, and so did the crowd of men and women who had gathered around to gawk at the Rebels and their mighty machines of war. "Are you people originally from this town?"

"Only a few of us," a woman answered. "Most of the residents either moved out or were killed a long time ago. A lot of them, those that were young enough, took to the hills to form militia groups to fight the cannibals and the thugs and the like. We don't know what happened to them.

But those of us here now, we figure God will take care of us. You see, none of us believe in the taking of a human life."

"Is that a fact?" Ben said. "Well, we're going to be using your old airport for a few days. We'll try not to bother you. If any of you need medical care, we have doctors who will see to your needs. We'll be set up at the airport." He turned to his team. "Let's get the hell out of here."

The Rebels stayed in the area for a few days, first making the local airport useable, then resupplying. The doctors saw to the needs of the few citizens who showed up (it was obvious that the locals did not trust the Rebels, which suited Ben just fine; he didn't care for the citizens either), and then the battalions moved out toward the east.

Ike kept his battalions south of Ben, but staying just far enough north to avoid the ruins of Washington. Georgi's battalions stayed to the north, stretched out north to south, working from the shore line of Lake Ontario, down to near Ben's more central route through the state.

At Altoona, Ben found several thousand people who had refused to let their town die. They had fought off punks and creeps and rebuilt out of the ashes until they had a thriving community of shops and farms. The roaming gangs of thugs left their area alone, as did the creeps. They wanted no part of the Rebel philosophy, and Ben didn't push the issue. There, the Rebels had medical supplies flown in for the residents—they had doctors, but few medicines—rested for a time, then moved on.

Ben pulled in several other battalions, until they had created a wall of troops, running north to south, giving the creeps and thugs no escape except to the east. Scouts, ranging far ahead of the main body of Rebels, reported that the punks were on the run, hardly stopping anywhere except to rest and then keep on running.

Ben got in touch with several Canadian militia groups

and told then what was happening. The Canadians then stretched their people out along the St. Lawrence, patrolling day and night, preventing any large number of gang members from crossing over.

Ben was herding the creeps and punks and thugs like cattle, moving them slowly eastward until the day they had the ocean to their backs, and Raines' Rebels facing them.

Then would come the final showdown.

"We're going to hit New Brunswick and Nova Scotia in the fall or early winter," Beth pointed out one day. "I am not looking forward to wintering in that climate."

Ben smiled. "Before that happens, we'll stretch out in towns north to south running from the Canadian border down to the Atlantic to keep the punks from slipping through, and wait them out until spring. But I don't think we'll have to wait that long. By that time the punks will be short on supplies and many of them will surrender rather than starve or freeze to death. We'll deal with the hard core in the spring. What's left of them," he added with a grim smile. "After the winter, they won't be in very good shape to put up much of a fight."

Ben had long had the reputation of being one of the dirtiest guerrilla fighters on the face of the earth. He would offer his enemies surrender and hope (or a quick death), but if they chose to fight, he would show them absolutely no compassion.

"Scouts reporting a small band of outlaws five miles ahead," Corrie said. "Forty to 50 men and women and a few children. They've stacked their weapons in the middle of the road and stuck up several white flags. They've reported by CB radio that they've had it. And they know of several other groups who want to pack it in."

"What about a set-up?" Ben questioned.

"The scouts say negative. They're in rough shape. And the scouts have been in contact with our people in records. This bunch is not on the list as being hard core."

"It's beginning," Ben said, after a moment. "And it's happening much sooner than I expected. We're pushing them so hard they can't rest and do much scrounging for food. Tell the scouts we're on the way." Ben chuckled. "By spring we'll have the entire eastern half of the nation relatively clean of gangs."

"And then, boss?" Jersey asked.

"We turn around and head west, and deal with Mister Simon Border."

Four

In his Rocky Mountain home, Simon Border frowned as he stared at a map that traced the movements of Ben Raines and the Rebels. Raines was moving fast, much faster than Simon had ever imagined he would, or could.

Simon's frown turned into a bitter smile as he thought, *You underestimated the man, and you knew never to do that. It's dangerous to underestimate Ben Raines. People who make that mistake usually end up dead.*

Simon relaxed a bit. The fleeing thugs would be forced to turn and make a stand sometime, possibly this late fall or winter. Simon had at least that long to make up his mind what to do about Ben. Simon knew his followers wanted a fight. But picking a fight with Ben Raines was very low on Simon's priority list. People who picked fights with Ben Raines and the Rebels always lost.

But, Simon reflected, perhaps the non-aggression pact he had signed with Ben would be honored.

Then Simon chuckled.

He knew as well as Ben that document was worthless the instant the ink dried.

But . . . if he could keep his people from making forays across the border into the NUSA and the SUSA—*especially* the latter—he might be able to prolong the inevitable for months, or even years. By that time, his own army would be so powerful Raines might be forced to think twice before attacking.

That was certainly something to hope and pray for.

And there was something else Simon would pray most fervently for: the death of Ben Raines.

As the Rebels advanced slowly but steadily eastward, they encountered only a few pockets of resistance. Citizens who came out to greet them said there had been a mass exodus of gangs of thugs for over a month, all of them heading east. The gangs had been stealing all the canned goods and dried and smoked meat they could find.

Ben offered to replenish what had been stolen, but the people politely refused.

"We're just glad to see you folks," was the usual response. Then, with a smile, "Actually, when we heard the gangs were coming, we hid most of our food."

The Rebels set up MASH tents and gave shots and prescribed medications and did what they could. The people were grateful and gracious, but the majority made it clear they did not want to adopt the Tri-States' form of government, preferring to stay with the NUSA. Ben respected that. He also made it very clear to the locals that he would tolerate no interference from them when it came to the Rebels' methods of dealing with criminals. They were cleaning out the Northeast, and that was that.

Some of them did not approve of the Rebels' harsh methods, but they were wise enough not to interfere.

The Rebels moved on.

Ben swung several more of his battalions around to beef up the battalions working north of him, leaving the ruins of Philadelphia, and the states of New Jersey and Delaware to the battalions of Ike, Greenwalt and Buddy.

For months Rebel intelligence had been receiving reports that what was left of New York City and Long Island were crawling (in some cases, literally crawling) with the most despicable types of humanity. Die-hard creeps, gangs of murderers, rapists, child molesters, and worse. Many, if not most, of the gang leaders that had attacked Base Camp One while the Rebels were in Europe had chosen to make the ruins of the city their last stand.

And Ben and his 1 Batt were on a collision course with the sprawling ruins of the city that used to be called the Big Apple.

Just west of the ruins of New York City, Ben brought his battalion to a halt and radioed in for resupplying. Those men and women in Ben's beefed-up 1 Batt smiled and exchanged sly glances.

They were going to peel the Big Apple, once and for all.

Inside the ruined city and out on Long Island, the gang leaders met, as one put it, probably for many of them, for the last time.

"We got no place left to run," a gang leader said. "We made our choice to fight it out here, and here we are."

For months, while on the move east, the gang leaders had been stealing food from locals as they passed through their towns. They had stockpiled containers of water. When they reached the city, they had worked around the clock reloading brass and making homemade bombs to use when their supply of grenades ran out. They had stolen millions of rounds of ammo during their brief occupation of parts of the SUSA, especially Base Camp One, in addition to grenades and mortar tubes and base-plates. When they had arrived at what for most would be their final destination, many had gone out on Long Island and planted gardens, canning the food for later use. They were ready for a siege.

"The creeps won't align with us," Craig Franklin said. "They prefer to fight Raines on their own."

"Which is fine with me," Rob "Big Tits" Ford, one of the few female gang leaders, said.

Her brother, Hal, nodded his head in agreement. "I ain't runnin' from that son-of-a-bitch Raines no more," he said. "I've had it."

"We've all had it," Jack Brittain commented. "The only choice we have left us is how we choose to die, and I choose to die fighting that bastard Raines and his Rebels."

Ray Brown, the gang leader Ben had sworn to personally kill with his bare hands, said, "Our patrols all say that Raines is heading his 1 Battalion dead at us. This is gonna be nose-to-nose and personal between us and them." He smiled, exposing surprisingly good teeth; most of the gang leaders had a mouth filled with rot. "I'm looking forward to it."

"Then you're a fool, Ray," Dale Jones said. "Ben Raines has swore to kill you personal, and he'll do it, too."

"Best thing for you to do, when the time comes, and it's coming, is to eat a pistol," Thad Keel suggested. "Of us all, Raines is gonna be lookin' hard for you."

"I won't be hard to find," Ray said. "I hope he does try me hand-to-hand. Ben Raines is a middle-aged man. I'll take him apart."

Sandy Allen spat and said, "And you'll shit if you eat regular, too. Raines ain't no pussy, middle-aged or not.

He'll as soon cut your guts out as look at you. Especially you, Ray, on account of you killin' his pet dogs.''

Ray gave the speaker a dirty look, but let that part of the subject drop. Ray wasn't afraid of Ben Raines. The man had to be at least 50 years old. Shit! Who the hell was scared of some 50-year-old? Not him. Over-The-Hill Raines, Ray thought with a smile. Yeah. That was a good name for Ben Raines. Over-The-Hill.

"Raines and them will be here in about a week," Sandy Allen said. "Ten days at the most. So any of you wants to cut and run, you'd better do it now."

That was met with cold stares from the several dozen gang leaders present in the underground chamber. Above them, the ruins of New York City lay in piles of twisted steel and rubble. The once towering skyscrapers had been halved by the relentless onslaught of Rebel artillery of years past. But an underground culture flourished beneath the piles of rubble, as Ben had suspected it would. Even though the Rebels had blown closed as many entrances to the miles and miles of tunnels beneath the old city as they could find, Ben knew that for every one they had sealed, supposedly trapping the punks and creeps, there was another entrance they had missed.

Fly-bys clearly showed that hundreds of gardens had been cultivated out on Long Island, keeping the tunnel-dwellers beneath the city supplied with vegetables. The fly-bys also showed pens for hogs and cattle from one end of Long Island to the other. The rubble of the city and in the towns on Long Island might well have been filled with the absolute dregs of society, but the gangs weren't stupid.

And the gangs in the city and out on Long Island had laid aside any personal differences and banded together to fight the common enemy: Ben Raines and the Rebels.

For one last time.

* * *

"Tanks will be useless in the city," Ben told his company commanders and platoon leaders. "The streets are impassable for anything other than motorcycles and bicycles. We're going to have to go into the city on foot, and slug it out on foot, taking the city block by block."

The faces of the COs and PLs remained impassive. The news came as no surprise to any of them; they just wanted to do it. All of them had lost friends and loved ones when the gangs invaded the old Base Camp One, and this was personal for them—intensely personal.

"I've pulled in two companies from Buddy's 8 Batt," Ben continued. "Plus platoons from other battalions. Now, this is going to be a son-of-a-bitch, people, and I won't kid you about it. Artillery will be practically useless, as will air support. This is going to be 'grunt' all the way. Some of these gangs have had years to get ready for us— and you'd better believe they are ready. Intel can't give us any accurate number of the creeps we'll be facing. We're practically going in blind. We're going to cross the river by boat and land in Battery Park, establish a firm foothold and a hospital, and then we spread out west to east, and start working north. And we're going to do it slowly. If we gain 50 feet a day, that's fine. But we're going to do it right.

"Ike has cut a path for us across New Jersey two miles wide and Tina's people are holding the docks for us while boats and barges are on the way. Georgi's people have cut off any escape to the north and they're holding." He smiled. "Manhattan and Long Island are all ours. Start drawing supplies and resting up. Because when we step ashore in Battery Park, there won't be time for much rest."

Everyone present had noticed that Ben had replaced his old Thompson with the Colt M4 Carbine, 5.56-caliber.

Empty, it weighed about half what his old Chicago Piano weighed, and thus enabled him to carry a lot more ammo. The M4 didn't have the brute knock-down power of the old .45-caliber Thompson, but for this type of fighting, it was much more practical.

No one made mention of it, but all had also noticed that Ben had sent Smoot back to Base Camp One for safekeeping. That was a clear sign that Ben expected a very vicious and prolonged fight.

The way Ben felt about the gangs he was going after—the most vicious, cruel, and degenerate gangs left in North America—it might well turn into a slaughter.

Craig Franklin, Frankie to his friends. Youngest son of a naval officer who turned bad before he was ten years old and started torturing to death neighborhood cats and dogs. Frankie felt the greatest thing ever to happen to him was when the world fell apart. Has spent the past few years raping and killing and torturing. His gang numbers several hundred strong.

• Foster Payne, Fos to his friends. Now in his mid-thirties, Payne was a spoiled brat as a kid. His parents gave him everything he hollered for and more. When he was 15 he killed them both with a shotgun because they wouldn't buy him a new Corvette. His gang numbers about 500 men and women.

• Thad Keel, Killer to his friends. Killed his first victim when he was 12, a neighborhood girl . . . after he raped and sodomized her. He was 16 when the world blew apart and working on his fifth victim. He had never been caught. His parents suspected he had something to do with the killings, but they just couldn't turn in their darling precious wonderful little dickhead to the cops. Just wasn't done, you know? Killer's gang numbers about 300.

• Les Justice, not his real name, but if Les even remembered what his real name was, he never mentioned it. A natural-born cold-blooded killer out of northeast Louisiana. His gang numbers about 400 scum of the earth.

• Jack Brittain, again, not his real name. Claimed to be from England, but no one believed him. Jack was vicious and cruel with his victims. His gang numbers about 300.

• Jamal Lumumba, not his real name either. No one knew where Jamal was from, and few cared. He was a troublemaker even among his fellow gang members—about 400 of the most worthless dregs of humanity ever assembled in one place.

• Beth Aleman, nicknamed Tootsie. A man-hater who ran a gang of the most vicious bunch of women ever gathered together. They all shared one thing in common, other than the obvious—they hated Ben Raines.

• Abdullah Camal, the only friend of Jamal Lumumba, which was good for the both of them, because nobody liked Abdullah any better than they did Jamal. Camal the Camel, as many gang leaders called him, led one of those gangs Ben and the Rebels had run out of Los Angeles years back. Abdullah blamed society for what he was. He had once filled out (more or less) an application for work with a high tech company in Southern California. When they wouldn't hire him, much less make him a vice president (which was the position he wanted), he changed his name and vowed to make war on the racist government of the United States. About a month later the whole world fell apart and Abdullah was left wondering where his next meal was coming from. Didn't take him long to figure out that stealing was a hell of a lot more fun than working. Abdullah's gang numbers several hundred.

• Karen Carr was the leader of one of the largest of all the gangs, numbering about 700 men and women. If Karen had any endearing qualities, none had ever been found during her relatively short but very violent tenure as a gang leader. Karen was so vicious and unpredictable, her male counterparts walked light around her.

• A brother-and-sister team, Hal and Robbie Ford, ran another gang. Robbie was known affectionately as Big Tits. Both had been born and reared in a Christian home, by loving parents, in Memphis, Tennessee. When the world blew apart, Hal and Robbie were at a summer church camp. That same day, Hal and Robbie killed one of their camp counselors, stole his car, and left. Hal and Robbie had found their niche in life. Their gang numbers about 300.

• Dale Jones, as a cop once observed, was a walking advertisement for the total legalization of abortion. By the time Dale was 15, and the world erupted in war, he had been arrested so many times the local police had a separate file cabinet just for his rap sheets. Dale's gang numbers about 400.

• No one knew where Mysterious Sandy Allen (not his real name) was from. His nickname was Spooky. Spooky bore a startling resemblance to a corpse, and had just about the same personality. Spooky liked to drink the blood of his victims. His gang numbers about 350.

• Dave Holton was originally from Michigan. When the Great War shattered the world, he had been serving time for rape and murder, and was in the midst of being tried for other crimes. He killed a deputy sheriff with a homemade shank, took his gun, killed the judge, and split. His gang numbers close to 400.

There were numerous other gang leaders in the ruins of Manhattan who fronted gangs that numbered from ten to 50, with names like Big Mac, Leadfoot, V-8, Blackie, and so forth.

Manhattan was about to become a killing ground— again.

Five

Ben expected a lot of gripes from his batt coms about leading the fight into the ruins of New York City, and they were not long in coming. He listened impassively to each of his commanders vent their spleens, then smiled and said, "Thank you for your concern. Your complaints are duly noted. I am still leading my battalion into the ruins. Good day."

"Hard-headed asshole!" Ike told him.

Ben smiled sweetly at his long-time friend. "I don't see you making any plans to leave the field, Ike."

Ike blustered about, then threw up his hands in disgust and left.

"You are getting too old for this type of silliness, Ben," Dan Gray, the former British SAS officer, told him.

"I'm only about five years older than you," Ben reminded him. "Would you like me to recommend you to be relieved of field command?"

Dan pursed his lips, cleared his throat rather loudly, then wheeled about and marched out of the office.

Ben's kids, Tina and Buddy, said nothing to their father. They both felt that Ben would someday die in the field, and kept silent about his constant chance-taking because that was his wish.

Doctor Lamar Chase flew into New Jersey and was taken by Hummer to the docks, where Ben and his beefed-up battalion were waiting to load the boats that would take them across to Battery Park.

"You damned fool," Chase told him. "When are you going to realize that you're the commanding general, start acting like it, and stop behaving as a spoiled child?"

"Nice day, isn't it, Lamar?" Ben responded with a smile.

"Goddammit, Raines! There are anywhere from 10,000 to 50,000 punks and creeps waiting over there in those ruins. And all of them hate your guts. I—"

"I have decided to forbid you from crossing over and taking charge of your medical teams, Lamar."

"You've *what?*" Chase roared. Rebels within earshot scattered in all directions. "Why, you pompous asshole, you can't forbid me a damn thing. I'm the chief of medicine. I can put *your* ass in bed for the duration, though."

"Try it!" Ben growled at his old friend.

The two men stood nose to nose, making faces at each other until Anna pushed her way between them and held them apart at her arms' length. "Silly," the young lady said. "This is silly. Neither one of you is going to do anything except make noise. I wish there was a stick around here so I could whack you both!"

The idea of Anna doing that startled both men and then caused Ben and Chase to burst out laughing.

"You're right, Anna," Ben finally said, wiping his eyes. "But you've been with us long enough to know that this is something Chase and I do at the start of every campaign."

Anna fixed him with those cold, pale eyes of hers and said, "And General Ben, it could be the doctor is right."

."Owwee . . . hee hee hee hee," Chase cackled, walking away. "Oh, ho ho ho ho, hee hee hee hee! Oh, did she get you good that time, Raines."

"Oh . . . shut up, you old goat!" Ben called after him.

"Hee hee hee hee!" Chase waved a hand and continued walking. He called over his shoulder. "I'll be ready to go over with the first wave, Raines!"

"You'll be ready to go over when I tell you to!" Ben shouted after him.

Chase flipped him the rigid digit and walked away, chuckling.

Ben looked down at Anna. "I should send you back to Base Camp One. You should be attending public school and having fun."

"I am being tutored quite well with the battalion, thank you," Anna replied sweetly.

Ben grunted. He really couldn't argue that, because his adopted daughter was being tutored quite well. Whenever the battalion was standing down, one of half a dozen former teachers would spend hours with her. Ben had never figured out a way to make her leave the battalion and try a normal, peaceful life away from combat. Fighting was all the young woman had ever known and she was a natural at it.

"Draw supplies, Anna," Ben told her. "We make the crossing tomorrow."

She flipped him a very sloppy salute and walked off.

Ben motioned for an officer from the special ops battalion to join him. "Your Zodiacs ready, lieutenant?"

"Yes, sir."

"Shove off at midnight and establish a toehold for us. We'll be joining you at dawn."

The young officer grinned. "Yes, sir!"

Ben walked over to where his team was relaxing in the shade of a warehouse. "We shove off in the morning. First wave." He walked over to where Chase was talking with several of the battalion doctors. Chase noticed the serious look on Ben's face and did not offer up one of his usual caustic verbal barbs. "Dawn tomorrow, Lamar. Your combat medics are checking supplies now. You and your people will go over on the second wave."

"All right, Ben," Lamar's reply was softly offered.

Ben walked over to a mess tent where his company commanders were sitting at a bench, drinking coffee. He paused long enough to say, "Dawn tomorrow."

Ruth Wiseman, CO of Bravo Company smiled and said, "We're sittin' on ready, general."

"Good enough," Ben said, and kept on walking.

He walked down to the shoreline and looked across at what used to be known as the Big Apple. "If you're over there, Ray Brown, you better eat a pistol now," he murmured. "Because if I find you alive, I'm going to beat you to death with my bare hands."

In the ruins of Manhattan, the gang leaders made ready for what those with any sense at all knew would be their last fight. They had sent patrols north, and found any hope of escape that way had been sealed by several Rebel battalions, under the overall command of the Russian, Georgi Striganov. Beginning at the northernmost tip of the Bronx, Georgi had stretched his battalions out from the Hudson River in the west over to Long Island Sound, from the College of Mt. St. Vincent over to the very edge of Shore Road.

Several more battalions, under the overall command of Ike, were ready to move into Brooklyn, and then onto Long Island. But the Big Apple belonged to Ben.

*   *   *

Misting rain and very foggy at 0500 hours. For early summer, there was a damp chill in the air. But the meteorologists said that in a few hours, the rain would stop, the fog would dissipate, and the temperature would rise to a comfortable high in the upper 70s.

"Special ops people have met little resistance," Corrie reported. "But they're stretched out thin as paper from Pier A over to the corner of the New York Plaza. They couldn't take a major push."

Ben shook his head. "If there was any kind of build-up it would have been observed. The punks showed their lack of planning again. They should have been ready to throw everything at us at landing." Ben smiled. "But since we know the bastards stole plenty of mortars and rounds from us down at Base Camp One, I've ordered the boats to maintain a zing-zap course during the crossing . . . just in case the punks try to get cute."

Standing nearby, Jersey frowned. She had a tendency to get airsick and seasick.

Cooper tried to put an arm around her. Impossible to do with the loaded packs they all had strapped on. "I'll take care of you, my little desert flower."

"Cooper," Jersey replied. "You can just barely take care of yourself. Now quit trying to grope me."

Cooper did his best to look hurt. He couldn't pull it off.

"In the boats," Ben ordered. "Move."

"I won't even be able to see the Statue of Liberty this morning," Anna groused. "I wanted to see that up close."

Nobody had the heart to tell her the welcoming lady with the torch had been heavily damaged during the last assault on New York City, a few years back.

The battalion was unusually silent as they all boarded the boats of various sizes for the transport across the fog-shrouded waters. They all carried two full canteens of water on web belts, plus three days' field rations in their packs, in addition to ground sheets and blankets, first aid kits, flashlights with extra batteries, knives, entrenching tools, grenades, full magazines for their weapons, extra socks, clean underwear, and maps of the city. In addition, many carried a round or two for a rocket launcher or mortar, cans of ammo for SAWs or M-60 machine guns, and their cargo pockets were stuffed with hi-energy candy bars, chewing gum, and boxes of cigarettes. They wore body armor that protected them from crotch to neck and state-of-the-art helmets had replaced berets as headgear.

All knew they could very easily be cut off from reinforcements the instant they touched the shoreline of Manhattan.

The chaplains had held a short prayer service just before the Rebels boarded the boats.

"Special ops people report no sign of the enemy," Corrie said after listening for a few seconds to her headset. "Sensors are showing no warm bodies anywhere close to our objective."

Ben nodded in understanding and began to breathe easier. The shoreline of Manhattan was coming up fast through the fog.

"I don't feel good," Jersey moaned.

"Puke in your helmet," Cooper told her.

"Gross, Cooper!"

Ben smiled. "We'll be on solid ground in two minutes, Jersey," he assured her.

"Thanks, boss. But I found an empty pocket in Cooper's jacket. I can barf in there if I have to."

Cooper moved as far away from her as he could, which was not far with the crush of bodies on the deck. Jersey smiled.

Ghostly figures suddenly appeared on the docks, out of the mist and fog.

"All clear, boss," Corrie said.

Ben moved to the front of the old tugboat and when the bow gently nudged the dock, was the first one off.

"Beachhead established, general," the young woman said. "Resistance has been practically nil."

"It won't be in a few hours," Ben replied.

"You got that straight, general," the young woman with her face camo-ed in urban colors replied.

Ben smiled and walked on, his team off the tug and surrounding him in a protective circle, the young woman taking the lead.

"We got you a CP all cleaned out over here, general," she called over her shoulder. "Not that you'll be using it for long," she added knowingly.

"Hospital?" Ben asked.

"Got a place all picked out and cleaned up for that, too," she said.

"Very good."

Rebels were running past Ben and team, disappearing into the fog and mist, heading for positions picked out by the special ops people. The Rebels would dig in hard in anticipation of attack from the punks.

Minutes ticked past and no attack came. The first wave of Rebels were ashore.

"Bring in the second and third wave," Ben told Corrie.

Doctors, support personnel, supplies, and additional combat troops.

"How big is this place?" Anna asked.

"About 23 square miles," Ben replied.

"Actually it's 22.6 square miles," Beth the statistician replied.

Ben smiled.

"At one time, one of the most densely populated areas

in North America," Beth continued. "There are hundreds of miles of tunnels and sewers and subway systems beneath the city."

"And that's where most of the punks and the creeps will be hiding." Ben picked it up. "Waiting for us."

One of the special ops people approached Ben and held out a small cardboard box. "Found this, sir. Thought you might like to see it."

Ben glanced at the familiar-appearing box. It had once contained a state-of-the-art gas mask, perfected by the lab boys and girls down in Base Camp One. One of hundreds stolen by the punks when they invaded that area.

Ben nodded. "Well, we suspected they had them. So much for the use of gas to drive them out of the tunnels. They also stole full-body protective suits. Hell, that gear will withstand radiation. This is going to be grunt all the way."

Ben unfolded a map of the city and spread it out on the hood of a long-abandoned, old rusted-out vehicle. "We're here, Anna." He pointed to the south end of the narrow outline of the city. He traced his finger northward all the way up to whatever might be left of the old Columbia-Presbyterian Medical Center. "We end up here."

"All city?" Anna asked.

"Except for Central Park," Ben told her. "And that's about 850 acres in the center of the city."

"Big job," the teenage warrior replied.

"Yeah," Ben said, folding the map and putting it away. "A hell of a big job."

In those states east of the Mississippi River which had chosen not to align themselves with the Tri-States philosophy, even now that the majority of the criminal element was gone from their lives, thanks to the efforts of the

Rebels, getting things back to even a small semblance of normalcy was proving very difficult.

Without the Rebels' expertise, even such things as setting up and maintaining clean water systems and sewer filtration plants were proving difficult. Before the Great War, very few people realized just how much they depended upon the central government. Now it was all coming home to roost.

In the several years since the Great War, in those areas outside of Rebel control, conditions had deteriorated to the point of total collapse. Millions of people were without jobs, living hand-to-mouth at best. There were no proper medical facilities and very few medicines. Factories were turning to rust, and the majority of the larger cities had been virtually destroyed after years of fighting.

To sum it up, with the exception of the SUSA, under Rebel control and laws, the rest of the nation was flat on its face and just barely kicking.

Six

The Rebels split up into squad-sized teams, spread out east to west, and advanced about 50 yards northward. They saw absolutely no sign of human life.

Ben and his team were on the eastern edge of Battery Park, picking their way slowly through the litter and rubble. Except for the faint cry of sea birds that circled and hovered at water's edge in a constant search for food, there was nothing to be found but an eerie silence in the ruins.

"Come on, come on, you bastards!" Jersey muttered, just loud enough for Ben to hear the words. "Let's mix it up."

"Not yet, Jersey," Ben told her. "We're too concentrated down here. The area will start widening out when we reach Battery Place. We'll be spread thinner. That's when we'll start seeing some action."

"Third and fourth waves are ashore," Corrie said. "Chase is setting up his hospital."

Battery Park, situated on a landfill at the extreme south

end of Manhattan, had not taken the pounding that other areas of the city had suffered several years back when the Rebels launched their all-out assault against Manhattan. The park consisted mostly of monuments and sculpture, and much of it was still standing, silent sentinels and tributes to the dead. The sun had not yet broken through the fog and the light mist continued to fall, giving the park a ghostly, surreal look.

Gunfire suddenly shattered the quiet and everyone hit the damp ground and lay still.

"Contact," Corrie said. "Of the hit-and-run type. Some punks tried an ambush that didn't work. One Rebel slightly wounded and several dead punks. To our northeast, between the park and State Street."

"Damn fog," Ben muttered, heaving himself up to his knees and squatting there trying in vain to see through the soup. "We're chasing ghosts out here."

"Meteorologists have now changed their minds," Corrie said. "A front is moving in and colliding with another, or squeezing it, or whatever those things do. They're predicting heavy rains today and tonight."

"Break out the ponchos," Ben said, disgust in his voice. "What a miserable way to start a push."

"Scouts report movement along Battery Place and that intersection where State runs into Broadway," Corrie said. "You called that one right, boss."

Ben rose to his boots. "Let's go mix it up, gang. Lousy weather or not, we came to do a job."

The clatter of M-16s, the stutter of machine guns and the occasional boom of a grenade reverberated through the rain and the fog as the Rebels slowly began their advance. Usually, the gang members would turn tail and run when the Rebels got close. But not this time. This time, the Rebels were going to have to buy every foot of real estate they gained.

By mid-morning, the thick, soupy fog had lifted but the rain had intensified, coming down in gray sheets. The Rebels were stretched out in a line running west to east from just south of First Place over to the Vietnam Veterans Plaza. And the punks were holding.

"Sixteen-hundred meters," Beth said during a break in the fighting.

"Beg pardon?" Ben asked, looking over at her.

The team was crouched under the overhang of what was left of an old business establishment on the south side of Battery Place. The punks were just across the street, almost close enough to touch.

"That's how far it is from the Hudson to the East River," Beth replied over the drum of rain. "That's how long the front is."

Ben grunted and cut his eyes to Anna. She had gone off, vanishing as silently as the now dissipated fog, and returned a few minutes later with several Rebels in tow, two of them lugging a Big Thumper, two more burly Rebels dutifully toting cases of 40mm grenades. Anna thanked them and began setting up the Mark 19–3 40mm automatic grenade launcher.

"Where did you get that?" Ben asked.

"I stole it," the young woman said matter-of-factly. "I'm going to knock a hole in that line across the street."

"Are you now?"

"Yes, I am."

"All by yourself?"

Anna flashed a grin. "I might require some small amount of help, thank you. Are you volunteering, General Ben?"

"Oh, why not?" Ben replied, as the rest of his team chuckled.

The Mark 19–3 grenade launcher, affectionately known as a Big Thumper, was belt fed and could spit out approximately 35 to 40 40mm grenades a minute, with a range of about 1750 feet and with a killing radius of about 16 feet. The cases the Rebels had lugged over for Anna contained loaded belts of M383 High Explosive grenades.

Beth crawled over and positioned herself on the left side of the Big Thumper, and locked a belt into place. Ben backed off a few feet to avoid getting hit by the ejected casings and waited.

"Everybody ready?" Anna asked.

"Let it bang," Ben said, an amused look on his face. The kid was certainly inventive, he thought, and didn't mind at all taking the initiative.

Anna sure as hell let it bang. She thumbed the trigger, working the muzzle left to right, and began clearing half a block of real estate.

"Open fire!" Ben shouted, and all along the line, Rebels opened up with weapons on full auto.

"Jesus friggin' Christ!" someone yelled from across the street, the shout filled with panic, as every Rebel within firing distance opened up.

Through the hard falling rain, the Rebels could see indistinct shapes—those that were still able to move—running and crawling away from the lethal hail of grenades and bullets that seemed to be coming at them as fast as the rain was falling.

"Smoke!" Ben yelled. Then, to Corrie, "Both ends move out and flank as soon as the smoke is thick enough. This weather will keep it close to the ground."

The Rebels started hurling smoke grenades. A few minutes later, the punks along Battery Place were on the run, having no stomach to fight angry Rebels close up and personal. The Rebels to the east used the same tactics and within minutes everything south of a line stretching from First Place over to Bowling Green Park and then to the Vietnam Veterans Plaza was in Rebel hands, the punks' first line of defense was broken, and the punks were running for their lives.

"No pursuit!" Ben told Corrie, and she quickly radioed the message. "This could be a planned move on their part. Although I doubt it. We'll hold what we've got and wait."

Two hours later, the rain had stopped coming down in sheets; now it was a slow and steady fall. Scouts had moved forward and found no trace of the creeps or the punks; they had pulled out when the incoming got hot.

Ben gave the order and the Rebels rose from their positions and slowly began their advance. They encountered no resistance in their cautious move forward. Fifty yards, a hundred yards; Ben and his team were moving straight up Broadway, pausing and then climbing over the piles of rubble and using the many burned-out and mangled hulks of automobiles for cover.

A block south of Exchange Place the punks made their second stand of that day, and this time they held. From West Thames Street on the Hudson River side over to Old Slip to the east, the gangs of punks held firm and stopped the Rebel advance cold . . . and wet.

Ben had ordered in as many snipers as the other battalions could spare just for moments such as this. He told Corrie to get on the horn and get the long-distance shooters into place and start taking out punks.

Artillery was a terrifying experience for the Grunt; the sniper surely came in a very close second. One second you were whispering to a buddy and, depending on the type of weapon the sniper was using, the next second your buddy's head was splattered all over you and you were wiping off blood and brains. Heavy artillery was demoralizing; a mine field was terrifying; a sniper could cause brave men to shit their pants. And Rebel snipers were the best in the world.

One of Dale Jones' gang members stuck his head out

of cover to take a peep and a 7.62 match ammo round, fired from 800 yards away, took him in the throat and sprayed the punk crouched next to him with blood. A punk from Dave Holton's gang stuck his head out from behind a pile of rubble and a sniper using a specially built .50-caliber rifle blew half his head off from a hidden position almost 2500 yards away. The punk was dead and cooling before the sound of the rifle's report reached those punks who had shared the pile of rubble with him.

For two days prior to the assault, Ben had asked for the punks' surrender by voice and by leaflets dropped from planes. He had warned them repeatedly that once the assault began, surrender would not be an option. The punks who didn't believe that did not know Ben Raines very well. Ben would give almost anybody a second chance, providing they took his initial offer to surrender. If he had to chase them all over North America before they decided that surrender just might be a good idea, they suddenly found the offer withdrawn. It had been oftentimes repeated by the press—back when there was a press—that when it came to war, Ben Raines was not a nice person.

The punks had plenty of mortars and rounds for the tubes, but they were useless against snipers, for the long-distance shooters were unseen; sudden death coming out of the gray falling rain followed only the crack of a rifle heavily muffled by the lousy weather.

The Rebels sat behind piles of rubble, behind what was left of the walls of burned-out and blown-up buildings, behind long-rusted hulks of trucks and automobiles, and sipped water, ate field rations, smoked cigarettes or chewed gun and let the snipers work.

And as had been the case in wars since the beginning of time, the Rebels found puppy dogs with whom they shared their rations and dried off with a spare shirt or towel, then tucked inside their field jackets to make pets out of them. Ben had long tried to discourage that practice, but without much enthusiasm on his part or success in the field. Soldiers will do what soldiers will do. Besides, Ben loved dogs.

As he watched a Rebel—veteran of a hundred countless battles on several continents—feed and pet a small dog he'd found among the ruins, he thought of his own beloved Huskies, the dogs that Ray Brown had brutally killed back at Base Camp One. Ben stared through the silver falling rain and once more silently vowed that he and he alone would deal with Ray Brown.

Ben looked forward to beating the man to death with his fists.

"Punks beefing up their lines," Corrie said, breaking into Ben's dark thoughts.

"We have all the time in the world," Ben replied. "Let the snipers have fun."

For two hours, the Rebels rested and stayed out of the rain under whatever cover they could find and let the snipers—some of them shooting from almost three quarters of a mile away—pick their targets and bring down their quarry.

"They're pulling back," Corrie said. "They've had enough of this long-range shooting."

"How many kills?" Ben asked.

"Sixty-one confirmed. 'Bout a dozen unconfirmed."

"Let's move out."

Rebels moved north, pausing only briefly to look at the dead punks sprawled in the dirt and rubble and rain. Crews moved in right behind the main body, collecting weapons and ammunition, searching the bodies for maps of the punks' location, scraps of paper that might contain strength numbers, anything that could aid them in this fight. The bodies were then carried to a predesignated area for disposal. Usually they were buried, but in Manhattan they would be burned.

The Rebels crossed over into what was left of the financial district, pulling up and digging in as best they could on the south side of Wall Street.

The Rebels were surrounded by devastation; the few tall buildings remaining had huge holes knocked in them from Rebel artillery of a few years past. Some of the piles of rubble on the sidewalks and in the streets were higher than the Rebels' heads, and behind each pile might be an ambush waiting to be sprung.

Ben halted the slow advance when the ruins of the World Trade Center came into view. "I'm guessing that in the bowels of those buildings is where we'll find the first of our creepies, gang. Send scouts up to take the nose test."

Scouts advanced slowly toward the ruins, expecting an ambush from the punks. None came.

"Another sign that we've entered creepie territory," Ben said.

"Reports from our left and right flanks indicate the punks split up just south of our present location," Corrie said, after listening to her headset for a moment. "They avoided this area and cut east and west, then cut north two blocks from here."

"That confirms it," Ben replied.

"Scouts report a strong odor coming from the ruins," Corrie added a moment later. "Rubble had been moved and entranceways cleared."

"Oh, boy!" Jersey muttered, grimacing. "Nightmare time."

For once Cooper didn't have a smart-assed reply. To a person, the Rebels hated fighting the creepies. The smell alone was enough to cause a goat to puke.

"We halt our advance right here, people," Ben said, surprising his team. "Contact Base Camp One and have an engineer battalion gear up. I want them up here ASAP. Tell them to bring all the three-inch pipe and hose they've got. And all the heavy duty pumps.

"Pumps?" Corrie questioned.

"Pumps," Ben repeated. "We know the punks and the creeps have gas masks, so we can't use gas to drive them out. We've got the Hudson on one side and the East River on the other. Plenty of water." He laughed. "We're going to give the creepies a bath!"

Seven

"I don't think there's enough water in both rivers to fill up all the tunnels under this city," Ike radioed to Ben.

"Oh, I don't intend to fill them up, Ike. Just put about a foot or so in the tunnels."

"What good is that going to do?"

"Then we pump in a mixture of oil and gas," Ben replied with a slight smile.

"Ahhh . . ." Ike said. "Then you toss in a match, so to speak."

"Something like that."

It was the third day after the landing of the Rebels in Battery Park and the big transports had brought in the engineers and equipment from Base Camp One. The pumps were howling, as they poured hundreds of thousands of gallons of river water into the labyrinth of tunnels under the ravished city.

Rebels had moved into positions several blocks north of the World Trade Center, stretching out in a line from the

Hudson River over to the East River. Those troops to the east were just north of the South Street Seaport Historical District . . . or at least what was left of it.

Ben had ordered a very volatile mix of oil, gas, and other highly flammable chemicals. The mixture was stacked in 55-gallon drums, ready to be pumped into the tunnels.

Ben was under no illusions about this operation; there was no way he could pump water and mix into every tunnel that lay under Manhattan—that would take years. But this would give the Rebels a firmer hold on the ruins of the Big Apple and get rid of a lot of creeps without endangering Rebel lives.

"Engineers say it's getting sloppy down there, boss," Corrie reported, pointing downward.

"All right. That's enough river water. Let's give them the mix."

By three o'clock that afternoon, the 55-gallon drums were empty. "Everybody back away," Ben ordered. "I don't really know what this stuff is going to do."

"You going to let the fumes dissipate, general?" an engineer asked.

"No."

"Oh, shit!" the engineer muttered.

"When everybody is clear, drop the charges and get the hell gone," Ben ordered.

"Don't you worry about that, sir," the officer in charge of the engineers said.

Ben grinned at him. "Think it's going to go boom?"

"I certainly do, sir."

Ben and his people backed up.

Cooper asked, "Exactly, boss, how do we know the stuff isn't going to blow our boots off?"

"We don't," Ben replied. "So I would advise you to get off that old manhole cover." Ben pointed. "As you can see, the creeps have broken the welds we did a few years back.''

Jersey pulled Cooper off the manhole cover and vacated the area.

"Hit the charges," Ben ordered.

For about a ten-block area, there was first a low rumbling, then the ground roared and shook as the fumes ignited. Manhole covers went flying several hundred feet into the air. Several buildings collapsed as the earth opened up and swallowed them. Flames shot out of the street.

"Son-of-a-bitch!" the normally quiet Beth muttered.

When the grumbling and rumbling had ceased under the Rebels' boots, thick smoke began pouring out, along with the stench of burning human flesh.

"I think," Ben said, "we can forget about any creeps in this area of the city."

Just a few blocks north, the punks who waited for the Rebels looked at each other and shook their heads, letting their eyes follow the thick trail of dirty smoke that was slowly gathering over that part of the city.

"Ben Raines is sure living up to his reputation," Spooky Allen said.

"I wonder if it's too late to surrender?" another gang member questioned.

"You want to try it and find out?" Spooky asked.

The gang member shook his head.

"I didn't think so."

"Now what?" Fos Payne asked.

"I'm pullin' my people back."

"We got to stop and fight somewheres," Dave said.

"Oh, we will," Spooky assured them. "But now ain't the time or place. If this is gonna be my last go-'round with Raines, I want to make it a good one."

"Let's get with Ray Brown," another said. "Someone said he had a plan."

Spooky thought about that, then slowly shook his head. "All right. Let's get the boys and girls out of here. This place is gonna be crawling with Rebels in a minute."

"Thing that bothers me," one of Dale Jones's lieutenants said, "is this—how come it has to be our last battle with Raines? Whose idea was that, anyways?"

The leaders and co-leaders of a dozen gangs lay behind cover and looked at each other. Finally, a member of Robbie Ford's gang said, "I think it was someone . . . no, it was Ray Brown. I remember now."

"That figures," someone else said. "Ray's the one Ben Raines has really got a hard-on for."

"Why you askin?' You thinkin' 'bout surrendrin'?"

"I might be. Beats dyin', don't it?"

"And once we surrender, then what?"

Many of the others had drifted away, including Spooky, leaving only a handful of gang leaders and members.

"Raines ain't gonna shoot us down in cold blood," a gang members said. "Lots of folks think the Rebels do that, but we all know different. If we was to walk out with our hands raised, we'd live. We ain't had no NBA testin' done on us—"

"DNA," someone corrected.

"Whatever. Most of us hidin' out in this pile of rocks ain't even been fingerprinted or had our pitcher took. Look, people, I ain't real anxious to die. I figure I could live straight if I tried. An' I'd kinda like to try."

"Me too. So let's pass the word around, real quiet-like, you know? We don't want to get shot by our own people for talkin' 'bout this. And some of them would do it, too."

"Damn sure would. Most of them is known to the Rebels; they ain't got shit to lose, one way or the other."

"Pass the word. We'll talk more tomorrow."

* * *

The morning after the underground explosions, the Rebels moved north without resistance for several blocks. They now stretched out, running west to east, from the Washington Market Park over to what was left of the NYC Police Headquarters building.

Not one shot was fired from either side that morning.

"They can't keep moving back forever," Cooper remarked during a rest break. Even though the Rebels had advanced several blocks, it was still very slow and nerve-wracking work: advance a few feet, hunker down behind cover and wait for a few moments, then dart forward a few more feet, all the time expecting a sniper's bullet to come screaming at them. "They have to stand and fight somewhere, sometime."

The sky was a clear cloudless blue and the temperature warm.

"Something weird is going on," Jersey replied. She was sharing the same small bit of cover with Cooper. Although the two argued and bickered and groused and bitched and picked at each other, they were as close as brother and sister. Scratch one and both felt it.

"Something weird is always going on in your head, Jersey. You want to explain what it is this time?"

"Almost funny, Coop. Ha. How the hell do I know what it is? I just think something weird is going to happen, that's all."

"Hey, Corrie!" Coop called. "You hear anything from the scouts?"

"Nothing," she returned the call. "They're back and said it's deserted for two blocks ahead."

"Let's go," Ben said, rising to his knees. "One more block and then we knock off for lunch."

"General Ben!" Anna said, peering through binoculars. "Someone is waving a white flag about two, three blocks ahead."

Beth looked up from an old map of the city. "That would be Foley Street, I think."

"I'm getting reports from all units," Corrie said. "White flags are showing up all over the place. Somebody over west of us is waving an old pair of longjohns. They need washing," she added drily.

Beth was handling the portable CB scanner and she shook her head. "Nothing coming over any of the forty channels."

"They might be afraid to broadcast," Ben said. "Many of the gang leaders know we'll hang them on the spot for past crimes. Those are the ones who have nothing to lose and will fight to the death."

"Scouts are out," Corrie said.

"Tell them to stay a full block away from the flag-wavers," Ben ordered. "This could be a trap."

"Units to the west report punks are surrendering en masse," Corrie said.

Before Ben could respond, Corrie added, "The scouts are reporting that the punks say their own people will kill them if we don't accept their surrender pretty damn fast. Their words, boss."

"Tell the scouts to wave the punks in. Tell them to keep their hands over their heads. If they drop their hands, they get a bullet."

All across the southern end of the ruins of Manhattan, the dregs of society began surrendering to Raines's Rebels. Within an hour, almost a thousand punks had turned themselves in, throwing their fate on the doorstep of Ben Raines, all of them doing so with no small amount of trepidation, for they knew that with just a nod of his head or a simple hand gesture, Ben could hang them—and would, if they gave him the slightest excuse.

The punks were searched, then marched back half a dozen blocks to a secure area and lined up, ten deep, in the littered street, crowded in close due to the lack of space.

Ben walked slowly down the line, eyeballing those who would meet his hard gaze. After a moment, he sighed and shook his head. "Get them out of here and across the river to Ike. We're still within mortar range of the gangs and it would be like them to kill any of their own who surrendered."

"Oh, they would, General Raines!" one gang member blurted. "They sure would."

Ben fixed him with a hard look and under the young man's dirty face, he visibly paled.

Ben walked away a few yards, his team with him. "They didn't steal any of our laser range-finders, boss," Beth reminded Ben. "Or our latest sights."

The hand-held laser range-finder could accurately range up to 10,000 meters, thus enabling the mortar crews to direct-fire at a target without first firing ranging rounds. With the new sights, developed by Rebel scientists, the 60mm mortar had an accuracy of plus or minus ten meters at extreme ranges.

"They probably wouldn't have been able to understand how they worked anyway," Ben muttered. He cleared his throat and said, "Get me Ike on the horn, Corrie. I've got to warn him what's coming his way and we've got to talk about what to do with them."

"What *are* you going to do with them, Ben?" the question came from behind him.

Ben turned and looked at Doctor Chase. He sighed. "Lamar, what the hell are you doing away from your hospital complex? This is very close to the front."

"I know where I am, Raines. The question still begs an answer—what are you going to do with the prisoners?"

"I don't know, Lamar. But I am certainly open for any and all suggestions."

"Well, first of all they have to be showered and fumigated, then given physicals. We'll test for TB and so forth." He smiled. "Beyond that, I don't have the vaguest idea what to do with them."

"You're a lot of help, Lamar."

"Anytime, Raines."

"All right, Corrie. Have our people march them down to the docks. You have Ike on the horn?"

"His CO says he's momentarily out of pocket."

"That means he's up with his grunts. The old goat."

"You're a fine one to talk about old goats, Raines," Lamar said, not about to let an opening like that pass.

"I'm in better shape than Ike," Ben came right back. "Hell, why don't you put him on a diet, Lamar? He's 50 pounds overweight."

"Twenty-five pounds, Raines. I keep an eye on him." Chase winked at Anna, standing a few feet away. "Just as I do with all you doddering old warriors."

"Screw you, Lamar!"

Anna laughed.

"You're not my type, Raines. See you." The chief of medicine walked over to a group of Rebels guarding the prisoners and chatted with them for a moment.

Ben turned away just as his ears picked up a familiar sound. "Mortars!" he shouted. "Incoming! Hit the deck, people!"

The words had just left his mouth when the first round struck, landing right in the middle of the prisoners. The screaming of the wounded joined the fluttering of incoming mortar rounds.

Ben jumped for cover, sliding under the rusted hulk of an old car. "Damn set-up," he muttered. "They knew about the surrender and set up mortar crews and waited us out. Son-of-a-bitch!"

Anna squirmed under the car with him. "We got had, General Ben," she said, speaking between exploding rounds, and they were coming in hot and heavy.

"We sure did, kid." He looked at the clearing where the prisoners had been lined up. He guessed over a hundred dead and at least that many wounded littered the street. But there was nothing he could do about the dead, dying, and wounded.

Ben pulled Anna close to him. "There will be a break in the incoming, Anna. Get ready for it and when it comes, make a dash for that building over there—" he cut his eyes, "—and join the team."

"But what about you, General Ben?"

"Don't argue with me, Anna. Just do it. Now slide toward the edge of the cover."

The rhythm of the enemy mortar crews was broken as the Rebels began returning the mortar fire. "Go, Anna! Now!"

Anna scooted out from cover and scampered for the safety of the building. Ben watched her disappear into the old storefront and smiled. He shifted his gaze toward the north and worked his way out of the cover, cussing as his right canteen hung briefly on something. He worked his way clear and scrambled for an open doorway, just making it before the incoming began dropping in.

Ben settled in, his back to a wall, his long legs stretched out in front of him, and took a sip of water. He had just slid the canteen back into the holder when what seemed like half a dozen mortar rounds struck the old building in rapid succession, the concussion knocking his helmet off his head. The entire front of the building collapsed all around him; several bricks bounced off his head.

Ben was slammed into unconsciousness, half buried under a mound of debris.

Eight

Ben slowly came to his senses in a world of darkness and pain. His head pounded fiercely and his back and shoulders and arms ached from being struck by falling bricks and other debris.

He briefly wondered where he was, then the memories of the mortar attack came rushing back. He wondered if his team had made it out? How many Rebels had been killed in the attack?

Ben tried to move his legs and found them pinned solidly by bricks and beams and other junk. His arms were free and he looked at his watch. Miraculously, it had remained intact. It was 1800 hours. He had been out all afternoon. It was full dark outside. Slowly he began to work to free himself, careful to make as little noise as possible, for he could hear only silence from the outside and had a pretty good idea his people had been overrun by the punks. As he worked, the stiffness and some of the soreness left his arms. But his head still throbbed.

After a few moments of work, Ben freed his legs. Before attempting to stand, he carefully moved his legs to check for broken bones. His legs were numb from being pinned for so long, but worked just fine. He felt around in the darkness for his rifle and found it several yards away . . . smashed. A beam had fallen directly on the M-16. But he still had his sidearm belted around his waist. He found his helmet, the top crushed by a falling beam.

Ben checked his canteens; one was full and the other nearly full. He took a small sip of water then rose carefully to his boots and began picking his way soundlessly through the shattered store. He stopped abruptly when the toe of his boot touched a lifeless, stiffening form.

Ben knelt down and inspected the body. It was a Rebel. The man had been shot in the throat and face and apparently had fallen into the open doorway of the store.

Ben removed the man's web belt and battle harness and felt around for a weapon. Found it—a CAR. He took the dead man's magazine pouch, which held six full 30-round mags and moved slowly toward the open door. He almost stumbled and fell over another dead body which lay just off the littered sidewalk. The whiteness of naked flesh caught his eyes in the almost nonexistent light. A Rebel. The body had been stripped of everything except his underwear.

We took a real beating this day, Ben thought.

He backed up until he touched the storefront and stood for a moment, getting his bearings and gathering his thoughts. To his right, which would be south, about two blocks away, he could see the flickering glow of dozens of small campfires. He could hear the faint sounds of hollering and laughing. He knew instantly the campfires did not have Rebels around them. No Rebel would be that stupid.

Under cover of the mortar attack, coming in right behind it, the punks assaulted our positions, Ben concluded. Gutsy move on their part. And they probably shoved us right off Manhattan.

Shit!

So if I can't go south, Ben thought . . .

He began moving out slowly and carefully, staying on the littered sidewalks as much as possible, making his way west. He inspected each body he found. They had all been stripped down to their underwear. Using a tiny penlight that each Rebel carried, but using it sparingly to save the batteries, Ben shone the tiny beam of light into each store opening, door or shop window. Two blocks from where he'd lain unconscious, Ben found another Rebel. The man had crawled into the store, behind an overturned counter. Ben spotted one boot sticking out.

Ben took the man's full magazine pouch and pack, which contained several grenades and three days' supply of rations, first aid kit, and several other items of survival, and added those to his own small supply.

He could not find the dead man's rifle, but he now had a dozen full 30-round mags for his 5.56 CAR. Three Beretta sidearms with nine full 15-round mags. Nine grenades. Ground sheet and blanket. Nine days' supply of food in the form of those damnable hi-energy bars dreamed up by the lab boys and girls. They tasted like shit smelled but would keep a person reasonably full and alive, if not happy. He had six canteens of water, his own long-bladed and very sharp knife, and was wearing a just broken-in pair of boots.

He had matches and extra batteries for his flashlight and three small plastic bottles of water purification tabs. He had extra socks (the ones found on the first dead Rebel were too small for him). He could not find an extra helmet, but he had a first aid kit.

None of the dead Rebels had carried a walkie-talkie.

Ben sat and rested for a time, gathering his strength

and washing down two aspirin with a long, much-needed drink of water.

Ben silently cursed when he heard the scurrying of dozens of tiny feet above him and in the rooms behind where he sat on the dirty floor. The rats were coming to feed, but there was nothing he could do about it. He didn't like the idea of the rats eating on dead Rebels, but he didn't blame the large rodents. Just as he was struggling to stay alive, so too were they.

He made up his mind to move west, to the waterfront, and try to somehow signal his people on the Jersey side. Tomorrow he would look for a broken piece of mirror to use to send some Morse in the afternoon when the sun was in the west. The trick would be to get over to the waterfront and stay alive in the process.

He ate one of his candy bars and tried not to dwell on how bad it tasted. But he had to admit, reluctantly, although he would never tell Doctor Chase, he did feel better after he'd eaten.

He didn't need a map to tell him where he was. When the attack came they'd been holding the prisoners in the block just south of City Hall Park, in what used to be called Park Row. Pace University would be due east of his location and the old Woolworth Building due west. He might try for the ruins of the old Woolworth Building that night. He tried to remember if Rebel artillery had brought it down years back, but couldn't recall.

Ben looked all around him, then stood for a moment, listening. He could hear nothing. Blocks south, the campfires of the punks still winked at him. Ben turned and walked away, picking his way carefully through the debris.

"Settle down!" Ike roared at the gathering of batt coms who had flown in when word of Ben's disappearance had been verified. "We've all been through this before. And you all know what Ben has said about it—don't jeopardize a lot of Rebel lives coming after him. If Ben has been taken prisoner, the punks will try to buy their way out of this jam with him. If they don't contact us within 48 hours . . ." He sighed. "Well, then we'll have to assume the worst."

"We all knew something like this could happen at any time," Ben's son Buddy said, standing up. "Father took terrible chances but loved every minute of it. He lived for combat. But he also told both Tina and me, more than once, that his odds for catching a bullet were just as high as anyone else's, and if that happened, the movement had to go on. Personally, I don't believe he's dead. He might be captured or wounded, but I don't believe he's dead."

Ike cut his eyes to Doctor Chase. "Ben's team, Lamar?"

"They'll all recover. Their wounds were numerous, but none of them life-threatening. I'll repeat this for any who missed it before—Anna said the last time she saw Ben, he was entering what was left of an old building. Then the mortars really started coming down thick and fast. She said the building took about half a dozen hits. That's when she got hit, one bullet striking her helmet and knocking her unconscious. The next thing she remembers, she was crossing the Hudson. What I would really like to know is, what happened?"

"We grossly underestimated the strength of the gangs," Ike replied. "And more importantly, their ability to fight and to plan. We now know they are massing in three different locations outside this area. If we don't stop them now, we'll be the ones in a box. Not a very secure box, one that we could punch through almost at will, but it's a situation we have to deal with . . . ah, before we can once more tackle Manhattan."

There was a low grumble of discontent from the ranks of the batt coms.

"Be quiet!" Ike shouted, holding up a sheet of paper. "Those are Ben's orders. Right here!" He waved the sheet of paper. "You all know that Ben spells out every contingency before a battle. Well, here it is. And I'm not about to go against his orders. Now just settle down. Georgi, have your people start laying out mines in the southernmost part of your section, then back up and wait. All we can do is contain the gangs in Manhattan until we deal with the new fronts."

The Russian growled something in reply but reluctantly nodded in understanding.

"The rest of you have your orders," Ike finished. "Prepare to move out. Dismissed."

Ben was hunkered down behind a wall of rubble, waiting for a large patrol of punks to pass by. It was the tenth patrol he'd seen since leaving his original position . . . four blocks back.

"Damn shore kicked their asses this day," one punk said, then laughed. "Them Rebels ain't much, you ask me."

"And we got enough food and medicine and guns and ammo to last us for a long, long time," another said. "Maybe even long enough for us to hold out until the Rebels give up and move on."

When pigs fly, Ben thought.

"An' enough prime new pussy to las' us for a long, long time," another said. "If our leaders will ever get done pumpin' and hunchin' an' wallerin' it out."

"Ah, hell, Royal. Pussy bein' what it is, that snatch'll snap right back and tighten up. We'll get our turn."

"Nice thing about it all—" Ben caught the words from the last man in the patrol as they passed "—is the Rebs done us a favor by killin' off a bunch of them stinkin' creeps.''

"That's about the only favor them assholes ever done for us," another said.

The patrol rounded a corner and was gone.

Killed the men and took the women prisoner, Ben thought. *Well now. I don't know what I can do about that little situation, but I can damn sure raise some hell with the punks.*

All thoughts of escape from Manhattan left Ben as he crouched behind the pile of rubble. He did not realize it, but his lips had curved back in something that resembled a snarl.

Ben Raines, the ol' curly wolf of the Rebels, was about to go on the prowl.

Ben began once more working his way toward the west. But he wasn't as interested in reaching the waterfront as he was in reaching a couple of gang members who might be taking an evening stroll among the ruins.

If he found a couple, he could guarantee them it would be the last stroll they would ever take.

Before he had gone half a block, Ben almost stepped on an object lying amid the rubble. He knelt down. It was an old piece of half-inch lead pipe, about two feet long. Ben smiled and picked it up, hefting the pipe. It would make a dandy shillelagh to bounce off someone's noggin.

And he didn't have to worry about cracking the skull of a friendly. On this terrain, there *were* no friendlies.

Ben heard a low murmuring of voices and stepped back into the darkness of a building stoop and waited.

Two voices. Two men. Ben smiled as their words grew louder, filled with ugliness and profanity. When they reached his position, he stepped out and busted the closest one across the forehead with the heavy pipe, cracking the man's skull. The punk dropped as if hit with a pile-driver.

"What the hell!" the second one managed to say.

Ben stopped all further conversation by slamming the lead pipe against the side of the punk's head. He fell in a heap on the littered sidewalk.

Ben had hit a gold mine. One of the men was carrying a full medic's pack, and the other was carrying a rucksack filled with grenades. Both were carrying Rebel M-16s, with full magazine pouches and Rebel web belts with two canteens.

The first man Ben had hit died while Ben was removing the web belt. The second was still alive, but bleeding from the nose, mouth, and ears. Ben dragged both of them into a building and left them.

Ben now had one hell of a heavy load, actually too much of a load for him. The canteens of water alone probably weighed 25 pounds. But he managed to go two more blocks before deciding he had to stash some of the gear. He hid the two M-16s, four of the canteens and some of the ammo in the ruins of a building and moved on, his load much lighter.

Two more blocks, and he ran into a line of punks. Somebody in the leadership was getting smart, for they had stretched the punks out in a line running south to north, effectively cutting off Ben's access to the waterfront. Every street and alley was blocked, and the punks were digging in for a long stay, fortifying every position.

"Interesting," Ben muttered to the night. "Why would they be doing that now?"

He thought about that for a moment, then concluded that the gang leaders suspected some Rebels had escaped the mortar attack, but had not been evac-ed from Manhattan. They were attempting to block as many avenues of escape as possible . . . and doing a pretty good job of it.

Ben cut back east and made his way to what he felt sure was Broadway. A plan was taking shape in his mind.

He might be blocked from escape, but he sure as hell

wasn't blocked from taking action. But he couldn't just jump in and start shooting. That would be signing his own death warrant. He had to hole up somewhere out of sight and formulate a plan of attack.

It was doubtful that the two punks he'd killed would be missed. But when he started head-hunting in earnest, the leaders of the gangs would know they had a situation and come looking for the troublemaker.

That meant he must behave like a bunny rabbit and have several exit holes.

He had carefully marked on his map the location of the cache of weapons, ammo, and water. He did not want to leave food, for he knew the rats would find that. A rat might actually enjoy Chase's hi-energy bars.

Nine

Gangs of thugs that had been hiding out in small groups all over the northeast massed and attacked Rebel positions. Ike called in every battalion in the Rebel army. But until reinforcements arrived, he could not worry about whether Ben was dead or alive in the ruins of Manhattan; he had a fight for survival on his hands.

Ben knew nothing of this. He had no radio and was cut off from the outside world. On the day he awakened in the gray light of his first early morning of isolation, he was hungry, thirsty, pissed off, and ached all over from bruises the falling debris had inflicted on his body.

Ben ate half of a hi-energy bar and thought longingly of bacon and eggs, home fries, biscuits and oatmeal and a pot of coffee.

He washed down a couple of aspirin with sips of tepid water and stood up, suppressing a groan as his battered body protested the movement.

He walked over to what used be a window on the second

floor of the building and looked out. He could see smoke from hundreds of cook fires, some of the smoke distressingly close to his position.

Ben packed up his gear and struggled into the pack, then picked up his CAR and his lead pipe club and carefully made his way down the rickety stairs to the ground floor. Just as his boots touched the floor, he froze as a man's voice reached him. The man appeared to be muttering to himself.

Jesus! Ben thought. *It's a good thing I'm not a restless sleeper or I'd be dead.*

The man walked into view and in the gloom of the old building, Ben could see that he was armed with an AK-47 and wearing a blue bandanna tied around his head. Ben wondered if those were gang colors, for the two men he'd bashed on the head hours before had been wearing the same color bandannas.

The man stepped closer and Ben whacked him on the noggin. The punk dropped unconscious to the floor, losing his grip on the AK. The AK bounced and clattered to the floor.

"Hey, Willie!" The shout came from the outside. "What's the matter, boy? Did you trip over your dick?"

Ben slung his CAR, shoved the lead pipe behind his web belt, and picked up the AK, checking it. He tore the ammo pouch off the man and slung it over one shoulder, straightening up just as the doorway filled with men.

"Goddammit!" one of the punks yelled, the sight before him registering in his brain.

The gang member didn't have long to think about it. Ben leveled the AK and pulled the trigger, clearing the archway of all living things.

Ben whirled around and was out the back door and in the alley before the echoing of the gunfire had died away. He ran up the alley and ducked into another building, silently hoping the building's other entrances and exits weren't blocked by debris.

In the semi-darkness of the building, a man rose up from dirty blankets and said, "What the hell's going on?"

Ben butt-stroked him under the chin, scooped up a rucksack by the man's rifle, and kept on running. He had no idea what was in the canvas rucksack, but hoped it was something he could use. The man fell back in his blankets for an additional and totally unexpected snooze.

Ben cut to his left and emerged in a courtyard between buildings. He cut to his right and stepped into the gloom and ruins of another building, then paused for a few seconds to catch his breath and look into the heavy rucksack. It was filled with grenades.

"The gods of war must be smiling on me this day," Ben muttered. He heard a shout, followed by running feet. Several punks had entered the courtyard. They paused, looking all around, trying to determine who, or what, was causing all the commotion.

Ben popped the pin on the grenade and chucked it, the mini-bomb landing right in the middle of the knot of punks.

Ben didn't wait around to see what carnage he caused; he turned and ran toward a stream of dim light pouring through a blasted hole in the wall. He could see empty street beyond that. He wished he had some thin black wire, and some time, so he could rig up booby traps for the unwashed.

He also wished for a pot of coffee.

His wishing abruptly vanished as a huge woman stepped in front of him. The woman was not fat, just big. About six feet tall and a good two hundred pounds.

"Who the fuck are you?" the woman asked, her extremely bad breath fouling the air. Ben also caught a whiff of body odor that would stop a stampeding ox.

"Jesus, lady," he said. "Did your mother forget to introduce you to soap and water?"

"Haw!" the near-amazon said.

Ben kissed her with the butt of the AK and the big woman hit the floor. "I really would like to stay and continue this sparkling conversation, lady, but I have pressing matters elsewhere," Ben muttered.

The big woman farted in her unconsciousness, and that put wings on Ben's boots. He headed for the light and, he hoped, a breath of fresh air.

What he got, standing in the light of the side street, was a half dozen punks. Ben ran into them, knocking several off their feet and sprawling in the dirty alley.

Ben recovered first, not due to any skill on his part—he just ran into a wall that stopped his forward motion. He spun around and leveled the AK, holding the trigger back and spraying the lead.

When the magazine emptied, Ben didn't wait to see how many gang members were out of action permanently; he just took off running into the next building, into an alley, into the next building, changing magazines on the trot. His face was throbbing from the impact against the brick wall and he could feel the blood trickling down his face from several cuts.

He exited that building and found himself in a brick-walled courtyard of some sort with no way out.

"Shit!" Ben said, and entered the building he'd just exited. This time he headed, he hoped, for the front of the building and the street, but he couldn't be sure—his sense of direction was all screwed up from the twisting and turning he'd done.

Ben slowed when he saw the blown-out shop windows pouring light into the gloom of the interior. Squatting in the stoop of the doorway for a moment, he caught his breath and listened.

All of the shouting seemed to be coming from his right, several blocks down. He did some fast figuring. He must have traveled, since the evening before, about eight or ten blocks north and two or three blocks west. He pulled out his map and studied it. He was on West Broadway, and the street directly to his left was Canal.

But why no punks in this area? Why hadn't they pursued him?

He thought about that for a moment.

Then the answer came to him.

Night People.

He was in creepie territory.

"Oh, hell!" Ben muttered.

He slowly rose to his boots and looked behind him. Nothing there but rubble. He stepped out onto the sidewalk and turned to his left, jogging up the street. If his calculations were correct, he was just south of the SoHo historical district—smack in the middle of creepie country.

Not a very comfortable situation.

He crossed Canal and ducked into the ruins of a building. The familiar smell assailed his nostrils. Grimacing, Ben backed out of that building, turned to his left, and kept walking for several blocks. He saw no punks but smelled plenty of creeps.

He stopped to rest, for his head still throbbed slightly and his body ached form the pounding of the bricks. Once more, he consulted his map. Useless, for the map didn't list all the smaller streets. Ben wasn't sure where he was.

Rested, he continued on north, moving cautiously. After several blocks, the smell of creepies faded and Ben guessed he was once more in punk territory. He slipped into a building and carefully inspected the ground floor, the only floor that remained. It was clear of punks and there was no telltale odor of creeps. Ben sat down on the floor, took a sip of water, rolled a cigarette, and pondered his situation, which was not good, no matter from which side he mentally approached it.

He was holding the unlit cigarette in one hand, lighter in another, when a voice behind him said, "You're no punk, mister. I can tell that much. But that doesn't mean you're not the enemy. You just sit still and don't move. You move, and I'll kill you."

A woman's voice. Not old, not young. "Do I have your permission to light this cigarette?" Ben asked.

"Yeah. I guess so. But do it slowly."

Ben lit up. "I'm going to put this lighter back in my pocket—okay?"

"All right."

The voice moved around to one side and Ben cut his eyes, following her movement. His eyes widened at the sight. A very attractive lady stood holding an M-16, and Ben had no doubt she knew how to use it—and would. Black hair cut short, unreadable dark eyes. Maybe five feet, four inches tall. Jeans that fit her very snugly and a man's shirt that was too large for her. Boots that had seen better days.

Ben guessed her age at about thirty.

"You a Rebel?" the woman asked.

"Yes."

"Aren't you kinda old for a Rebel?"

Ben laughed and the woman's eyes narrowed. "There are those in my command who would certainly agree with you, lady. You have a name?"

"Judy."

"I'm Ben Raines."

"You're a liar, mister! Ben Raines runs a whole country down south. Probably lives in a big mansion with servants and all that."

Ben chuckled. "Actually, my house is rather average. And I have no servants. Just a person who comes in once a week and cleans up—when I'm home, that is, which isn't often."

"You got some I.D.?" She moved closer.

"I sure do. Dog tags around my neck."

"Take them off and toss them to me."

Ben slipped the tags off his neck and tossed them on the floor about two feet in front of the woman. When she bent down to retrieve the tags, Ben jerked the rifle out of her hands and shoved her backward. She landed on her butt on the floor, spitting like a cat.

"Now just calm down," Ben told her, grabbing up his dog tags and slipping them around his neck. He moved back a comfortable distance and sat down on an old wooden box. "My name really is Ben Raines. The punks hit us with a surprise attack yesterday. I got cut off from my team and pinned down in a building. Knocked out. I came to about 1800 hours last evening and have been dodging punks even since." He smiled. "And killing a few whenever possible."

The woman slowly nodded. She pulled herself up to a sitting position, her back against what was left of a counter showcase. "How'd you get through the Uglies south of here?"

"The Uglies?"

"Most people outside of the zone call them Night People."

"Manhattan is the zone, I presume?"

"Yes."

"I walked through the creeps' territory. But did so very cautiously when I started smelling the bastards."

She smiled, and her teeth were startlingly white against her face. "They do stink, don't they?"

"You have a last name?"

"Miller. When my husband got killed several years ago, I went back to my maiden name."

Ben held up the M-16, hesitated for a few seconds, then tossed the weapon to her.

She caught it deftly. "Thanks. You really are Ben Raines?"

"In person. And wondering how the hell to get off this piece of real estate."

She laughed softly. "Forget it, General Raines. As soon as the punks launched their attack on you people 'way south of here, they began shifting people around. There are patrols everywhere. I couldn't get back to my people because of the patrols."

"Your people?"

"Yes. We hold Central Park and a few blocks all around the area. We have just under two hundred people . . . men, women, and children."

Ben dug in his pack for one of the hi-energy bars and tossed it to her. "They don't taste very good, but they're packed with all sorts of stuff the doctors say we need to stay alive."

Judy tore off the wrapper and took a bite. "Not bad," she said. "You ever eaten rat, general?"

"Call me Ben. No, I've been spared that."

"We have. Gulls, pigeons, you name it. We won't eat dogs or cats. We draw the line at that. But compared to some of the things we had to eat when we first banded together, this is great."

"How have you managed to keep the punks and the creepies out of your area?"

"We booby-trapped it. We had an ex-army man with us for several years who was some sort of guerrilla fighter. He showed us all about man-trapping and so forth."

"What happened to him?"

"He was killed by the punks just about a year ago. He went out on patrol with a couple of others and the punks ambushed them. Only one made it back and he died the next day."

"You going to invite me to your fort?" Ben asked with a smile.

She looked at him for a moment, then nodded. "Sure. But we can't go during the day, it's too risky. It's jumping with punks out there."

"I'm sure you know best."

"You people have radios?"

"Oh, yes. CBs."

"That'll work. I've got to get in touch with my people and tell them to hold off shelling the city until we can get you and your bunch out of here."

"We've wanted to make a run for it for some time. Head down south to the SUSA." She sighed. "But that's such a long way. And we've got some elderly with us that . . . well, I don't know if they could stand the trip."

"We'll get you out of these ruins, Judy. Are there any more groups like yours?"

She shook her head. "No. There used to be dozens of little groups of survivors scattered about. Some made it out, most were killed by the punks or the uglies."

"You're sure? For when I turn my people loose, it's going to get real grim in a hurry."

"Yes. I'm sure."

"How about boats, Judy?"

She smiled and shook her head. "Not a chance, general . . . I mean, Ben. And believe me, we've looked."

"You people must have moved into the ruins just after we pulled out, several years ago?"

She shrugged. "I suppose so. We're from all over. We've just got one thing in common."

"Oh?"

"Yes. Staying alive."

Ten

Several times that day, punk patrols walked past the building where Ben and Judy were hiding. Once a man stuck his head inside, looked around for a few seconds, then left.

"How many punks on this rock?" Ben asked.

"Thousands. We estimated five or six thousand up until about six months ago. Then they really started pouring in."

"That's our fault, Judy. We put them on the run and began herding them in this direction."

"And you're going to wipe them out?"

"Right now to the last person, if they don't surrender."

"And you'll let us become a part of the SUSA?"

"Sure. Once we're off this rock, I'll call in for transports and fly you and your people down south." He smiled. "What'd you do before the Great War?"

"I was just out of college. A teacher. One morning I

woke up and . . . everything was topsy-turvy. You know what I mean?''

"Yes. I know exactly what you mean.''

"My dad used to read your Western books, Ben. He had a whole collection of them.''

Ben chuckled. "Where was home?''

"Really not that far from here. Massachusetts. Little town on the Cape. Real pretty place.''

"No desire to go back and live there?''

"Not really.'' She laughed softly. "I was a real go-getter activist before the Great War. What you used to call in your books a hanky-stomping liberal. I'm afraid I could never fit in again back in that little town.''

"It's amazing how many converts I've run into since everything collapsed.''

She smiled. "I'm sure about that. Oh, I sobbed for the poor criminals in prison because of abusive childhoods. I wept for the poor misunderstood wretches imprisoned because of a racist society. I don't think you would have liked me very much back then, Ben.''

"Oh, I probably would have just laughed at you.''

Her smile faded. "Not too much to laugh about now, though, is there?''

"Not in this part of the country.''

"Down in the SUSA?''

"Last report I got said we were getting back to normal. At least as normal as things can get at this time.''

"There is nothing normal around here.''

Judy and Ben talked of many things during the long afternoon. Ben noticed that she talked very little of her past, and evaded mosts questions he posed about it.

She was educated, Ben knew that after speaking with her for only a few minutes. She had come from an upper middle class family where both parents worked. She had a brother and a sister, but had no idea what had happened to them. And that was it. Whenever Ben tried to shift the conversation back to her, she skillfully moved it right back to the SUSA, the Rebels, Ben's writing career, his travels, or any one of a dozen other areas.

He did not believe the woman was lying to him, pretending to be what she was not, but her past was private, and she was determined to keep it that way.

Perhaps, Ben concluded, events had been so traumatic she had blocked out the terrible memories. Ben had known of people who had done that. Jersey had practically no memory of her past as a child.

When the afternoon began casting long shadows among the ruins, Ben got to his feet and stretched some of the stiffness out of his muscles and joints. His head had stopped its throbbing, and considering the situation, he felt pretty good.

"You ready to travel, Judy?"

She stood up and stretched. "I guess so. But this is the part I hate."

"Why so?"

"We seldom lose people going out of our area. It's always coming back."

"They get careless and anxious. We won't do either." Her words had triggered a silent alarm bell in Ben's head. And the bell rang out one word: informant. The punks or the creeps, probably the former, had a plant among Judy's people. As she was gathering her meager possessions, Ben asked, "How long has this been going on?"

"What do you mean?"

"Your losing people on the way back in."

"Oh . . . about a year. Why?"

"Just curious, that's all. You ready?"

"Yes. Let's go. Stay behind me, Ben. Especially when we get close. Just remember what I told you about the booby traps."

Ben held up a hand. "Just hold on for a minute. This

ex-army man you had with you . . . was he the first to get killed coming back in?''

''Ah . . . as a matter of fact, he was. What are you getting at, Ben?''

''And how many team leaders or whatever you call them have been killed since?''

''Several.''

''You've got an informer in your ranks, Judy.''

She looked at him for a moment, her eyes narrowing in suspicious thought, then sat back down on the old packing crate. She nodded. ''Yeah. Only we never thought of that,'' she said softly. ''Everyone is so close. We all count on each other. It's like a big family.''

''Except this family has a bad seed among the relatives. Come on. Let's go.''

It was almost full dark when the two of them stepped out of the building, exiting the back way. Judy was carrying part of Ben's original load, and the traveling now was much easier. The one thing Ben had deliberately not asked her was why she was out by herself, lone-wolfing it in the middle of bogie country. He had hoped she would tell him, but she had not.

She stopped at the edge of the street and looked up at Ben. ''In case you're wondering, and you probably are, Jim—that was the ex-soldier's name—and I were lovers. We were going to be married if or when we got to a safe locale. He was about twenty years older than me, but I didn't care about that. Since his death, I haven't cared much about anything, except killing punks. That's why I go out by myself into the zone. To kill punks.''

''I have been wondering. Well, that's a pretty good reason, Judy.''

''You don't think I'm nuts for doing that?''

''Not at all. Revenge is something I understand perfectly well.''

''You've lost a loved one in this war?''

"Yes. Several years ago. A long way from here."

"Then you understand what drives me?"

"Oh, yes. I sure do."

"Some of the others in the group think I'm crazy."

Ben chuckled. "I know that feeling too, Judy. Believe it or not, I like to lone-wolf it."

She smiled. "I think we'll get along, Ben Raines."

"I'm sure of it."

They walked on into the gathering night.

They had not gone a block before Ben heard the faint murmur of voices and jerked Judy into what was left of an old building. The voices grew louder, and both knew it was no small group of punks.

"Too many for us this far away from home," Ben whispered, his mouth close to her ear.

She nodded in agreement, her hair brushing gently on the side of his face.

It was a temptation for the both of them; a real struggle to keep from blasting the night and clearing the street of crud. But they pulled back into the shadows and were still until the 25 or so men and women had passed and could no longer be heard.

"I wanted to kill them all," Judy whispered.

"So did I. But that would have been suicide for us. Come on, let's go."

Two blocks later, both of them knew that getting to Central Park was going to be a real challenge. Everywhere they looked there were groups of punks.

"What's going on?" Ben whispered. "Is it always this way?"

"No. They're probably looking for me. I told my people I'd be back tonight. This proves you're right about there being an informer in our bunch." She cursed very softly but very heatedly for a moment. "We're going to have to go the long way to get out of the zone. But even then, it's going to be risky."

"You're leading this parade, Judy."

It was long hours later when Judy halted them at the edge of Ninth Avenue and West 60th Street. It had taken them almost an hour to thread their way through a maze of booby traps. "Almost home," she said, weariness evident in her voice. She softly whistled three times, then paused and whistled three more times.

Somewhere in the darkness, someone answered with two whistles.

"Two of us coming in," she called.

"Two of you?" a man's voice called.

"Me and General Ben Raines!"

"Good God Almighty. Come on."

"We change the sign and countersign every time somebody goes out," Judy told Ben as they walked toward the north side of Columbus Circle. "Sometimes it's a lip whistle, sometimes a word, sometimes a tin whistle."

A man stepped out of the shadows and said, "Welcome back, Judy. We were getting worried."

"This is General Raines, Greg."

"My God, but it's good to see you, general," Greg said, grabbing and pumping Ben's hand. "We knew your people were here, of course, but never dreamed you were among them."

A woman stepped up and hugged Judy. "Ben, this is Marie. Marie, General Ben Raines."

Then there were people all around them, and the names were coming so fast Ben knew he would not remember a fraction of them.

"Let's get you people inside," Greg said. "God, you both must be worn out."

"Just get me to a radio," Ben said. "I've got to talk to my people before they start shelling this place." He smiled. "And how would you folks like some real coffee?"

"Real coffee, general?" a woman Ben remembered

being introduced as Babe asked. "My God, sir! I've forgotten what that tastes like."

"Get me to a radio and you'll have coffee for lunch."

Since this was non-scrambled voice, Ben used one of the simplest but oldest codes the Rebels had. It was a mishmash of voice codes, some of them probably concocted by children back when the world was whole. The days of the week were easy: today was January, Monday was February, Tuesday was March, and so on. Then Ben used a mixture of pig latin and carnival talk to finish up his brief transmission. He opened a map, pointed to an area in the park, and looked at Judy and Greg, the only two people he had allowed to be present while making his radio contact. "We'll start getting supplies in about one hour. No time for rest. Let's go over to this area and get ready to receive."

Greg smiled. "You don't waste much time, do you, general?"

"Oh, I've just gotten started, Greg. Wait until I really get rolling."

The planes came in all at once and low, dropping the supplies Ben had requested, and then they were gone, catching the gangs by surprise. The drop was made at the southern end of the park, between the zoo and the lake. The supplies landed on target.

The hold-outs in the park worked quickly and within minutes, the carefully packed crates had been unhooked from their harnesses and carried off.

The first thing Ben did was set up the radio and get in touch with his people, on scramble.

"Are you sure you're OK, Ben?" Ike asked.

"I'm fine, Ike." Now that he could talk freely, Ben explained what had happened to him and all that had taken place since he woke up half buried under debris.

"We're fighting on three fronts, Ben," Ike said. "The punks are getting smarter and using hit-and-run tactics. They're not doing any damage, but it's keeping us busy. You want us to come in and get you?"

"Negative, Ike. But on the second drop this afternoon, give me all the claymores you can spare. By that time I will probably have ferreted out the informer and can begin really booby-trapping the perimeters of this park."

"We'll keep you supplied with whatever you want, Ben, whenever you want it. Ben, the pilots said they reported no SAMs coming at them."

"I know. If they have them, and that's a big 'if' in my mind right now, I don't think the gangs know how to use them. Personally I don't think they have any surface-to-air missiles. But we'll know this afternoon. Have the fighters up and circling before you make the drop."

"Will do, Ben."

"Then that about does it. Ike, I don't want any heroics from any of my people on my behalf. I want that firmly understood. When it comes time to once more invade this hunk of rock and rubble, we can scatter and keep our heads down."

"Your people aren't going to like that, Ben."

"Well, they're going to have to live with it. Those are my orders and I expect to have them obeyed."

"You got it, partner."

"All right, Ike. Eagle out."

Ben laid the mic down and stood up, looking at Greg and Judy and two of their most trusted lieutenants. "Now then, people. Let me set up this PSE equipment and then we'll find your informer."

"What happens when we find the person, general?" Babe asked.

"We shoot him."

Eleven

But Ben didn't have to test anyone. As soon as word about the PSE equipment spread, and that there was at least one, possibly two informants within the survivors' midst, who would be shot as soon as they were discovered, a man and a woman vanished.

"I would never have thought in my wildest dreams it would be that pair," a woman called Nell said.

"Nor I," a man named Don said.

"They joined us right after we all banded together," Greg added. "It just doesn't make sense to me why they would do something this . . . awful. We called them friend. Shared what we had with them."

"Did anybody ever see them actually kill a gang member?" Ben asked.

The members standing by exchanged glances and one by one slowly shook their heads.

"No," one of the co-leaders said. "As a matter of fact,

I didn't. But looking back, I can remember several very odd things about them."

Ben waved a hand. "It makes no difference now. They're gone. Let's start gearing up for the next drop. This one will be much larger than the first." He smiled. "But first, let's brew up some of that good coffee."

Over the first real coffee most of them had tasted in years, Ben told them about his army and what they were doing. He told them about life in the SUSA and about Simon Border's ultra-religious nation out west. He told them about the NUSA being formed here in the North and East.

"When this is over," a man said, "I don't ever want to have to pick up a gun again."

Ben smiled sadly. "Those days are going to be long in coming, my friend. Probably not in our lifetime."

Only a few of the Manhattan survivors professed any doubts about moving down to the SUSA. The majority of them were eager to get on the way.

"No crime in the SUSA?" a woman who'd been introduced as Joan asked.

"Practically none," Ben assured her. "We just don't tolerate it. Kids are taught the difference between right and wrong in school. They're taught values and morals."

"And the Bible?" one of the doubters asked, a smile on his lips.

"Not in public schools," Ben surprised him by answering. "That's up to the parents and religious leaders. I believe in a very wide separation of church and state."

"Then how do you teach creation?" another asked.

"That the world was created. It just came to be. Once a child has grown into adulthood and is in college, then all sorts of theories are taught. But by that time, the student is old enough to form his own opinions."

"Do you believe in a supreme being, general?" Cliff asked.

"Yes, I do. Very much. There is no way anyone will ever convince me that all the wonders of nature just 'happened.' I don't believe that; I'll never believe that."

"But after all the tragedy that has occurred in the world, you can't believe God is a merciful god," a woman called Linda said.

"I believe that God gave us a brain, Linda. He later gave Moses a tablet with His basic laws, laws He would like for us all to try, and I stress *try*, to live by. God didn't ask that any of us be perfect, just to try."

"And do you try, general?" a man asked.

Ben smiled. "I do try, Red. I'll give anybody a chance if they'll cut me just a little slack."

"And do you read the Bible, general?"

"General George Patton was asked that question one time, during the Second World War. He supposedly replied, 'Every goddamn day.' "

Ben went off to catch a few hours sleep.

The second drop that day went as smoothly as the first one, with no surface-to-air missiles fired at the planes. Ben was convinced now that the gangs did not have SAMs.

The early afternoon drop brought the park survivors more food and medical supplies, thousands of rounds of ammo, several hundred M-16s, half a dozen Big Thumpers, cases of grenades, uniforms and boots and socks, underwear for the male and female genders, and dozens of other articles necessary for survival.

"Marvelous!" Doctor James exclaimed, eagerly ripping open the cases of medical supplies. He turned to the woman who acted as his nurse. "Round up the kids and get them in here, Claire. Let's get to work. Then we'll start with the adults. Everybody gets a quick once-over and then we start the shots." He smiled up at Ben. "This is like manna from heaven, general."

"Enjoy," Ben told him.

Ben began a walking inspection of the park's perimeters and knew very quickly that anytime the punks wanted to rush the area, they could do it. It would cost them dearly in terms of human life, but they could overrun the park.

There were too few survivors and far too many gangs for them to effectively defend such a large area. If they were going to stay within the confines of the park, their area of defense would have to be cut down to a more defensible size.

Ben consulted a sheet of paper Judy had given him. There were 162 adults of reasonable fighting age in the group. Sixteen children. Twelve elderly people. The park comprised 840 acres. Not nearly enough people to defend such a large area.

Besides, the gangs had mortars, and Ben was sure, now that they knew he was inside the park confines, they would start using those mortars. Once they started that, it would be slaughter for the survivors.

But where else could such a large group of people hide in the city?

He didn't know. But there had to be a place.

Ben sighed and Judy cut her eyes to him. "What it is, Ben?"

"The park. The gangs could overrun you anytime they wanted to."

"But the booby traps . . . ?"

"A couple of dozen grenades or sticks of dynamite would blow a path right through them. The punks would pour through. I think the only reason they haven't done so before now is because of the informants they had planted among you."

Judy opened her mouth to protest and Ben held up a hand. Greg and some of the others stood close by, listening. "Before we began herding all the gangs in this direction, back when your army man was still alive, how many punks were there in the city? Take a guess somebody."

"Two or three thousand," Judy said. "And maybe that many creepies."

"And there were other small bands of survivors scattered all over the city, right?"

"That's right. Dozens of them."

"Well, the other groups supplied the food for the creeps, and you all were too well fortified for the small unorganized gangs to rush. But all that has changed now. There are now thousands more gang members in the ruins, well armed and well equipped. As soon as they realize they can overrun this park, they'll do it."

Ben paused and listened for a moment to the distant Rebel artillery fire. The heavy bombardment was coming from the north, south, and west of them. Ben wished he knew what Ike was doing.

"What do you suggest, general?" one of the men in the group asked.

Ben looked at him—couldn't remember his name. "If we stay inside the park, we're eventually going to be slaughtered. That artillery fire tells me that my people are very busy out there. This is a last-ditch effort on the part of the punks. It's do or die time for them. Most of them are beyond caring; they just want to take out as many Rebels as they can before we kill them. You see, the majority of the gang members we've pushed up here know all they've got to look forward to is a bullet or a rope. They are the absolute dregs of society and have committed crimes against humanity of a nature that would make a maggot puke. They have absolutely nothing to lose."

"We'll do whatever you tell us to do, general," a woman spoke from the group.

"Then let's get packed up and make plans to get the hell gone from here."

Ben bumped Ike on scramble and told him what they were planning.

"I was just about to tell you to get out of the park, Ben. Aerial recon shows the punks appear to be massing for an attack against your position. For some reason, they're mainly coming at you from the west."

"All right, Ike. We're out of here. Eagle out." Ben turned to Judy. "You people know all the rabbit holes in and out of the park. I'll follow your lead."

"How much time do we have, Ben?"

Ben shrugged. "When you hear the mortars incoming, we're out of time."

She put serious eyes on him. "I don't know where to take us."

"This park is going to be first blown all to hell, and then filled with punks. And you know what they're going to do if they take you women alive. Just get the people out of here."

Ben figured they had probably less than a hour before the gangs struck. He looked up at the sky. About four hours of daylight left.

Ben packed up his gear just as Judy walked up, wearing a heavy pack. "We're going to go out the east side, Ben. Through an old drainage tunnel we found. That will lead us underground, into the tunnels."

Ben stared at her for a moment. "The creeps—the uglies, as you call them?"

"There may be seven or eight hundred of them. As compared to thousands of punks."

Ben nodded. "We'll take our chances against the uglies, then."

"There is a chance there won't be any in that area. When the punks started arriving, we noticed the uglies began pulling out."

"We can always hope."

"You ready?"

"Anytime. I just want to activate a few more claymores before we pull out. I want to leave a few surprises behind for the punks."

"Go ahead. I'll pass the word to keep this area clear."

Ben spent a few minutes carefully placing claymores and then backed away, joining the others. "Let's go."

The lead-off men led the group single-file into thick brush, the elderly men and women and the small children placed in the middle of the column to reduce their chances of being separated. It was not a long walk to the edge of the park, but it was tough going through the thick underbrush that had been deliberately allowed to grown wild. There, the group halted for a moment's rest.

"The drainage pipe is over there," Judy pointed. "In all that brush. It wasn't in use for years before the Great War. Not many people know it's there."

"Where the hell does it lead?" Ben asked.

"Originally, it flowed to the sewer under the city. But the uglies, I guess it was them, knocked out the brick wall and enlarged the whole thing. I'll be honest with you— we really don't know where it comes out. It's a maze under there. But we do know that if you get lost, just keep walking and looking up. There are manhole covers and exits into buildings the uglies knocked out long ago. I've been lost in there several times. The first time, I thought panic would give me a heart attack. Then I learned it's practically impossible to get really lost." She looked away from Ben to nod at Doctor James. "Go ahead," she said quietly.

Ben watched as the doctor and his nurse began giving the younger kids shots to knock them out, and he knew why it was being done—there were rats in the tunnels as big as small dogs. This would insure the kids' silence. Ben had questioned the doctor's request for the drugs when he had first called in to Ike, but had done so silently, figuring the medical man had his reasons. Now he knew why.

The group rested quietly for a few more minutes, until the drug started taking effect and the kids began yawning. When they could no longer keep their eyes open, they were picked up and held while others tied them in place on the adults.

"Let's do it," Judy said, standing up.

One by one, the people began disappearing into the darkness that loomed just a few feet inside the wide drainage pipe. Ben brought up the rear, and there he placed several claymores outside and just inside of the huge pipe.

Then he stepped into the darkness and the unknown, walking down the slight slant into the maze of tunnels that lay under the city.

Twelve

They all carried plenty of extra batteries for the flashlights Ben had requested from the aerial drop, and candles to be used if they had to spend more time than anticipated in the darkness of the tunnels.

They had gone only a few hundred feet in the oppressive darkness when the nearly overpowering stench of rotting human flesh hit them like a hammer blow. Even the drugged and sleeping children stirred in the arms of those carrying them, wrinkling their noses against the sickening smell.

Judy halted the column and called for Ben to join her up front. "They've come back," she whispered. "They haven't been this close in months."

"We probably pushed them this way," Ben told her. "Pass the word, no candles or open flames of any sort. There might be methene down here."

"You can bet the uglies know we're here," she responded.

"Put someone else in the rear. I'll stay up here with you."

Judy assigned two other men to bring up the drag, and she and Ben took the point, working their way slowly eastward through the huge drainage pipe. Stinking dark water slopped at their boots and often the powerful beams from their flashlights would catch huge, beady-eyed rats glaring at them, their hairless obscene tails trailing behind them in the filth.

Light suddenly flooded the chamber ahead of them and Judy said, "Open manhole cover. Pass the word— absolutely no noise as we pass under it."

"Does that mean we've passed one block?" Ben asked.

"Yes. At least three more to go."

The column began passing noiselessly under the open manhole cover, with two people counting each head as it passed. When the last person went by, they passed the word: everybody accounted for.

Around a bend in the tunnel, and darkness once more swallowed them. Silence, except for the scratching of tiny clawed feet as the big rats reluctantly gave ground before them. But some of them gave no ground, squatting on the ledges and glaring balefully as the humans passed by.

"I hate rats," Judy whispered.

"Join the club," Ben returned the whisper.

Two blocks later, and Ben and Judy each threw up a hand to signal a halt. The beams of their flashlights had flicked over, then quickly arced back and settled on a scene out of a horror writer's nightmare: several thousand rats were blocking the tunnel. The mound of moving, hairy, filthy rodents was several feet tall and several feet wide. From under the disgusting ever-moving mound, Ben and Judy could see the gnawed-on hands, feet and arms of once-human beings. White glistening bone now, with only a few scraps of meat still remaining.

"Sweet Jesus Christ!" Judy gasped.

"Back up," Ben said. "Back to the last manhole. We can't go any further in this tunnel."

Judy pointed a shaky finger at the moving mound. "But that . . ."

"What's left of the uglies' dinner," Ben replied, trying to keep the disgust and horror out of his voice. "This is where they put the leftovers, I guess. Come on, back up. Let's get the hell out of here."

Slowly the column backed up, with many wondering what was going on, for the majority of the men and women who made up the small band of survivors had been spared the sight of the rats feeding on dead human flesh.

"We're going to be a couple of blocks short, Ben," Judy said.

"Do we have a choice?"

"No."

"No point in discussing it then."

The smell had caused several people to lose their lunch. The sounds of gagging and retching filled the tunnel for several moments.

"Watch your step," Ben advised drily.

Ben did not lose his lunch. He had seen worse over the years. But at the moment he would be hard-pressed to recall it.

"Who . . . ?" Judy gasped on the way back to the last manhole cover.

"I don't know. Maybe punks the creeps waylaid over the past few weeks. The bodies haven't been there long. Maybe there are more survivors in the ruins than you think. We'll never know, Judy, so put it out of your mind."

"I hate those damn uglies!"

"You're at the end of a long list, dear. Move!"

Two of the younger survivors went up the ladder and out the manhole cover. They were gone for a couple of minutes before one called down, "It's all clear. Come on and be quick about it. The men carrying the kids up first. Untie the ropes and pass them up, then follow. Head for the ruins to the east. It's what's left of a church, I think."

The words had no sooner left his mouth when the unmistakable sounds of mortars came to those in the tunnels.

"It's started," Ben said. "That's why there are no punks around here. They've all massed around the park for the final assault. They'll probably soften up the park for an hour, concentrating first on the areas they know are rigged with booby traps. Then they'll hit the park. It won't take them long to discover we're gone." Ben reached out in the dim light and brushed several large roaches off Judy's back.

"What was that?" she asked.

"Very large, ugly roaches, Judy."

She shuddered in revulsion as Ben picked another roach out of her hair.

"There are roaches on the island of Madagascar that grow to four inches in length and stand up on their hind legs and hiss and spit," he said.

"Now, I really could have done without that knowledge!"

Ben chuckled.

"But so far they're found only on that island."

"Unless you're just trying to make me feel better, thank God for small favors."

"Kids are clear and in the ruins across the street, Judy!" Greg called.

"The elderly next," she returned the call. "Then we go as we're lined up."

"A squad of men out, Judy," Ben gently corrected. "Throw up a defensive line. Then the elderly."

"You're right, Ben. I'm not thinking." She corrected her orders.

"Clear!" The word was called after a few moments, as the defensive line got into place street-level.

"I'll go last," Ben said.

Ben waited until the last man had climbed up the ladder, then took a final look at his surroundings. Several dozen rats had left the huge mound of rotting cadavers and they squatted along the sides of the tunnels, glaring hate at him, their eyes glowing wickedly in the gloom.

Topside, he breathed in and out deeply, several times, clearing his lungs if not his nostrils of the dreadful stench of the tunnels. Then he moved over to the ruins of the old church and squatted there behind cover, listening to the punks' bombardment of the park. He lifted his handy-talkie.

"We're clear of the park," he radioed. "To the east side as planned. Four blocks east. Start dropping them in, people, and good shooting."

Across the Hudson River, Rebel gunners manning 105s and 155s began lobbing in a variety of rounds with deadly accuracy and effectiveness. The 155s were using anti-personnel rounds, each shell filled with from 36 to 60 high-explosive anti-personnel grenades. Some of the 105s were using a mixed bag of rounds, from HE to anti-personnel. Whatever they used, the rounds were falling dead on with devastating results, and it stopped the punks' advance into the park cold.

Ben climbed up on top of a building that had, miraculously, remained virtually intact during the Rebels' assault several years before. Using binoculars, he peered over the several blocks of ruins and rubble and began calling in rounds. Ben smiled, thinking, *You might call me an RO, for rear observer.*

Judy climbed up to join him. "You thought of where you might take us?" Ben asked.

"No. Wherever we go on this rock, we're still going to

be within mortar range of those bastards." She jerked her head toward the park.

"Yes, but when my people are through today, there will be considerably fewer of the species known as punk, you can be assured of that."

"That will help us right now. But the question is—can we survive until your people take this damn rock?"

"Oh, we'll survive, Judy. Put any doubts about that out of your mind. Even if we have to go down into the old subway system to do it."

"More of that remains than you might think, Ben. I'd say at least a hundred or so miles. Your people wrecked about half of it."

"And only God knows how many miles of other long forgotten tunnels are under the city."

"Hundreds of miles of them, Ben. But what uglies are left live down there. And the rats."

Ben grimaced. "Well, we'll go into the drainage tunnels only as a last resort. But the subways . . . that might be our salvation."

She shuddered. "I don't like the underground."

"Neither do I. But the prospect of getting captured by punks appeals to me even less."

"You do have a point."

"Is anyone in your group familiar with what remains of the subway tunnels?"

"Oh, yes. Several of the men."

Ben looked at her for a moment, neither of them speaking. Finally, Judy nodded in agreement. "We don't have much choice in the matter, do we?"

"Not a whole lot."

"I'll get Mike, see what he says about it. I honestly don't know where the nearest entrance is. I do my best to avoid those places."

Ben stood alone on the roof for a time, watching the

Rebel gunners blast the punks on the west side of the park. He sensed Mike coming up to stand quietly beside him and turned.

"Judy says you're thinking about moving us into the tunnels, general."

"You have a better plan?"

"Not really, sir. We've got emergency rations to last us for a time but water is going to be a problem."

"You know where there is some seepage?"

"Yes, sir. But I sure as hell wouldn't want to drink that stuff."

"We can boil it and then purify it with tablets. Believe me when I say my people have drunk water that at first glance would gag a maggot."

Mike smiled. "All right, sir."

"How far are we from a subway entrance?"

"About two blocks."

"Then I guess we'd better do it, Mike. It'll be uncomfortable, but we'll be alive. And my people are gearing up to once more assault this rock. A few more days, and we'll be home free." *I hope,* Ben silently added.

"Then I'll get the people ready to move, sir."

"Send a patrol to check out the subway entrance first, Mike. Use the walkie-talkies from the drop. The punks don't have the equipment to intercept any transmission from them."

"Yes, sir. Sir?"

Ben cut his eyes.

"Is it true that there is no crime down in the SUSA?"

"It's true, Mike. We have zero tolerance for crime and criminals."

"What a wonderful place that must be to live and raise a family."

Ben smiled. "You'd be surprised. I figure about half of your group could make it down there."

"This bunch? Are you kidding?"

"Not at all. It takes a very special person to live down there, Mike. When your people are out of this box and free to make choices, you'll see."

"Well, count me in as one who will make it, general."

"Oh, you will, Mike. I have no doubts about that."

"I'll send that patrol out now."

"We don't have much daylight left," Ben reminded the man.

"Where we're going, general," Mike replied grimly, "that won't make a bit of difference."

Thirteen

Ben waited topside and stood guard with a small team of survivors while the others disappeared into the darkness of the old subway system. Ben waved the others down until he was alone at street level.

"All right, Ike," he muttered. "We can last about a week if we're both careful and lucky. So get it in gear, boy."

Ben stood up and took one last look at the outside world, then walked down the rubble-littered steps, being careful not to disturb the war-torn look of them.

"This way, general," a man called. "To your right."

Ben joined the man and together they walked past the turnstiles and out to the platforms, where over the years millions of people had waited for transportation to and from home and work—back when the world made a little sense.

Ben hopped down to the tracks and began following the bobbing beam of the survivor's flashlight as the man walked deeper into the tunnel.

"I don't like it either, general," the man called over his shoulder, as if reading Ben's mind. "Nobody in their right mind likes the tunnels."

As he walked, Ben sniffed the air. There was not the slightest whiff of creepie. He said as much.

"They're spotty throughout the city," the man replied. Ahead of them, Ben could see the darting beams of flashlights. "As you know far better than me, there used to be thousands of uglies in the city. After you people got through with them a few years back—before any of us got here—there were only about a thousand or so left . . . at least that's how we figure it. But they had done a lot of work down here in the tunnels. You'll see. Some of us, before we banded together, used to hide out down here."

They caught up with the main group just as a man stuck his head out of a large vent of some sort, about six feet off the tracks and about three feet up from a concrete walkway. "All clear, folks," he said. "Hand the kids up." The iron grate to the vent lay off to one side, propped up on the ledge.

One by one, the kids began disappearing into the side of the tunnel. Once during a rest break, Ben stepped up onto the ledge and looked inside. He stood for a moment, astonished. There was a walkway about six feet in diameter that opened up into an enormous cavern. The room was as large as a gymnasium.

The man who was helping the kids and the elderly into the cavern smiled at the expression on Ben's face. "There are places like this all over Manhattan, general. This big rock is honeycombed with natural caves and tunnels. I don't know when this air vent was put up, but I'll wager this cavern has been long forgotten."

"Probably," Ben said, climbing in and relieving the man helping the others inside. He looked behind him and was startled to find that he could not see the cave.

The others around him laughed. "It's like one of those trick rooms you used to find in carnivals along the midway, general," one said. "You can only see the entrance when standing in one narrow spot. Anywhere else you stand, it's blocked."

"Well, I'll be damned," Ben muttered, angling around several times and still unable to see the second entrance to the huge cavern.

Once everybody was out of the subway tunnel and in the cavern, Ben prowled around the enormous room, finding half a dozen smaller caves around the base of the large one.

"Be careful about going in any of those, general," Greg warned from across the cavern. "They're endless, and we have lost one person in them." He grimaced. "He never came out."

"I will certainly keep that in mind," Ben said, peering into the darkness of the smaller cave.

Ben did not stick his head out of the cave for nearly 36 hours. He could neither transmit nor receive by radio, so he did not know what was going on up top. Finally, just after noon on the second day in the tunnels, he could take no more of it.

"I'm going topside," he told Judy. "I've got to find out what's going on."

She nor any of the others made any move to stop him, but Ben could tell none of them thought much of the idea.

Ben picked up his CAR and backpack. He looked at the group. "Don't send anyone out looking for me. If I don't return, write me off. But stay safe."

Ben left the cave without another word. He walked the tracks until he came to the old station. There he squatted down for a few moments, listening. He could hear nothing and could smell no telltale odor of creeps.

Ben walked through the silent and littered old station and climbed the steps to ground level, emerging into a very overcast day, the low clouds threatening rain. There, he squatted down again and listened, breathing deeply of the air. Truth was, Ben despised caves. He had always suspected that he might be a bit claustrophobic.

The late afternoon air smelled of smoke; the park had really taken a hammering from Rebel artillery.

Ben slipped into the ruins of an old building and climbed the rickety steps to what remained of the second floor. There he knelt down under the open sky and called in.

"This is Eagle. Come in."

"Go Eagle," came Corrie's familiar and welcome voice.

"Everything OK here. Give me a report from your end."

"Plans to assault your position delayed due to build-up of punks on mainland. Don't know where they came from. Believe they may have been in hiding, waiting to spring the trap on us. Can you hold?"

"For a few more days."

"Are you in a position to receive a drop?"

"Negative. What about the park?"

"We creamed it. Aerial recon shows hundreds of punks dead and wounded. Can you give me a position?"

"East side of the park. About five or six blocks from the waterfront."

"Can you and your group make it to Roosevelt Island?"

"Negative. Too many kids and elderly. Too risky."

"Understood, Eagle."

"I'm going to do some recon. I'll get back to you in a few hours."

"That's ten-four, Eagle."

"Eagle out."

Ben spent the next twenty or so minutes scanning everything he could see through binoculars. He picked up the thin tentacles of cook fires north, east and south, but none very close to his position, and that puzzled him. He thought about that for a moment, then shook his head, unable to figure it out. He carefully climbed back down the steps to ground level, and staying in the ruins of the old building, he secured everything on his person that might clink or rattle and stepped into the alley.

He walked east until the alley ended on what was left of a street. Ben slipped through the ruins of long-deserted buildings until he reached the end of the block. There, he looked hard for anything that might be left of a street marker. Nothing.

"Shit!" he muttered, thinking it would be really nice to know his exact location.

The Rebels had really done a number on Manhattan several years back. Their artillery had leveled some blocks down to street level, but surprisingly, other blocks had survived, with some buildings virtually unscathed.

Ben entered one of the buildings that had survived— at least several stories of it had—and began an inspection of the place. There was no odor of creeps to be sniffed out, and he could detect no other sign of human inhabitation.

"Interesting," he muttered. "Odd, but interesting."

He spent a good 45 minutes carefully going over the four stories of the building. The top two floors on the west side of the structure had great gaping holes blown in them, so inspecting that part of the building didn't take long.

Looking around on the second floor, Ben was amused to find the front section of the Sunday edition of a New York newspaper. He sat down and read all the news that was fit to print from a decade past. Even though the news was over ten years old, the writing still did nothing to enhance his opinion of the newspaper.

Ben laid the paper aside just as he heard footsteps on the floor below, then voices.

"I tell you I seen somebody movin' around, man."

"I think you're full of shit, Ned. I think you're seein' things that ain't there."

Ben had not brought his lead pipe and now looked around for something to use as a club. He did not want to open fire unless it was absolutely necessary, for that would bring the punks running from all directions. He spotted a broken length of two-by-four amid all the crap on the floor and scooped it up, pressing back against the wall and waiting.

"I hope it's one of them cunts from the park," the first voice said in a whisper, as he stood on the second floor landing. "There was some fine lookin' pussy in that bunch."

"Now that I agree with you about."

"And this one ain't armed, neither."

"How do you know that, smart-ass?"

" 'Cause they'd be shootin' at us by now if they was."

"Good point, Ned."

Ned stuck his head into the room and Ben whacked him in the face, sending the man sprawling back onto the landing and tumbling down the old steps.

"Shit!" the second man yelled, just as Ben stepped out of the room and swung the two-by-four from right to left. The heavy board caught the punk on the side of the head and he dropped like a concrete block, one side of his head indented.

Ben did not need their weapons, but he took them anyway, along with their full magazine pouches. He left the men for the rats and exited the building out the back. A block away he cached the weapons in a building and kept on walking.

He stopped and was looking over the devastation of the

city when his eyes caught movement in the ruins of a building. A blown-out window on the second floor. He quickly slipped behind the cover of a jagged fence that had once been a brick wall and slipped along behind it until reaching the back of the building. Ben chanced a quick look and sure enough, his eyes had not fooled him. There was the figure of a person looking out, but looking out toward the front of the building, not toward the rear.

The figure disappeared and Ben ran across the alley, through the ruins of another building, then out the back. He began a slow and careful circling until he had reached the rear of the building where the person—or persons, he cautioned—was lying in wait.

They had the high ground, and with that advantage, they could take Ben down with one well-placed shot. He had to take them out. Providing, of course, "they" were hostile. And at this point, he didn't know that for sure.

Ben slipped carefully through the destruction, every few seconds lifting his eyes to scan the rear of the suspect building. He had not seen any further movement. The rain had turned to a light drizzle, not much more than a mist.

There were half a dozen rusted-out and burned hulks of cars in a parking area in the rear of the building, and about 50 or so feet of relatively clear area between Ben and the cars. Ben caught his breath, then ran to the protection of the old vehicles. There, he scanned the rear of the building from top to bottom, then ran to the rear wall. He could hear the faint murmur of voices coming from inside, one of the voices definitely female. The voices seemed to be in argument. After a moment they faded into silence.

He heard the careful whisper of feet, then a female head popped out of the window about a foot from him. Ben stuck the muzzle of the CAR against her face and said, "Just take it easy, lady, and talk to me."

"I'll talk to you, you bastard!" a man's voice came from behind Ben. "I'll blow holes in you."

"Then she's surely dead," Ben replied, as calmly as possible, considering the circumstances. "My finger's on the trigger. No matter how many times you get lead in me, reflex will still pull this trigger. Think about that."

"Don't do anything stupid, Jeff!" the woman with Ben's CAR stuck in her ear said. "Easy, now. This guy doesn't look like a gang member to me."

"I'm not," Ben said. "But who the hell are you people? Talk to me, dammit!"

"OK, OK!" the woman said. "Back off, Jeff. Back off, I say!"

"Backing off," the voice behind Ben said.

"Come around front so I can see you," Ben told him.

Ben guessed the woman to be around thirty, and when the man stepped into view, Ben could see he was about the same age. Both man and woman were reasonably clean, considering how they had to live. Their clothing had certainly seen better days and they both wore black scarves around their necks. Gang colors? Ben questioned. He thought not. But he'd give them a test.

"Damn punks!" Ben snarled at them.

"No, sir," Jeff said. "We're not gang members. Well . . ." he hesitated. "There is a group of us, but we're not part of any of the thugs who have taken over the ruins."

Ben did some fast visual checking. Jeff was carrying a bolt action rifle; at first glance it appeared to be in the .270 range. The muzzle of the rifle the woman carried, sticking out of what used to be a window, appeared to be no larger than a .22.

Ben took a chance and lowered his CAR, stepping back a couple of feet. "My name is Ben Raines, commanding general of the SUSA Rebels. You people want to talk to me?"

"Holy Mother of God!" the woman whispered. *"Ben Raines!"*

Jeff stared at Ben for a moment. Then nodded his head. "It's him, Sue. It's really him! I've seen his picture."

The sky opened up and the rain began falling; a cold rain for this time of year. Ben looked up, the fat drops splashing on his face. The raindrops felt good. He cut his eyes to Jeff. "I've got some real coffee in my pack." He smiled. "How about we step inside and have a cup?"

"Honest-to-God real coffee?" Jeff questioned.

Ben smiled. "Honest-to-God real coffee."

"General, you're a saint!" the woman said.

Ben laughed. "I know some chaplains who would give you an argument about that."

Fourteen

Jeff and Sue savored the odor of coffee for a few seconds before taking a sip. "My God, that's good," Sue said. "That's the first real coffee we've had in years."

"Good," Jeff agreed, a smile on his face. He held up one of the hi-energy bars Ben had given him and the smile faded. "But these . . ."

Ben laughed at him. "They really don't taste very good, do they? But they will keep you alive, if not happy." Ben looked at the couple for a moment. "Want to tell me about yourselves and how you got on this rock, and why?"

"Getting into Manhattan is easy," Sue said. "We came over by boat. About six months ago."

"You have boats?" Ben asked.

"Not anymore," Jeff replied. "We did have five. Five pretty good-sized boats we found over on the Jersey side. We landed and came ashore. Thirty of us. We just wanted to look around some. We've been hiding out up in the New Hampshire White Mountains for several years. Then we heard the wars were over and the country was being split up into political sections. We came out of hiding and got this far.'' He shook his head. "Truth is, we got stupid, I guess.'' He lifted his tin cup and Sue took it.

"We didn't leave guards behind with the boats. And when we got back to the waterfront, the boats were gone. We were stuck. Then the gangs started pouring in here and we've been running and hiding ever since. We knew there was a large group of people living in and around the park, but we didn't know how to approach them. We didn't know what kind of people they were. One of our people surprised a group of them out on some kind of patrol one day, and they opened fire on him. Since then, we've stayed far away from them.''

"There are thirty of you?''

"Yes,'' Jeff replied. "All adults. There are six couples, married. Well . . . paired off, I guess you'd have to say. We had a ceremony, but not with a minister.'' He smiled. "We took turns marrying each other.''

"That'll work,'' Ben said. "But we have chaplains with us if you'd like to do it over sometime.''

"We'd like that,'' they both said.

Ben stood up and stretched. "Let's go meet your people and make some plans.''

"About getting out of Manhattan?'' Sue asked.

"About staying alive until we can,'' Ben replied.

The members of the newest group of survivors were all about the same age, in their early to mid thirties. Ben guessed—as it turned out, accurately—that the bunch had been together for years, probably since their teens, and that most were from the same area of the country.

Ben had brought enough coffee with him so that each of them could at least have a couple of swallows of the real stuff. They trapped birds and squirrels for food, and had even eaten rat. They offered Ben some fried rat. He refused as politely as possible.

"How about other groups in the ruins?" Ben asked.

"There were about a dozen or so when we first got here," a man who had been introduced as Rob said. "Then the gangs of thugs began arriving and killing them off. They killed the men and took the women. I'd guess there are no more than . . . oh, 150 people left, max, who aren't aligned with the gangs."

"The women they seized, are they still alive?"

"If that's what you want to call it," a woman named Janet said. "They're slaves. The gangs trade them back and forth. The children too. There are . . . perverts among the gangs who prefer boys as sex objects. If you know what I mean."

Ben knew, and it never failed to fill him with the deepest of disgust. "I know," he said, his words soft but edged with rage. He looked at the group for a moment, meeting every eye. "I'm surprised you people have survived as long as you have."

"We move often," a man called Al said. "And we've been doing this for a long time, general. We've been on our own since we were teenagers. We were all attending private schools in the Northeast when the Great War hit us. The schools were about ten miles apart. We knew each other through dances and debating societies and so forth. We work well together. Leaving our boats unguarded was one of the few times we really acted stupid."

"You searched the waterfront area?"

"As best we could," Sue said. "We know they're hidden down there somewhere. But that's a big area to search."

"The punks didn't walk on water to get here," Ben said, as much to himself as to the others. "The boats are hidden somewhere. We just have to find them."

Ben stood up and paced the room for a moment, then turned to the group. "I'll level with you—we've got to get off this rock and do it quickly. When my people launch their next assault, it's going to be all-out. Those are my orders. When the assault starts, I can keep the artillery away from us, but it won't take the punks long to figure out our general location. We're also running out of supplies. I want to find as many of the survivors trapped on this rock as possible. I don't want innocent deaths on my hands. Can you contact these groups?"

"Some of them, sure," Jeff said. "But whether they'll believe us is another matter. They're pretty suspicious." He shrugged. "Who can blame them?"

"Then do it," Ben said. "I'm going to contact my people on the mainland and see just how much time we've got. In war, timetables are subject to revision very quickly."

They sure were. In only a matter of a few hours, the tides of war had shifted dramatically.

"We've got the punks on the run, Ben," Ike told him. "It won't be long, maybe two, three days max before we're ready to hit the ruins of the city. Do you want us to come get you?"

"Negative, Ike. The gangs are expecting something like that and they'll be ready, you can bet on it. What they aren't expecting is for us to locate the hidden boats and try an escape from this side. Give us three days, and then launch the assault."

"All right, Ben. But even if you find the boats, you're going to have a lot of open water to cross. In very small boats."

"I know. Continue with your plan to assault the ruins, Ike. Whether we make it out or not. That's the way I want it. OK?"

"All right, Ben." Ike's reply was tinged with sadness, but Ben knew the ex-SEAL wouldn't hesitate to carry out the orders. "But if you can't get out in time, I want an exact location from you."

"I'll try, Ike. I can't promise anything. Just stay ready for anything. You hear me?"

Ike could read a lot in that last remark. "All right, Ben."

"Good luck, Ike."

"Same to you, Ben. Shark out."

At dark, Ben led the second band of survivors to the various places where he had earlier cached all the weapons and ammo he could not carry. On the way, he showed them the fine art of silent killing by taking out two more punks. Now a full third of the new people were armed with either M-16s or AK-47s, and had ample ammunition for those weapons.

Whether or not the new people knew how to use the weapons was something Ben would learn soon enough, although they all said they did.

Then he led them to the subway tunnel and told them to stay within the confines of the old station. He wasn't about to lead them to the cave until he had the OK of the people there. This was their show, not his.

Judy, Greg, Dr. James, and several more of the survivors walked back up with Ben to meet the new people. Within minutes, the scene resembled old home week. Ben stood off to one side, amused at the sight.

When the conversation finally took a break, Ben said, "All right, people. Listen up. Red, you take someone and get back to the cave, draw two days' rations for ten people, and get back here. Judy, you and Greg, Babe, Bud, and Joan. You're with me. Sue and Jeff, Paul and Sally. That makes ten by my count. We're going boat hunting. Cliff, you monitor the radio. I'll try to broadcast twice during the day, at 1000 hours and 1800 hours. That means you've got to chance the outside to pick me up. Use the headset to reduce the chances of being heard."

Cliff nodded in understanding and looked at his watch, one of many that Ike had included in the emergency drops.

Ben smiled, thinking, *Simple things like a wristwatch that the Rebels have taken for granted for years. This country has a hell of a long way to go on the road back.*

Ben looked at the group for a few seconds, then made up his mind. "We've got five days," he deliberately lied, adding two days to what he and Ike had discussed. "So pack up everything that isn't absolutely necessary and be ready to move at my signal. And when you start moving, don't stop. Just come on to our location, wherever it might be. And people, when I give you the word, don't turn back for anything or anybody, because you won't have time to recover if you do."

Red returned a few minutes later, several men helping him carry the food and water and ammo. When everyone was supplied and their packs filled, Ben preset the radio frequencies and picked up his CAR. He looked at Cliff. "I'll do a radio check in one hour, Cliff."

Cliff nodded. "I'll be waiting, general."

With Ben leading the way, the group marched out of the tunnel and up to ground level. Ben halted them while he checked in all directions, then waved them forward.

Somewhere along the waterfront there were boats that would take them off the rock. Ben intended to find them. If not that, then he planned to kill a lot of punks.

On the mainland, Ike was rapidly wrapping up his offensive against the punks. The gang leaders had planned well, Ike gave them that, but anytime one planned war against the Rebels, it was best to plan for the totally unexpected, for the Rebels did not adhere to any set rules of engagement. The Rebels had not taken many prisoners, for as Ben had said, these were the hardcore of the criminal element, and they had nothing to gain by surrendering. They knew what awaited them at the hands of the Rebels.

Ike met with the batt coms and told them of Ben's decision. "He gave us three days, folks. Then ordered me to let the hammer down. And in so many words; he asked that no rescue attempt be made on our part. If he's not off the rock in three days, he's going to try to radio us his exact location and we'll keep artillery away from there." Ike waited until the low murmur of disapproval had died down. Then he spread his big hands. "The boss's orders, gang. What can I say?"

The only batt com who had not groused was Ben's son, Buddy. He stood up. "Dad's got something up his sleeve, Ike. If he didn't, he wouldn't issue those types of orders."

"I agree, Buddy," Ike said. "But *what* has he got working in that devious mind of his?"

The handsome and muscular young man shrugged his shoulders. "I don't know and we're not going to know until the last moment. It's my belief that Dad doesn't fully trust someone in the bunch he's aligned with. He's playing his cards close."

The others in the room nodded in agreement.

"Ike sat down on the edge of a folding table that groaned under his weight. He ignored the smiles from the others. Ike was in excellent physical shape; he was just . . . well, large. "Ben hasn't said anything about creeps on the rock. I think perhaps the majority of them have moved on. God alone knows where. But you can bet we'll meet them again along the way. We've killed a lot of punks, but many of them have also moved on. We've still got a hell of a fight looking at us somewhere along the way." He sighed. "Then there is Simon Border to deal with. I'm rambling, people, trying not to think about the fact that Ben is trapped on that goddamn rubbled-up piece of real estate over yonder."

Tina, Ben's daughter, stood up. "Ike, Dad is lone-wolfing

it. He's doing what he loves to do . . . with no restrictions placed on him and no one nursemaiding him and bitching at him and watching him like a hawk looking at a rabbit. He's enjoying himself. And you all know that. Dad probably has a plan he's not telling us about. He's usually got an ace up his sleeve. But he's given us orders, and we've got to obey them. Like them, or not.''

"I guess that is the bottom line,'' Ike reluctantly agreed. He expelled air and then stood up. The table sprang back into its normal shape. "Start repositioning the artillery. Let's get ready to take that rock over there.'' He looked at his watch. "We start shelling the objective in 80 hours. That's all, people.''

Fifteen

The rain continued to come down in a steady fall as Ben let Greg take the point and lead them toward the waterfront. They skirted the park in silence and then cut due west. The rain was obviously keeping the punks under cover. Greg kept the group in the alleys as much as possible and the going was slow but safer. After an hour had passed, Ben signaled for a halt and called in. Cliff answered immediately and the signal was clear and strong, then the group pushed on through the rain.

When they reached what a member assured Ben was Tenth Avenue, they cut north and continued for a number of blocks before Greg called for a rest break.

"This will take us to Pier One," he told Ben. "When we get there, we'll start working south. If the boats aren't hidden somewhere along there, I don't know where to look."

"We'll give it our best shot. But I've got to say we've been damn lucky so far this night."

"I've never seen a creep out in the rain. They don't like water. I don't know where the gangs are, or why they aren't out patrolling. It's . . . sort of weird."

Ben thought he knew the answer to that, but he keep his opinion to himself, and his eyes on one member of the group. He'd been watching him since first arriving in the park.

The rainstorm began to blow itself out as the front pushed eastward, out into the Atlantic.

Another block, and Bud said, "I know a shortcut, Greg. It'll save us time. I'll take the lead if you don't mind."

Ben smiled in the darkness. "Oh, I don't think that will be necessary, Bud."

"Sir?" Bud asked, turning to face Ben.

"I've been trying to figure out how you tipped off the punks." Ben lifted his CAR as Joan started to slip to one side. "Stand easy, Joan. Take her weapon, Greg."

Confusion on his face, Greg jerked the weapon from Joan's hands and backed up.

"Put your rifle on the ground, Bud. Slow and easy. That's good. Now back away from it."

"You're making a mistake, general," Bud said. "I haven't been tipping anyone off."

"That's right, Bud. But only because you couldn't figure out how to do it. You couldn't leave the park to warn your buddies; you couldn't leave a message for fear it would get destroyed in the mortar assault. All you could do was hope we'd send out a patrol and you could be a part of it . . . so you could lead us straight to your punk friends."

Joan suddenly whirled around and started to make a run for it. Judy gave her the butt of a rifle to the back of her head. The woman dropped like a brick to the wet alley.

Bud's shoulders sagged, his eyes on the still form of his woman. "You couldn't have had any proof. You had to be guessing it all,'' he said. "You were running a bluff and Joan panicked. Shit!"

Ben smiled. "I'm a pretty good guesser, Bud. You see, every time I looked up, either you or Joan were standing close to me, listening very intently. I thought the both of you were going to have a heart attack when I suddenly decided to leave the tunnel and go scouting. That's when I pulled Cliff aside and told him to never let the radio out of his sight. The punks seized radios when they overran our position; didn't take a genius to figure that out. That's why I changed frequencies. That's also why I told a few other little lies. Just in case you'd somehow find a way to leave a note, tipping off your punk friends."

"You can't prove any of this!" Bud flared. "Hell, Joan just panicked a minute ago, that's all. Doesn't prove a thing."

"But your coming back from every patrol damn sure does," Greg said. "Everybody else would be suffering everything from gunshot wounds to scrapes. But not you. You never got so much as a scratch. But what was the point, Bud? What did you gain from it all?"

"Food," Babe said, open hate in her voice. "While the rest of us were eating rat and anything else we could get our hands on, losing weight, Bud and Joan never lost an ounce. Look at them. They haven't changed in months. Jesus, I must have been blind not to see it. You two had food cached in the park. Goddamn you both!"

"I always thought you two were just lovers who wanted to be left alone," Judy broke her angry silence. "That's why I never gave it a second thought when you'd go off by yourselves and stay gone for hours. You were meeting the gangs and telling them about upcoming patrols and then chowing down while the rest of us were walking around hungry. Especially the kids, who really needed nourishing food. Damn you to hell!"

Bud grinned at the group, his smile macabre in the misty night. "Go ahead, general. Kill me. Fire your weapon. And when you do, you'll have a thousand people around you in five minutes. Come on, pull the trigger, kill me. I'll at least go out knowing you're a dead man. None of you will ever get off this rock. You'll all die here. I can at least take some satisfaction in that. You'll never find the boats. They're too well hidden and too well guarded. Fuck you, Ben Raines!"

"You're not my type, Bud." Ben took a step forward and buried the blade of his knife in Bud's belly, muscling the blade upward. Bud fell backward and hit the concrete of the alley. He twitched several times, then lay still.

"Take his weapons and food and water. Then do what you want to with Joan," Ben said. "Just do it quietly."

Judy reached down and cut the unconscious woman's throat with her own knife. She stared down at what she had done for a moment, then took a couple of steps to one side and vomited.

Ben waited until she had regained her composure. "Drag the bodies into a building. Let's get moving. We've still got a long way to go."

As the group neared the waterfront, still about three blocks away, Ben slowed their advance. They moved forward one at a time, darting from cover to cover. The rain had stopped, but the skies were overcast. The gangs had yet to make an appearance.

"72nd Street," Greg whispered to Ben, as they crossed the street.

"I'm glad somebody knows where they are," Ben muttered.

Greg smiled at the remark and waved the others behind on across the street.

A couple more long blocks and they were at the waterfront, the Hudson River looming dark and ever-moving just ahead of them.

"What now?" Jeff whispered to Ben.

"We get a few hours sleep and then start looking. We can't search at night, so we'll have to risk daylight. We'll break up into two-person teams at first light. I know it's risky, but that's the only way I see to do it."

"They sure won't be expecting us during the day."

"That's my thinking."

Ben assigned guards and then stretched out on the concrete of what remained of a warehouse and surprisingly dropped off to sleep within minutes. Babe shook him awake at 0400 hours.

"Everything quiet, general," the woman whispered. "Nothing has been moving out there."

"That's the way we like it."

The pre-dawn was filled with mist and fog when Ben awakened the others. They wandered off for what privacy they could find for their toilet and then gathered around Ben. Ben broke them up into four teams of two each. He made sure everyone had a map, a walkie-talkie, and knew where they would meet just before noon. They all said that from noon to dark was the most dangerous time, for the punks seemed to sleep late and then prowl all afternoon. Ben sent them out at 15-minute intervals, he and Judy the last ones to pull out.

"We're in real trouble if we don't find these boats, aren't we, Ben?"

"Let's put it this way—I don't want to be on this rock when the Rebels start their assault."

"But we've got five days to that, right?"

Ben smiled. "We've got about two and a half days, Judy. I lied."

She looked at Ben for a moment, then returned the smile. "Then I guess we've better find those boats, Ben."

The gangs had left guards along the waterfront, but they were unevenly spaced and not located in every pier. They were also careless and not very attentive. During that morning's search, there were a least a dozen times when Ben could have silently taken out the guard. He let them live, for to kill them would have given away the survivors' presence.

Ben checked in with Cliff at 1000 hours and then called off the so-far fruitless search at 1130 hours that morning, telling the teams to hunt a hole for the day and stay put. The teams had worked their way down to Pier 97 with no luck. Ben sat off to himself in the ruins of a warehouse and studied a map of the waterfront.

"Too much territory and not enough time," he muttered. "We're not going to make it."

"You say something, Ben?" Judy asked, walking up.

"We've not going to make it." Ben folded his map. "Even if we found the boats on the last day, it would take too long to get the people over here. You know where we are; you know how much territory we've covered and how much we have to go. I think the best thing for us to do is head on back and get ready to ride it out."

"What are our chances, Ben?"

"Fifty-fifty. My people can pinpoint their targets. It's not the artillery we have to worry about. The punks may be lowlifes of the worst degree, but they're not stupid. After a few hours they're sure to spot what area is being avoided. Then they'll come after us. They have nothing to lose."

"So now we. . . ?"

"Wait for dark and head on back. Unless you've got a better idea?"

She shook her head and silently mouthed the word, *No.*

"Well, let's see what the others have to say about it."

The group took the news in silence. Babe cleared her throat and said, "What are the chances of our riding it out, general?"

"Just like I told Judy. About fifty-fifty. It's not the artillery, it's the punks. Once they figure out our gunners are deliberately avoiding a certain area, they'll come swarming in there."

"We could booby-trap the tunnel," Jeff suggested.

"Well, we could," Ben replied. "But on the other hand, if I were doing the searching, that would be a dead give-away. But it's up to you folks."

"Let's head on back at dark," Paul suggested. "I don't think we could find where those boats are hidden if we had a month to look."

"I'm afraid I have to agree with you," Ben said. "That agreeable with everyone?"

It was.

"Let's get some rest then. We'll head back at dark."

Ben went outside and bumped Ike, breaking the news to him. Ben had figured out the exact location of the subway where the survivors were hiding, and gave it to him.

"I hate this, Ben. I'm going to be right up front with you."

"We don't have a choice in the matter, Ike. You try to assault this rock without first softening it up, we'll lose a lot of Rebel lives. We'll keep our heads down, you can be assured of that."

There was a few seconds pause from across the river. "Timetable still firm?"

"It's still 'go'."

"All right, Ben." There was resignation in Ike's voice. "You're callin' the shots."

"Eagle out."

Ben joined the others in the old warehouse, made sure everyone knew their guard assignments, and stretched out on the floor to get some rest. There was no point in worrying about whether they could make it through a bombardment. They had no choice in the matter.

There was not a Rebel who wouldn't willingly give his or her life in an attempt to rescue Ben. Ben knew that. But there was no way he would ever allow it.

They would ride out the assault, or they wouldn't.

Ben closed his eyes and let sleep take him.

The others took the news of the deaths of Bud and Joan stoically, a few shaking their heads in disgust. Then Ben told them about the upcoming artillery bombardment. The survivors took that news just as unemotionally.

"Theoretically, my artillery people can pinpoint targets to within a few yards," Ben said, then paused and added very, very drily, "Theoretically. But we'll cut ourselves a bit more slack. I've ordered my people to keep the rounds from falling in this general area." He looked at his watch. "We've got about 50 hours to get ready for it. Let's start boiling the water from that seepage we found and purifying it with chemicals. Start dividing up the rations into small packets that are easily carried by one person. That's in case we have to leave the tunnels and get separated up top." *Or get lost in these tunnels that honeycomb the area,* he thought, but didn't vocalize it. "I want everyone to have flashlights, extra batteries, candles, matches and a couple of packets of extra rations. Make sure your canteens are full; keep refilling them as you drink. The youngest and strongest of the men will each be assigned a child to look after. All right, people, let's start getting ready for my people to get us off this rock." *Or make our peace with God before we die here,* he silently added.

Ben eyes touched Judy's steady gaze, and knew she was thinking the same thing. He smiled and she returned the smile as she walked toward him in the candlelit cave.

"You and me?" she asked softly.

"You and me," Ben replied.

Sixteen

Ben and the others did what they could to prepare for the assault, and then there was nothing else to do but wait. For many, that was the hardest part of all.

Then one morning, while many still slept, the ground above them began to rumble. The assault on the ruins of Manhattan was on.

Ben ordered all fires put out. Even though the huge cave had a natural ventilation system, the smoke filtering out through tiny cracks in the stone high above the floor, Ben did not want any telltale odor of smoke or food to linger in the old subway tunnel. He left a few of the candles burning, for he knew that utter darkness would only exacerbate an already bad situation for the adults, and besides, it would scare the children even worse than they already were.

The bombardment continued unabated for 24 hours. Ben knew that P-51Es were also dropping high-explosive and napalm on the city, and that the ruins of the city were burning.

During the middle of the afternoon on the second day of the artillery assault, the guards in the tunnel came rushing into the cave.

"The punks are all over the place," Mike panted the words. "Searching every grate and vent. They're removing the bars and really looking inside, general."

The grate over the opening, Ben knew, was held in place by only two bolts. Once the punks saw that, it would be all over. "How much time do we have?"

"They're moving slow. I'd say an hour."

"All right, Mike," he said. "Get the people out of here and past the rubble in the tunnel, toward the next station south. Just as we planned. Enforce noise discipline. Good luck."

One by one, the survivors quickly moved out. The children sensed danger and were silent. They were wide-eyed and frightened, but quiet.

The last of the survivors had left the cave and was out of sight down the old tracks when Ben saw the flashlight and torches of the punks heading their way. He and Judy were the last ones in the cave.

"Little late for us, Judy," he said calmly. "Any ideas?"

"I'm with you, Ben."

"I hate to say it, but it looks like we fall back into one of those smaller caves."

"People go in those caves and don't come back out, Ben."

"You have a better idea, my dear?"

She smiled at the "my dear," and shook her head. "I guess not."

"Pick one."

They were both wearing heavy packs. She turned slowly and pointed. "That one."

"Let's go."

They were deep into the cave when the punks were pulling the grate loose from the concrete wall of the tunnel.

Ben carried a small rock and used it to cut a mark into the right side of the cave every few dozen steps.

"What are you doing?" Judy asked.

"Making sure we can find our way out of here. Coming back, the marks will be on our left. Remember that. Be quiet and count your steps."

The punks entered the cave but only for a few moments. They soon gave up the search and returned to the main cavern, wanting no part of the dark, twisty tunnel.

After a half hour, Ben called a halt. "They're not following us. We don't need to go any further."

They rested in the darkness and sipped water.

"You think you can find your way out of this mess, Ben?"

"Yes, I do. There were only three offshoots to this main cave on the way here. Two on our left, one to the right. Going back they'll be reversed. Just remember that. And the caves are well vented; no problem with air."

She told him the number of steps they had taken.

"We didn't go far. About a quarter of a mile. I'm no spelunker, Judy. I hate caves. But just don't panic. I had a cave explorer tell me one time."

"I hate the darkness. I can't see my hand in front of my face. I want to light a candle or something."

"No. The punks would smell the candle burning and we don't dare use flashlights for fear of reflection. Try to get some sleep."

"The cave floor is cold, Ben."

"So is the grave. Be quiet and go to sleep."

After 12 hours, Ben had had all the cave he could take, and knew that Judy was about to come unglued. They both had heard the scurrying of tiny clawed feet, and knew that rats had found them. Neither of them wanted any part of hordes of rats.

"We've got to get moving, Ben," Judy whispered. "Head back and take our chances. I can cope with the darkness, but not the rats."

"I'm with you. OK. Let's stand up. Snug the rope and let's go."

Securely roped together, with about six feet between them, they started back, both of them silently counting steps and trying to be as quiet as possible. Ben used the flashlight sparingly, fighting an urge to keep the tiny friendly beam of light on constantly.

As they neared the count's end, they both heard voices, lots of voices.

"We've had it, Ben," Judy whispered, near defeat in her voice.

"Not without one hell of a fight," Ben returned the whisper.

They walked on, the voices growing louder.

Ben clicked on his flashlight, startling Judy.

"They'll see us, Ben!" she whispered.

"That's the idea, Judy I want them to."

"You *want* them to see us?"

"Yeah. Those are my people, Judy. Those are Rebels in the cave. One of those voices belongs to my son, Buddy."

Seventeen

Ike had seen a mutiny coming if he didn't at least make an attempt to rescue Ben, so he finally allowed Buddy and his special ops people to cross the river. They had smashed their way through the punk lines, opening up a hole. Ike then laid down smoke and several battalions of Rebels were now in the ruins of Manhattan.

"My people?" Judy asked.

"Safe," Buddy told her. "We found them about a mile down the tracks, behind a pile of rubble."

Although Buddy had not known it at the time, his people had hit the rock at the punks' weakest point, throwing the gangs back, sending them running in all directions. The next wave of Rebels hit practically no resistance for several blocks as they spread out, throwing up a protective line north and south of the old subway station.

Georgi Striganov and his people had crossed into Manhattan from the north and were pushing the punks south, trapping them between Rebel lines. Ike was pouring Rebels into the ruins, and the punks had no place to run and nothing to do except die, which they were doing in large numbers.

Ben sat quietly, smoking a cigarette, while Buddy made his report. He knew he should be angry, for his orders had been disobeyed, but he could find no anger in him.

"Doctor Chase has set up a hospital along the waterfront, Father," Buddy said. "He ordered us to bring you to him immediately."

Ben nodded his head, knowing it would be useless to argue. "Judy's people?"

"Already there, being checked out."

Ben stood up and smiled at his son. "If you ever learn to obey orders, you're going to make one hell of a commander, boy."

"Yes, sir," the young man replied, with no change of expression.

"Strip, bathe, put on this gown, and get your ass into bed," Doctor Chase told Ben. "You're out of commission for a couple of days."

"You're a mean old man, Lamar," Ben said. "And your disposition is not improving with age."

"You can always fire me," Chase shot right back, grinning wickedly.

"Then I wouldn't have anyone to argue with, you old goat."

"Well, you couldn't fire me anyway," Chase replied, shoving Ben toward the portable showers. "I'm too damn old for active duty, so I have no military rank and therefore I am acting under the orders of President Jefferys. Now put that in your mess kit and shove it."

"You're impossible, Lamar. Jesus! This gown is open

all the way down the back. I have never understood the reasoning behind that.''

''No play on words intended, I'm sure. Move, Raines.''

Ike came to see Ben several times during his hospital stay, bringing him up to date. Ben was kept in the field hospital for 36 hours, checked out from all directions by a staff of doctors. They could find nothing wrong with him, and that seemed to disappoint Doctor Chase.

''Are you happy now, you damned pill-pusher?'' Ben asked Chase.

''I have to release you, Raines,'' Lamar grumped. ''I need the bed for people who really need treatment.''

''Good.'' Ben swung his long legs off the cot and reached for his trousers.

''Although I really should keep you for another day or two.''

''Try it!'' Ben challenged him.

''No thanks. It isn't worth listening to you bitch. Get the hell out of here.''

''With pleasure.''

Ben dressed as quickly as possible and stepped out of the front part of the warehouse, which was all that was left standing. Rebels were all over the place, but none saluted the general, for the no-saluting rule in a combat zone was strictly enforced by the Rebels. Ben stood for a moment, content just to breathe the air and watch his surroundings.

He had been informed while in the hospital that Judy and her people had been transferred over to the Jersey side. Ben did not anticipate ever seeing her again, so he put her out of his mind.

He looked up and smiled at the sight of his team walking slowly toward him. They had all been to see him in the hospital, but could not stay for very long due to all the tests Chase was having run on him . . . all of which turned out to the good.

"Well," Ben said, pushing away from the building and walking up to the five of them. "You people look all fat and happy."

"It's been boring, General Ben," Anna said. "When do we go back to work?"

"How about right now?" Ben asked, picking up his pack and CAR.

Bullets pocked the walls behind Ben and his team, blowing dust all over them. Ben, face down on the floor, turned his head and smiled at Anna.

"You wanted to get back to work, dear?"

She spat out dust and grimaced. Ben had taken his team out for what was supposed to be a routine patrol. It had turned out to be anything but routine. They had been working at the northern edge of what used to be called Midtown, and had run into heavy fighting just east of the ruins of the old Museum of Modern Art. They were in no danger of being overrun, for there were Rebels all around them. It was just annoying being pinned down, however briefly.

Rebels on the left and right flanks of them tossed a couple of grenades. That was followed by sustained bursts of gunfire, then an unnatural silence settled over that little area of Manhattan.

"OK." The voice came from across the street. "We've had it. We're givin' up. We don't wanna fight no more. Understood?"

"Then leave your weapons on the ground and stand up," Ben shouted. "Hands in the air."

"And if we do that?"

"You'll live a little bit longer," Ben replied coldly.

"We got women with us. Not fightin' women. Women we grabbed or swapped for. What about them?"

"Send them out first."

Half a dozen women, most of them dressed in no more than rags, began climbing out of the rubble. When they cleared the piles of rubble, they stood with their hands in the air, frightened and confused looks on their faces.

Rebel medics called out to them and the women quickly moved out of the line of fire and disappeared into the ruins. They would be transported to Chase's MASH units along the waterfront, checked out, and given treatment.

"Now stand up and move into the street!" Ben called.

They were a sorry-looking bunch. It was the fifth day of fighting since Chase had kicked Ben out of his hospital and Ben had returned to the field. The Rebels had been fighting the gangs day and night for over a week, cutting them no slack, and the gangs were exhausted.

This group of gang members numbered 20, their ages ranging from early twenties to late forties, a mixed bag of black and white. Back in the old days, before the world fell apart, certain liberals would have immediately begun sobbing and moaning and making excuses for the behavior of the gang members. Some members of the press would have written and broadcast that their behavior could be blamed on a poor diet as children. Or perhaps they felt rejected while in school because the coach wouldn't let them play or the homecoming queen wouldn't date them or the next door neighbor's kid had a fancier bicycle or their father spanked them, or some such crap as that.

Ben didn't buy that nonsense back then and he sure as hell didn't buy it now.

Ben sat on a pile of rubble and rolled a cigarette. He didn't have to tell his people to question every prisoner about the whereabouts of Ray Brown; those were standing orders. But Ray Brown, if he was still on the rock, had proved to be very elusive. Ben was beginning to think the man had somehow managed to slip out of the ruins.

No matter. Someday he'd find him. And when he did, he'd kill him.

Ben watched as the prisoners' hands were tied behind their backs and they were led off to a Rebel interrogation point. There, they would be fingerprinted and blood would be drawn for DNA work-ups. Prints and DNA samples would be sent back to Base Camp One for possible match-ups.

Ben wasn't being soft-hearted. He just didn't want to be accused of shooting or hanging the wrong people.

Since the second assault on the rock by the Rebels, gang members had been surrendering in increasingly larger numbers, and that was something that Ben had not antici-pated. It led him to believe that many of the more hard-core gang leaders and their followers had somehow slipped out of the ruins and were on the run.

But so far not one prisoner had been able to confirm that suspicion.

Now, what to do with the prisoners was beginning to be a real problem for the Rebels.

The prisoners weren't giving their names, weren't admit-ting anything, and if they hadn't been mugged, finger-printed or had samples of DNA previously taken, the Rebels had no way of knowing the severity of their past crimes.

The surrendering gang members were getting to be a real pain in the ass.

Ben walked over to the ragged line of punks, all standing with their hands tied behind them. Most of them refused to meet his hard gaze, but a few were still defiant, open hate in their eyes as they glared at him.

"Aren't you going to tell me all about your terribly tragic childhood?" Ben asked one man. "I'm sure that's why you embarked on a life of crime."

"Screw you, Raines!"

It had long since ceased to surprise Ben that his face was so well known. Everything from gold to women had been offered for his capture over the years.

"I do wish you people would become a bit more original," Ben told him. "Although I'm sure that's due to a lack of something or another in your diet while young. It amazes me that Shakespeare ever managed to get a word written, considering the dietary fare of those days."

"You're really enjoying this, aren't you, Raines?" the man asked.

"Not especially. I'd much rather be home, to tell the truth."

"Me, too, if I had a home to go to."

Ben stared at the man for a moment. He shifted his gaze to a Rebel standing close by. "Cut him loose," he ordered.

The man rubbed his wrists for a few seconds, then asked, "You gonna hang me now, general?"

"No. I'm going to talk with you. Come on."

Ben turned his back on the man and walked away, toward the ruins of a building.

"Move!" Jersey told the thug menacingly, lifting her CAR. The man moved.

Ben shrugged out of his pack and sat down on what remained of a windowsill. He dug in his pack and came up with the Rebel's version of the old MRE—Meals Ready to Eat—and tossed the package to the man.

"I thought a condemned man got his choice of food for his last meal," the man said.

"Be glad you're getting that."

The gang member, in his late thirties, Ben guessed, opened the outer wrappings and selected a pack, tearing it open. He ate hungrily.

"You're old enough to remember what it was like before the Great War," Ben prompted. "So tell me your sad story about why you chose a life of crime."

The man chewed, swallowed, took a drink of water from a canteen, and said, "You know, Raines, you're a real asshole."

Ben smiled. "Oh?"

"Yeah. The whole damn world falls apart, and you go out and build yourself a friggin' nation. No big deal for you. You just do it. You shit on the Constitution and expect others to like it. Well, let me give you a news flash, there are some people, Raines, who just can't, or won't, live under your rules and laws."

"Millions of them," Ben agreed. "But while they choose not to be a part of the Tri-States philosophy, they do live under a basic set of rules and laws. You and your kind won't even do that much."

"Maybe not, Raines. But you can't kill us all."

Ben chuckled. "You want to bet?"

Eighteen

The group of survivors that Ben had stayed with during the days he was trapped in the ruins all agreed they wanted to be a part of the SUSA. They boarded the next transport plane south and were gone, out of Ben's life, to start a new life in the Southern United States of America. Ben had no doubts about their ability to make it in the SUSA. They were all good solid moral people who, to a person, believed in hard work and law and order.

Ben turned his attention back to the clearing out of Manhattan.

"Probably half the punks got away," Ben's chief of intelligence informed him. "They slipped away in small boats and then scattered."

"Ray Brown among them?"

"Yes. That's been confirmed."

"And no idea where they all went?"

"Not a clue, Ben. We believe they broke up into very small groups and scattered in all directions."

"They'll cause a lot of people some grief before they're finally stopped."

"Yes," Mike replied with a smile. "But only if they stay in those areas not aligned with the Tri-States philosophy."

Ben laughed. "For a fact."

"Another two weeks or so on this rock should do it." Mike stood up. "I'm heading up into the northeast part of the country. Check things out. I'll see you when you get there."

Mike tossed Ben a sloppy salute and was gone. Ben knew it might be weeks before he once more checked in, but when he did, he would have vital information he had gathered along the way. The man was like a chameleon, able to blend in anywhere.

Ben left the half-building he was using for a CP and walked along the rubble-littered street, down to where recently-taken prisoners were being interrogated. Some had been shipped back to the states where they had committed crimes; others had been hanged or shot. Still others, having had the shit scared out of them by being forced to watch executions, were, at least for the moment, all too anxious to start over and live a life of law-abiding productivity. Ben knew that for about half of them, that sudden desire to become law-abiding citizens would last until the Rebels pulled out.

And then it would be a return to punk business as usual.

But Ben wasn't going to order mass executions as a means of putting a stop to crime. He had executed those who the Rebels had proof were wanted killers, slavers, terrorists, and the like.

Now the final purge of the ruins of Manhattan was winding down.

There were some towns in the north and east that had managed to rise at least part of the way from the ashes of war and put together some semblance of a newspaper.

Their reporters were calling the siege of New York a slaughter. Ben just laughed at the newspaper accounts of how he was supposedly treating the hard-core criminals; he expected no less from those reporters and ignored their rantings and ravings.

Ben sat down on a pile of rubble and looked at the ragged bunch of new prisoners now being marched off to interrogation. They were a sad-looking lot. The Rebels were now flushing out the real dregs.

"A slaughter," Ben muttered. "If there has been any slaughter in the ashes it's been the roaming gangs slaughtering innocent people coast to coast. Or perhaps Simon Border and his people slaughtering people in their territory who don't agree with his philosophy. Hell, we just come along and clean up afterward."

"You say something, boss?" Jersey asked, walking up to stand by Ben.

"Oh, not really, Jersey." He held up the clipping. "Did you read this?"

"I read it. It's bullshit. There's been no slaughter here. The only slaughter has been the gangs killing innocent people all over the country. Fuck those cry-baby reporters."

Ben smiled. "I can always count on you, Little Bit."

"Well, it's the truth, boss. I visit the archives down at Base Camp One whenever we're home. I've read hundreds of old newspapers that we've salvaged and put on computer and microfilm. There were journalists back then constantly pissing and moaning about the rights of criminals. I read where law-abiding citizens were put in jail or sued because they used deadly force to protect what was theirs against punks and thugs and street crap. And that's the kind of society these assholes—" she pointed toward the clipping "—want to return to? Not me. Never."

Before Ben could reply, the rest of his team walked up. Corrie said, "This sector is clean, boss. Up north of the park, the gangs are surrendering by the droves. It looks like it's all but over here."

"How many gangs leaders are estimated to have gotten away?"

"About half of them. Including Ray Brown."

"All the heavy duty gang leaders got off the rock," Beth said. "With quite a few of their followers."

Ben stood up and brushed off his BDUs. "I'm ready to get the hell off this rock, folks."

"I been ready," Jersey said.

Ben handed the remaining clean-up of the ruins of Manhattan over to Ike, took his 1 Batt, and pulled out the next morning, heading first north, up into Connecticut.

They hadn't gone far before it became obvious that the gangs escaping from Manhattan had not traveled either north or east.

"We did have some criminal types hanging around, general," one resident of a small town said. "But they just up and pulled out about six weeks ago."

"Which way did they go?"

"West. I guess they heard you folks were on the way. You going to stay around here, general?"

"No. We're going to give you people a hand in getting back on your feet, and then pull out."

"You don't act like you're very happy to be up here, general."

"I'm not. And the sooner we can pull out the happier we'll all be."

"Anxious to get back to your gunpowder society, general?" a woman asked.

Ben looked at her for a moment, then laughed. The woman looked to be in her mid-fifties, and might have been on the fringes of the peace and love movement several decades back. Those wonderful people, among whose numbers were those who taunted and spat on American fighting men returning from Southeast Asia.

"If that is what you choose to call the SUSA, ma'am," Ben replied, with as much civility as possible.

"You execute people there by firing squad, don't you, general?" she asked.

"Well, actually, ma'am, we give them a choice of being hanged or shot."

"I find that disgusting and inhumane!"

"We find it quite a deterrent to crime." Ben was keeping a very wary eye on Jersey. He did not want her to get up in this woman's face.

"Ah, general." The man who seemed to be one of the leaders of the group of townspeople, seeing that the woman was about to let her ass overload her mouth, stepped in, and Ben silently thanked him. "I want to thank you for stopping here to offer us use of your fine medical facilities."

The man had to have been a politician before the war, Ben thought. "That's why we're here, sir. It's probably been a long time since your local doctors had access to serums and vaccines."

"Years, general."

"We'll take care of you. But after that . . ."

"I understand. There are a number of people in this area of the country who just don't understand the Tri-States philosophy. I do, and could live very happily under it. But I'm in the minority, I'm afraid."

The woman snorted derisively and walked off.

"You'd be welcome in the SUSA."

The man smiled. "This is my home, general. I was born and reared here. It would take something drastic for me to up and leave."

Ben returned the smile. "That something drastic might

be when you let the hammer down on a punk and these hanky-stompers you've got for neighbors have you arrested."

"Should that happen, general, you will see me cross the borders into the SUSA."

"Should that happen, sir, get in touch with me and I'll send Rebels up to get you. By force, if necessary."

"I'll remember that."

"Please do."

Ben and his people pulled out a few days later and headed east, over into Rhode Island. Not a shot had been fired in several weeks. Wherever the punks had fled to, they had done a good job of covering their tracks. The trip was turning into a real yawner.

"Boring," Jersey said.

"Are Buddy and his special ops people still tagging along behind us?" Ben asked.

"Laying back about 50 miles," Corrie replied. "I'm pretty sure that's Ike's idea, boss."

"Oh, you can bet it is. Well, nothing we can do about it. You can be assured Ike got his orders from Cecil . . . at Ike's suggestion, of course."

The citizens of Rhode Island were glad to see Ben and the Rebels and the medical teams traveling with them. They were open and friendly people, but most made it clear they did not want to live under the Tri-States philosophy.

The Rebels saw to their medical needs and moved on.

"The gangs have pulled out, so the danger is over," Ben said with a smile.

"But the criminal element is everywhere," Cooper said. "Without hard rules and laws, as soon as we're gone, they'll re-surface."

"Of course, they will," Ben agreed. "But the good citizens are seeing only the immediate relief. It's their state, they have the right to choose the type of government they wish to live under. We're doing the humanitarian thing this trip."

"But someday we'll have to come back and kick ass, boss," Jersey said.

Ben shook his head. "I don't think so, Jersey. Once we've put this trip to the Northeast behind us, I have no plans of ever returning. If the people in these areas want to bankrupt themselves with the same old legal and social systems they had before, that's their business. In a few months, I'm convinced we're going to have our hands full dealing with Simon Border. After that . . . ?" He shrugged. "I don't know. But I don't envision us ever coming back up here. Not in this role anyway."

The team exchanged glances and smiles. They knew what Ben meant. If they had to come back, it would not be in the role of humanitarian.

Three weeks after Ben and his 1 Batt pulled out of the ruins of Manhattan, Mike Richards caught up with the column.

"The Northeast is clean," he informed Ben. "The damn gangs are gone. I'm convinced they've broken up into very small groups and are laying low until we leave."

"Something I plan to do before the summer is over." Ben's words were offered very drily.

Mike smiled. "What's the matter, Ben? Aren't you receiving a warm friendly reception?"

"On the contrary, the people have been very nice. But somebody has duped them into believing the worst is over. I personally think they're in for a very rude surprise."

"So do I. Once you pull all your people out. But when you get up into Vermont, New Hampshire, Maine?" Mike shook his head. "Those are tough people, Ben. Pioneer stock. Oh, there are some cry-baby liberals among them, but not too many."

"What do you hear from those states, Mike?"

"Not much. The cities are a mess, but out in the rural areas the folks are doing all right. Not great, but making it. Very self-sufficient folks in those areas."

"And you and your people saw to it they know we're on the way?"

"You bet."

"Their response?"

"Welcome with open arms. They don't necessarily want to join us politically, but they're not our enemies." Mike smiled. "Besides, it's awful pretty country. And it damn sure beats getting shot at."

"First we have to get through Massachusetts," Ben reminded him.

"Or what's left of it."

"True."

"What are your plans for the ruins of Boston?"

"I have no plans for that city or any other city. I'm through with the cities, Mike. We'll do our best to stabilize the countryside. If the people in the rural areas want to deal with the crud and the crap in the ruins of the cities, that's up to them. I'm not going to waste another Rebel life in the damn rubble of the cities. Not the major cities, anyway."

"Was it that bad for you trapped in the ruins, Ben?"

"No. Not really. But I did have a chance to do some thinking. It isn't our fight, Mike. If these people here in the northeast were aligning with us, then that would be a different story. But for the most part, they're choosing to stay with the old system, even though they should know by now it didn't work. By their choosing the old way, that makes it their fight, not ours. I think, medically speaking, we do have an obligation to treat the sick wherever we can. If they'll let us. That is for our good as well as theirs. But as far as I'm concerned, it ends there."

Mike stood up. "That's the way I see it, too. What about Simon Border, Ben?"

"I need to know everything there is to know about the man and his army."

"I'll get right on it. Well, enjoy your stay in the Northeast, Ben. I'll catch up with you."

Ben nodded and Mike was gone out the door.

Jersey appeared in the open doorway. "We going to kick Simon Border's ass, boss?"

"Probably, Jersey."

"A religious war, boss?"

"Simon will surely call it that."

"I wonder what history will call it?"

Ben smiled. "Historians will surely paint us as the bad guys, Jersey. I think we've already seen to that."

"Yeah? Well, fuck 'em if they can't take a joke!"

Ben was still laughing when the rest of his team stuck their heads into the room to see what in the world was going on.

Nineteen

Ben and his people stayed well away from the ruins of Boston, heading toward New Hampshire on Interstate 495. Buddy sent some of his special ops people in to look over the city and they reported back about what Ben thought they would.

"About 5,000 or so people in the ruins, Father," Buddy said. "That's just an estimate, of course."

"Close enough for government work, boy."

"What?"

"Nothing, son. Just an old expression you wouldn't be familiar with. Any punks in the city?"

"No, sir."

"Any creepies?"

The handsome young man shook his head.

"No punks, no creeps," Ben muttered. "Where the hell did they go?"

"They certainly didn't head south. They didn't go north, for the Canadian militia is guarding all possible crossing sites. Scouts report that they didn't go east. So that leaves only one direction open.''

"Simon Border double-crossed them once. They're not stupid enough to fall for his line again.''

"I wouldn't think so. But he's a very convincing man, right?''

"Yes. He is. He conned thousands into following him west.''

"Then perhaps he did convince them to return.''

"The West is a vast country,'' Anna said. "According to what I have read. Much of it unpopulated. Correct?''

"You're right, Anna,'' Buddy said. "Even more so now.''

Ben groaned. "Don't tell me you think the punks might have gone to the ruins of Los Angeles and Southern California.''

"It's certainly a possibility.''

"Hell, we left that in worse shape than we did New York!''

"I'd opt for the deserts and the mountains.'' Jersey spoke up. "Lots of little towns dotted all over the place.''

"You mean you think the punks turned over a new leaf and went straight?'' Ben asked.

"Not necessarily,'' his son answered. "In this, the aftermath of the greatest disaster ever to strike the earth, what would a certain type of weak-willed, even lower-charactered person be looking for, other than food?''

Ben thought for a moment, then grimaced. "Oh, no, boy! Don't tell me that!''

"What?'' Anna asked.

"Drugs,'' Beth said. "I think Buddy's got it, boss.''

Corrie walked into the room holding half a dozen blown-up photos. There was a very puzzled look on her face. "Boss, we just got this transmission from Base Camp One. It's from several satellite passovers taken over the past few days.''

"What is it?"

"Motorcycles and dune buggies. Hundreds of them. All heading west. But not all together. They reached a certain point, then split up."

Ben looked at each of the photos for a moment, then flung them on the table in disgust. "Ray Brown is smarter than I thought. He had a secondary plan to fall back on. They hid motorcycles, dune buggies, alternate transportation, all over the place as they moved east. But why? Why even go east in the first place if they felt they were going to lose?"

No one had an immediate answer to that and neither did Ben.

"Diversion?" Jersey finally tossed the word out.

"From what? For what?" Ben asked.

"Maybe just to get us out of the center of the country, Father," Buddy said.

"All right, let's play that one out. Why would they want us out of the center of the country?"

No one replied and Ben finally shook his head and stood up, glancing down at the photos. "Oh, to hell with it. The punks slipped out of the net and are heading west. We know that much for fact. Maybe Simon Border's people will deal with them and that will mean one less problem for us."

"So we continue on with our humanitarian efforts?" Buddy asked.

"That's why we're here, son."

The Rebels moved on. They cleaned up airports and the big transports from the SUSA came roaring in, bringing medical supplies. In the SUSA, factories and research labs were running around the clock, producing medicines for the Rebels to distribute in the North and East.

Ben ordered leaflets dropped all over the Northeast, telling the citizens the Rebels were on the way and giving the locations and the approximate times they would be there.

Ben told his political officers to stand down and ceased all talk of anyone becoming a part of the SUSA. He wanted only to finish the job they'd started. The majority of the people they met and treated were friendly and open and glad to see the Rebels. Reporters from various small newspapers that had been springing up all over the eastern United States caught up with the columns and in general stayed out of the way, letting the Rebels work. After a couple of minor confrontations, those few reporters with a penchant for being obnoxious stayed clear of the Rebels. They learned very quickly that when they were told to get the hell out of the way, the Rebels weren't kidding, and they backed up their warnings rather violently.

West of the Mississippi River, Simon Border's people had either purged the "undesirables" from their territory or had demoralized them to the point where any dissidents were no longer a problem.

Only a few SUSA supporters were still active in the areas under solid control of Simon Border forces, with the exception of the Mormons. For a time it looked as if Simon would leave any Mormon-controlled area alone, but that soon proved to be false. The state of Utah was now completely surrounded by Border's troops and nothing got in or out . . . so far.

"The man is a bigger fool than I first thought," Ben said. "Corrie, get some people in there and see what we can do to assist the Mormons. Let me rephrase that—see if the Mormons *want* our help. No strings attached."

"What's that lunatic got against the Mormons?" Jersey asked.

"Simon Border is against anyone who does not completely subscribe to his wacky ideas of religion and worship.''

"I thought he was going to try to work with us?" Cooper asked.

"Simon lies," Ben told him. "He lies when the truth would serve him better."

Ben took a piece of paper from his pocket and unfolded it. "We got this early this morning. Our people in Simon's territory think something is up . . . involving us."

"But Simon has signed a non-aggression pact with us!" Buddy protested.

Ben smiled. "That document isn't worth the paper it's printed on, son. We knew that all along. I told you that someday we'd have to fight Simon and his people."

A runner from communications came into the room and handed Ben a communiqué. Ben quickly read it, then grunted. "Simon's been quietly recruiting people outside his territory. He's managed to convince thousands of ultra-religious people—of the very fanatical, off-the-wall types—to come over and join him."

"And that means. . . ?" Buddy asked.

"We wrap it up here as quickly as possible and start backtracking, taking the shortest routes."

"And run head-on into a religious war, Father?"

"I don't want one, son, that's for sure. But I've warned Simon to keep his nutty people west of the Mississippi. He agreed and also agreed to leave Utah alone. He's broken every promise he ever made to me." Ben shrugged. "Which I expected him to do."

"President Altman has managed to put together something of an army," Beth said. "The people we left behind as advisors say they're looking pretty good. It's a small force, but growing."

"It isn't growing fast enough," Ben replied. "The NUSA will never have much of an army because the goddamn liberals will never permit it to grow to any size. And whatever kind of police they finally do put in place will have their hands tied from the git-go." He grimaced. "Probably won't even allow them to carry guns."

Ben's team, including the usually straight-faced Buddy, all had to struggle to hide their grins. To say that Ben Raines had absolutely no use for cry-baby liberals was the same as saying a mule was stubborn.

"So we'll have to go back and clean out the punks and crud again," Jersey remarked. "So what else is new?"

"Simon Border and his people, Jersey," Ben replied. "I don't want us to get bogged down in a religious war. That is the absolute last thing I want. But I don't see any way to avoid it."

"Talk about history giving us a black mark," Cooper said. "That will sure do it."

"I'm afraid you're right, Coop," Ben agreed. "Well . . . let's get our humanitarian work done, and then we'll deal with the Most Reverend Simon Border."

"The word I get is that he'll screw anything that will stand still or lie down long enough," Jersey said. "How the hell can people fall for anything that comes out of the mouth of someone like that?"

Ben laughed. "Oh, Jersey, back before the Great War, there were any number of TV preachers just as bad as Simon Border. The airwaves were filled with them. There was one in particular I used to enjoy watching occasionally."

Buddy's mouth dropped open. "You enjoyed watching him, Father?"

"Oh, sure. Hell, he'd get the spirit and start speaking in strange tongues and doing the heebie-jeebie and the mashed potato and the twist and the slop-bop, jumping all over the stage. He was quite a sight to see."

"Whatever happened to him?" Beth asked.

"Some husband caught him in bed with both his wife and his 13-year-old daughter and shot him five times in the ass. He survived the shooting, but I don't know what happened to him after that." Ben waited until the laughter had died down. "I did hear that it messed up his dancing somewhat."

Ben didn't believe for a minute that all the criminal element had pulled out of the Northeast. What he did believe was that they were in hiding, lying low until the Rebels passed through. Then they would resurface.

It's not our problem, Ben thought. *The citizens can deal with it. And if they don't want to deal with it, then that's their problem.*

The Rebels stopped and offered medical treatment to every community who wanted it. If the people were reluctant to accept it, the Rebels moved on without another word. Ben had ordered his people not to discuss politics unless the townspeople brought it up . . . and most didn't.

It was so boring and so uneventful that most of the reporters who had been following the various Rebel battalions went back home. While waiting at what was left of an airport for supplies in northern Massachusetts, Mike Richards once more rejoined the column. He had been gone for a month.

"You were right, Ben," the spook said. "Simon Border is preparing for war against us."

Ben sighed. "Why, Mike?"

"Because you and the Rebels are godless, that's why. According to Simon, the SUSA is nothing more than a huge den of sin. If the United States is ever to be whole and moral and God-fearing, the SUSA must be destroyed."

"I'm sure he's telling his followers and faithful that God told him all that."

"Right. The man has visions where he actually talks with God."

"I seem to remember that another fellow, Jethro Jim Bob Musseldine, had similar visions."

"Jethro didn't have 20 million or so followers, Ben, all ready to do battle with the Great Satan."

"The great satan being me?"

"Exactly."

"And he's found 20 million Americans who actually believe that crap?"

"At least in part, Ben. Simon has provided them with hope. He's done some good things; we have to admit that. He's got some very smart people with him. They've rebuilt towns and communities and churches, got the sewer and water and lights working, raised crops, and gave the people a sense of worth."

"I'll grant you that, and did a good job of it. But add that we didn't interfere with him doing that."

"But we did aid the men and women in the hills and mountains who are fighting him, and Simon knows we did, and knows that we still are."

"He's guessing."

Mike shook his head. "No, Ben. The man has a pretty good intelligence network. Not yet as good as ours, and never will have because of his lack of satellites, but they're pretty damn good. I won't sell them short."

Corrie came running into the room, waving a piece of paper. "Boss! This just in from Cecil. Dozens of kids, maybe hundreds, they don't have an accurate count yet, were taken to area hospitals all over the SUSA. But mostly confined to Texas, Arkansas, and Louisiana. Someone laced the schools' water supply with some sort of mind-altering drug. Similar to LSD, but with much more horrible results. A dozen or more teachers are down as well."

Ben's face turned as hard as stone and his eyes became as flint. "Go on," he muttered darkly.

"Our people killed one man early this morning close to a school when he refused to stop at their command," Corrie read from the communiqué. "They're running both prints and DNA now."

Mike stood up. "I'm outta here. I'll bump you from Base Camp One."

Ben nodded, not trusting his voice to speak.

"Cecil says he'll contact you as soon as they know more," Corrie finished it.

Ben cleared his throat. Stood up and walked around the room for a moment. His team had gathered near the door, standing silently. "Down through the years people have done just about everything in the book in an attempt to stop us," Ben spoke, his words low and holding menace. "But to attack children is just about as vile as an enemy can get."

"Simon Border, boss?" Cooper asked.

"I don't know, Coop. But you can bet I'm going to find out."

"Might be Ray Brown, boss," Jersey said. "We know he got out of the ruins of Manhattan. And we damn sure know he hates you."

"That was my first thought, Jersey. I believe I read in his dossier that Ray was in trouble for manufacturing drugs just before the Great War, right?"

"Yes, sir. Among other things. I think he was still in the army when the drug thing came up."

"Pull in 7 and 10 Batts to relieve us here. Order all the rest of our people to stand by to pull out—"

"This might interest you, Father," Buddy said, walking into the room holding a newspaper.

"Is that Simon Border's publication?" Ben asked.

"Yes, sir. A front page article. It claims we are brainwashing children in the SUSA and by the time they are six or seven years old, they are beyond rehabilitation. It further states that since nits grow into lice, people of all ages living within the borders of the SUSA should be considered the enemy. There is more, but you get the general idea.''

"I sure do, son. I think we are going to find that Simon has elected to shake hands with the devil in order to try to defeat us—the devil being the punks that escaped from the East. Corrie, as soon as my suspicions are confirmed, order full-scale preparations for all-out war against Simon Border. Simon doesn't realize it, but he just opened Pandora's Box.''

Twenty

Ben stayed with his 1 Batt and waited for further word about the events taking place in the SUSA. It was not long in coming.

"Two of the teachers died, Ben," Cecil told him. "Looks like the kids are going to make it, but the psychiatrists can only guess what's going to happen further on down the road."

"Anything on the man killed by the school?"

"He's been positively ID'd as being part of Ray Brown's gang. And everything is pointing toward Simon Border allowing the gangs to come in and operate in his claimed territory, just as long as they leave his people alone."

"That sorry son-of-a-bitch!"

Cecil said nothing. He waited for Ben to finish venting his spleen. And that took awhile, for Ben cussed Simon Border loud and long.

"Close the borders," Ben finally calmed down enough to say. "Seal them tight. Double the patrols. Place your

battalions on middle alert. I'm on my way. I'll probably
cut west through Arkansas and enter Simon's territory that
way.''

"You're sure this is what you want to do, Ben?"

"I'm sure it's the only thing that Simon will understand,
Cec. Anybody who deliberately makes war on children is
too low to live.''

"Well, you'll get no argument from me on that. All right,
Ben. Give me a progress report from time to time.''

"You know I will, Cec. Eagle out.'' He turned to Corrie.
"Mount 'em up, Corrie. We're out of here.''

When the initial battalions that were to cross over into
Simon Border's territory linked up a few days later, it was
an awesome sight. There were five over-strength battalions:
Ben's 1 Batt, Dan's 3 Batt, Buddy's 8 Batt, Jackie Malone's
12 Batt, and Jim Peters's 14 Batt. The column seemed
to stretch out endlessly. People heard the rumbling long
before the trucks and Hummers and tanks and self-
propelled and towed artillery came into view. They gathered alongside the old highways to watch them pass, waving
at the Rebels.

Ben kept to the old interstate system as much as possible,
but even with that, the going was slow, for the highways
were in terrible shape.

The Rebels experienced no trouble on the way southwest. "This has to be the longest stretch of inaction in our
history,'' Ben said.

"Boring,'' Jersey replied.

"It won't be once we cross over into Simon's territory,''
Ben warned.

"Suits me, boss.''

Ben was under no illusions about the consequences of
crossing over into Simon Border's claimed territory. The

man had built a powerful army that not only was well-equipped but highly motivated. And Ben had spent more than a few sleepless hours weighing his decision to invade Simon's territory.

Simon would deny any connection with the deaths of the teachers and the mind-crippling of the kids, and he would be very convincing about it. He would paint the Rebels as the aggressors and any American citizen who disliked the Tri-States philosophy would be more than ready and willing to believe him. Cecil didn't have to bring that to Ben's attention; Ben was already well aware of it.

"Any word from Mike?" Ben asked Corrie, as the long column moved through the countryside.

"Not a peep, boss. Not from Mike, nor from any of his people in the field."

"Nothing from any of the resistance fighters in the mountains?"

"Nothing."

There were dozens of small groups scattered throughout Simon's territory who were violently opposed to Simon's off-the-wall ultra-religious rule. The Rebels supplied them as best they could, but since the guerrilla fighters were constantly on the move, it was hard to know exactly where they were from week to week. They managed to keep some of Simon's forces busy, but it was more like a man swatting at a pesky mosquito.

If the column made 200 miles a day, they considered that excellent time, for most of the time the roads were so bad, they were lucky to average 20 miles an hour. Equipment breakdowns occurred frequently.

Mike Richards radioed in on the Rebels' seventh day on the road. "The punks are in the Southwest, Ben. Running west from the Texas-New Mexico border over to the ruins of L.A., and then north up to the Utah-Colorado line. They're pretty well all over Nevada and in the California deserts. Mainly located in the ruins of small deserted towns where there is water.''

''They have drug factories going?''

''Affirmative, Ben. All sorts of drugs. I captured one gang member. After a few minutes, he was more than willing to spill his guts . . .''

Ben didn't ask how Mike had accomplished that; he really didn't want to know.

''They've worked out some sort of deal with gangs from Mexico, Central America, and South America. They trade women for materials—among other items. Blondes seem to be the favorite this month.''

''Slavers.'' Ben spat the word. ''Goddamn dopers dealing with goddamn slavers!''

Mike said nothing. He knew how Ben despised both.

''We can't cover the whole border with troops,'' Ben said, after catching his breath. ''That's several thousand miles.''

''Wouldn't do any good, Ben. They're flying the junk in and flying the women out.''

''But we can damn sure put our fighter pilots to work, though, can't we?''

''As long as they get them coming in and not going out,'' Mike warned.

''I'll make sure they understand that. What else can you tell me, Mike?''

''Simon is behind it all. I've got that nailed down tight and for a fact. He's going to deny it until hell freezes over, but everything Ray Brown and the others are doing is with Simon's approval. The women Ray and the others are swapping for the raw materials to make the drugs are not, according to Simon, 'Christian women.' They are, again in his words, 'the devil's harlots,' and beyond redemption.''

''That's very Christian of the sanctimonious son-of-a-bitch,'' Ben said, his words leaking acid.

Mike burst out laughing at both Ben's words and tone. "Sorry, Ben. But I needed that."

Ben smiled, some of his rage simmering down. "It looks like we'll be wintering in the desert, Mike."

"Beats wintering in Maine, Ben. See ya." Mike broke the connection.

Ben spoke with Cecil, bringing him up to date. He then bumped Thermopolis down at Base Camp One and told him to get his 19 Batt up and equipped for the field . . . again. Therm, the aging hippie-turned-warrior, and his wife, Rosebud, ran the headquarters battalion, seeing to the resupplying of the entire Rebel Army, logistics, food, everything from panties to ammunition, and the thousand and one other details involved in keeping thousands of troops on the go and ready.

"Emil Hite has attached himself to me, Ben," Therm warned. "What do you want me to do about him?"

"What does Rosebud have to say about it?" Ben asked, doing his best to keep from chuckling.

"Well, let's put it this way—the little con artist has promised to behave himself and Rosebud has agreed to give him one more chance."

"He is amusing to have around, Therm."

"You want him?"

"I didn't say that," Ben was quick to add. "No . . . I think he'll probably be an asset to your battalion. You keep him."

"That's very big of you."

"I always try to look after the needs of my people, Therm. See you in a couple of weeks."

Therm mumbled something and broke the connection.

Emil Hite had joined Ben's Rebels a few years back, promising to renounce his days as a con artist—something no one believed. The little man was a great big pain in the ass, but when the chips were down, he and his band of followers had proved themselves in combat time after time.

"Let's head for the New Mexico state line, gang," Ben told his team.

When Simon Border heard that Ben had turned his army around and was heading west, he immediately went to his sanctuary, fell to his knees, and began fervently praying. He asked God to strike Ben dead with lightning bolts, drown him in a flood, just do *something* to stop the paganistic godless heathen from reaching Simon's territory.

When no angels appeared to tell him that Ben had been destroyed, Simon reckoned that he'd just have to do it himself. He put every able-bodied man in his territory on full alert.

"The Great Satan is coming," he warned his thousands of followers. "Prepare to defend our homeland."

"We're going to stay out of Simon's heavily populated northern areas," Ben told four batt coms he was taking into Simon's territory. "Intel has solid evidence that the drug factories are located along the border with Mexico, so that's where we'll hit. If Simon doesn't interfere, and allows us to destroy the drug factories and wipe out the gangs, we'll leave him alone and get out of his territory once it's done. If he wants a war—" Ben shrugged his shoulders "—then we'll give him a war."

"What about the other battalions?" Jim Peters asked.

"They'll be stationed along the edge of our territory, ready to come in if needed. Really, I want Simon to see what he's up against. That may be all it takes to open his eyes."

"Do you believe it will, Father?" Buddy asked.

"No, son, I don't. But I want to give the man a chance to back off."

Dan Gray stood up. "Ben, this is not a holy war. The man is nothing but a two-bit dictator. He's about as holy as a rattlesnake."

"In the minds of millions of people, Dan, he's the next thing to Jesus. And many of those people live outside of Simon's claimed territory. His movement is nationwide, and it isn't getting any smaller."

"How did he happen, general?" Jackie Malone asked. "I mean, what's wrong with people to fall for a line like his?"

"People became desperate, Jackie. The nation was hammered to its knees twice in only a few years. Many thought perhaps God was signaling them the end was near. Many people lost all hope until they found Simon and his snake-oil message. They needed something to lean on, to prop them up, and Simon provided it."

"But we were the most stable force in all the world," Jackie insisted. "We had a working government, schools, hospitals, everything. Yet these people turned their backs on us, and went with a nut like Simon Border." She shook her head. "I just don't understand it."

Ben smiled. "My dad used to say—'Everyone to their own taste, said the woman who kissed a cow.'"

Buddy waited until the laugher died down and said, "What is the fascination with drugs, Father? I can appreciate an occasional drink to relax, but to destroy one's mind with chemicals is beyond my realm of understanding. It's . . . stupid."

"It really started back in the 1960s, son, when I was just a little boy. The peace and love generation. Tune in and drop out, I believe one of the slogans went. A lot of recording artists glorified drug use. As did many of the movies. It was a sad time in our culture. None of you people, with the exception of Dan and me, were even born then, and we were just little boys. Hell, most of the Rebels weren't born until years and years later. The government had very ineffective drug prevention programs . . ."

"Why didn't the authorities just shoot the dealers?" Ben's son persisted.

Ben chuckled. "Oh, that, ah, would have suited many Americans just fine, son. And there were countries who did just that. But if we wouldn't execute murderers, rapists, child molesters, and the like. . . ?" Ben shrugged his shoulders. "Well, it's all moot now. Any further questions?"

There were none.

"Well, let's go to war, people."

Twenty-One

Ben carefully studied the terrain through binoculars. He could see nothing out of the ordinary, which he knew meant absolutely nothing. There might be hundreds of enemy troops waiting in ambush.

"Scouts report nothing, boss," Corrie said. "No signs of life whatsoever."

The Rebel convoy was stopped just inside the Oklahoma line, on old Highway 70. Arkansas lay a few miles behind them. The Red River flowed silently on just to the south of them.

"How far in are they?"

"What is left of Broken Bow. No signs of life in the town."

"About 4,500 people lived there before the Great War," Beth said. "Next town of any size is Idabel."

"We may be too close to the Texas line for Simon's people to give us any trouble. I'm thinking he settled his

people some miles north of the line. We'll soon know
Let's push on. Mount up, people."

Idabel was a silent and deserted ruin, utterly devoid o
human life. The town had been looted and picked ove
so many times that nothing remained. The column pushed
on.

The Rebels bivouacked that night in the ruins of Hugo
another once bustling and prosperous town. Now it was
home to only the sighing of the wind and whatever ghosts
might have chosen to remain among its looted buildings

"Place is spooky," Cooper said.

"Cooper," Jersey replied. "You've seen hundreds o
deserted towns here and halfway around the world. What's
so special about this one?"

"I don't know. It's just gives me the creeps, that's all.'

Ben lifted his head and stared at Cooper for a moment
"What'd you say, Coop?"

"Huh, boss?"

"What did you just say, Coop?"

"I said I don't know."

"No, after that?"

"I said . . . this place gives me the creeps, that's all.'
Coop's eyes narrowed. "You think. . . ?"

"Maybe. I've been jumpy myself ever since we stopped
here. Creeps just might explain why we haven't seen any
people."

"Oh, crap!" Corrie muttered, reaching for her CAR.

The Rebel battalions were strung out for about 20 miles,
with several miles between each battalion, a long and very
formidable line.

"Put everybody on alert, Corrie," Ben ordered. "The
shit just may be getting ready to hit the fan. Let's get over
behind those ruins, over there."

There had been no breeze all afternoon, and it had
been hot and dry as summer began waning. Now the air

was beginning to stir with a slight breeze and the moving air brought with it the very faint smell of creepie.

Ben wrinkled his nose. "Smell it, gang?"

They smelled it. Anna said, "Wet sheep shit smells like perfume compared to that."

Ben smiled. "My, but you do have a way with words, dear."

"Wet sheep shit?" Cooper grimaced, bipodding his SAW and making sure he had another container of ammo ready.

"Thank you," Anna replied, and checked her CAR, laying out half a dozen 30-round magazines within easy reach.

"All battalions on alert," Corrie said. "Several sentries have reported what they were sure were sightings, but too far out to be sure."

"They can be sure," Ben told her. "Mortar crews ready with IMs?"

"Ready with illumination flares."

"Batt coms are on their own as to when to drop them in."

"Affirmative."

Lightning licked at the sky and thunder rumbled in the distance as a late summer storm built up steam in the West.

"This is liable to get interesting," Jersey muttered, her words tossed around as the wind picked up.

"At least the bastards will get a bath," Beth replied.

Jim Peters's 14 Batt was the easternmost bivouac, miles away from Ben's 1 Batt. "Batt 14 under attack," Corrie called.

"There must be a lot of the bastards to attack us at this strength," Cooper said.

"Now we know where the punks *and* the creeps went," Ben replied.

"Surely Simon Border didn't invite these cannibals?" Anna questioned.

"No. I doubt that even he would do that," Ben said.

"Heads up!" Corrie called. "Here they come."

"IMs up!" Ben said.

The cloudy night was abruptly filled with artificial illumination as the flares soared high and popped.

"They never learn," Ben muttered, his words too low for anyone else to hear. "Every time they try a frontal assault, we always kick their asses."

Then there was no time left for conversation as the night became filled with gunfire, screaming and cursing. The dark shapes of the creeps, appearing on the land as giant, hooded roaches, rushed toward the Rebel positions.

The Rebels opened up with everything they had at their disposal, which was awesome. The creepies went down in bits and pieces and bloody chunks of what once was more or less human flesh.

"Keep your eyes open for the bastards to pop out of the ruins," Ben yelled.

The words had no sooner left his lips when creeps began pouring out of holes they'd dug and then camouflaged in the ruins of the town, waiting patiently for a new food supply to come unsuspectingly along.

Those who were hidden in the ruins died just as surely as their brothers and sisters in perversion who were attacking the town from the weed-grown fields.

The firefight did not last long, although in combat seconds very often seem like minutes and minutes often seem like hours to those caught up in the noisy hell.

The IMs still filling the air with harsh light showed those creeps left alive and able to crawl, stagger or run doing so, away from the ruins of the deserted town, leaving behind them dozens of dead and dying.

Ben popped an empty magazine and slipped home a full one. "Start putting those wounded creeps out of their misery," he called in a cold voice.

Single, well-placed shots began ringing out in the bloody night.

"Report," Ben said.

"Except for those few hidden in the ruins, none of the creeps even got close," Corrie said. "We have no dead, two with non-life-threatening wounds."

"Not much of a fight," Anna groused. "I think the creeps are losing their punch."

"They're losing their numbers, dear," Ben corrected. "Over the years we've killed thousands of them. And I wouldn't think their recruitment numbers are all that high."

"Yeah, I would think they'd have trouble convincing any normal person to join them voluntarily," Beth added.

"I can just hear the recruitment ads now," Jersey said. "Come enjoy the pleasures of never taking a bath and dining on raw human flesh. Yuck!" She spat on the ground.

"I don't think they'll return," Ben said. "But double the guards just in case."

"Reports coming in from other battalions," Corrie announced. "One dead and a dozen wounded, most of the wounds not serious. Scouts report that while the creeps retreated north and south, they soon cut west.

"Durant's the next town of any size," Beth called. "About 15,000 before the Great War."

"Have fly-bys shown any signs of human life there?" Ben asked.

"Negative, boss. Nothing."

"So we have the creeps to look forward to from here on in. Wonderful."

"At least they don't profess to be something they're not," Corrie said. "Unlike Simon Border."

"For a fact, Corrie," Ben agreed. "For a fact."

*   *   *

The Rebels began massive daily daylight airdrops into Utah: medical supplies, food, and weapons, from M-16s to .50-caliber heavy machine guns, artillery pieces and mortars. Ben halted the airdrops only when the commanders of the various Mormon units in Utah radioed that with the new supplies, they could now hold their own against just about anything that Simon might throw at them.

The long Rebel columns moved on the morning after the firefight. They did not take the time to bury the creepie dead.

"Carrion birds have to eat, too," Ben said. "Let's get this show on the road."

"I hope they don't get sick and croak afterward," Jersey replied.

The column made the 50-mile run to Durant and found a dead town.

"It wasn't until recently," Ben said, looking over a cemetery filled with relatively recent graves. "I'd say these graves are no more than a year old." And in the town's business district: "Some of these stores have been repainted and fixed up. This was a thriving community until Simon Border and the creeps moved in."

"Scouts report that the bridge over the lake just west of here is gone," Corrie said. "At least part of it. We'll have to detour around it."

"Did we blow that bridge?" Ben asked. "I don't remember."

His team shrugged their shoulders. "Beats me, boss," Cooper said. "We've blown so many."

Beth had lost many of her valuable journals over the years in ambushes and attacks and could not help either.

"Doesn't matter," Ben said. "It's gone and that's that." He laid a map out on the hood of the big wagon. "We'll cut north up to this little town at the tip of the lake and bivouac there for the night. Advise the scouts."

"They're already heading that way," Corrie said. "Reporting no trouble and no signs of life."

"Where the hell did the people go?" Ben muttered. "What happened to them?"

The wind sighed its unreadable reply and Ben knew that was about as much answer as he was ever likely to get. He didn't like to think the creeps got them, but realized that was an option he had to consider.

"You better come see this, general," a Rebel said, running up to Ben's side. The young man pointed. "Down that way, about a block."

Ben and team and about 50 other Rebels walked the distance to an old church.

"It's inside, sir," the Rebel told Ben in a very quiet voice.

Ben looked at the young man, then nodded. "Lead the way."

The young Rebel hesitated.

"What is it, son?"

"Better get the chaplain, sir."

"All right." Ben looked at Corrie and she spoke into her headset.

"On the way."

"We'll wait until he arrives."

There were several chaplains assigned to each battalion, Catholic, Protestant, Jew, and all three drove up in a Hummer.

"What is it, general?" Rabbi Wassermann asked.

"I don't know, Gary. We'll see in a minute. Whatever it is, it's in that church."

"What denomination was this?" another asked.

"Don't know," the third replied.

"Let's go," Ben said. To the young Rebel: "Lead the way, son."

The scene that greeted them brought everyone up short. On the wall behind where the pulpit once stood, between a wooden cross bolted to the wall, were the bones of four people, rotting flesh hanging from the bones. They had all been crucified, spikes driven into their feet, knees, sides, and hands.

Ben heard all three chaplains mutter short and very fervent prayers.

Painted on the wall, in bright red, were the words: RAY BROWN RULES.

"Over here, sir." The young Rebel who had led the way touched Ben's arm.

Scrawled on another wall, in pencil, were the words: *God help us all. First it was the cannibals, now it's the hordes of criminals, acting under the direct auspices of Simon Border. They've taken the women and the young children. The screaming as they are being raped is terrible. The leader, Ray Brown, has told us what he has planned for us. He is a spawn of the devil. The personification of everything evil. Oh my God, give me strength to endure the pain.*

"Get the remains down from the wall," Ben said softly. "And do it as gently as possible. We'll bury them in the yard beside the church."

"This Ray Brown," one of the chaplains spoke, his words hard with anger. "This creature . . ." He shook his head, unable to finish the sentence.

"I know," Ben said. "We'll deal with him this run. I promise you that."

"We've found a pit, or a ditch, that is filled with the bones of people, general," a scout said. "Looks like they've been dead several months. All lined up and shot."

"Let's see it."

Ben stood over the long ditch and looked down at the remains of perhaps 75 people while a Rebel doctor quickly

examined the rag-covered bones. Ben noticed he was paying particular attention to the teeth.

"Mostly men," the doctor said, looking up. "And I
would say they were mostly old men."

"Old men?"

"Yes, sir. No young men here."

"What do you make of that, general?" an intelligence
officer asked.

Ben was thoughtful for a moment. "My guess would be
they've taken the younger men to use as slaves, or to trade
them as such."

"Trade them, General Ben?" Anna asked. "To whom
and for what?"

"I'll reserve comment on both those questions, Anna.
But I can't believe Simon Border is involved in any type
of slave-trading or the use of slaves."

"I can," Beth said, considerable heat in her voice. "If
these people refused to go along with Simon's wacky views
on religion, I wouldn't put anything past that bastard, or
his goofy-assed followers."

Ben smiled at her words, for Beth was usually the quiet
one of his team, then he sobered at the truth in her statement. Ben was convinced that Simon Border was insane.
Functionally mad, but insane nonetheless.

Ben again looked down at the ditch of death. "Cover
them," he ordered. "We can't do much more than that
for them now." He sighed. "Then let's get the hell out of
here."

Twenty-Two

The column spent the night stretched out along the eastern side of the lake, with 1 Batt at the northern tip. The next day they rolled into Ardmore, and found it deserted.

"Somebody put up a hell of a battle here," Buddy observed, as he stood with his father on the main street of town.

"That they did, son. For all the good it did them," he added.

"We've found another mass grave, general," a scout said, walking up. "The doc is looking over the bones now."

Ben and Buddy followed the scout over to the mass grave located on the edge of town.

"Just like the other one," the doctor said, climbing out of the ditch. "All old people. What about the churches, general?"

"I have people inspecting them now. But I am expecting the worse."

The bad news wasn't long in coming.

"Two men and a woman, general," one of Ben's company commanders reported. "Nailed up just like the others. Same message on the wall. Ray Brown left his mark here, too."

"Get them down and bury them with the others."

"Simon Border on the horn, boss," Corrie said. "And he appears to be angry about something."

"I wonder what in the world could have made him angry," Ben replied with a smile. He walked over to the communications truck and took the mic. "This is Ben Raines, Simon. Go ahead."

Simon started preaching, running his words together and gulping air. Ben listened until the man ran out of air. "I didn't understand a damn word of that, Simon. You want to back up and start all over?"

"You have invaded my territory, Raines. You have broken your word, as I knew you would. You cannot be trusted. You are evil. You are a pig, Ben Raines. You are a spawn of the devil, straight from hell."

"And you're an asshole, Border," Ben said calmly.

There was a long silence from the other end. Then Border screamed, "What did you call me?"

"An asshole," Ben repeated. "A hypocritical, lying, self-serving, mean-spirited dickhead. I wouldn't trust you if you swore on a stack of Bibles. You don't know what the word Christian means, Border."

"How dare you speak to *me* in such a manner, you, you . . . heathen!"

Simon then, very unChristianlike, began cussing him, and he knew all the words and got them in the right places. Ben waited until the man had wound down. "Simon, you really fucked up with me when you let Ray Brown and that bunch of scum into your territory and gave them the green light to do any damn thing they wanted to do."

"I don't know what you're talking about, Raines!"

"You're a damn liar as well, Simon."

Simon sputtered for a moment and then fell silent.

"You made a bad mistake when you declared war on kids, Simon."

"I didn't do anything of the sort!"

"Don't lie, Simon. When you gave Ray Brown and the rest of that scummy bunch sanctuary, you shook hands with the devil. You stay out my way, Simon. You keep clear of me and my Rebels. You understand?"

"You don't give me orders, Raines."

"I just did, Simon. Now you listen to me. I am going to rid this land of Ray Brown and his ilk once and for all. And if you interfere, I'll step on you like the big ugly nasty roach you are. Is that clear?"

"You're dead, Raines!" Simon screamed. "You're a walking-around dead man. Nobody, *nobody*, talks to me like that. Now then, do *you* understand all *that?*"

"I can answer that with two words, Simon."

"They had better be 'I'm sorry.' "

"No. Fuck you!"

The Rebel column resumed its march across the southern part of the state. Ben knew, just as Caesar had known when he crossed the Rubicon, that the die was cast. There no doubt had been many people listening when Ben last spoke with Simon, and the man had no choice now but to fight . . . especially after what Ben had said to him.

Altus was a deserted and looted town. Where once more than 20,000 souls had lived and worked and played and loved and hoped and planned, only silent ghosts now remained. And here, too, just as in the other towns of any size the Rebels had passed through in Oklahoma, they found where Ray Brown and his thugs had struck.

"Same thing, general," the doctors told him, after the

mass grave, which had never been covered, was found. "The bones are those of old people, and, ah, the bones of their pets were found, too."

"Killed the dogs and cats along with their owners?" Ben asked.

"Yes, sir."

"Well, the people and their pets are in a better place now. I guess that's the way we're going to have to look at it. The pets won't have to wait at the Rainbow Bridge for their human companions."

"The Rainbow Bridge, sir?"

"Never heard of that, doctor?"

"No, sir."

"Some people believe that is a place where animals, after death, wait for their human friends to join them. It's called the Rainbow Bridge."

"Do you believe that, General Ben?" Anna asked.

Ben shrugged. "Why not? It's a nice thought."

"You believe animals go to heaven, general?" one of the chaplains asked.

"Yes, I do. It would certainly be a sadder place without them."

Anna smiled. "Some of the people in the old country used to kill dogs and cats to eat. I would never let those few in my bunch who wanted to do that. Most of us agreed that it would be a sin. We would rather go hungry."

Ben touched her face with surprisingly gentle fingers, for Ben was not an emotional man and seldom allowed his feelings to surface. Then the moment was past and Ben turned and walked away.

"General Ben's bark is much worse than his bite, I'm thinking," Anna said, then smiled. "In most cases," she added, to the agreement of Ben's team.

* * *

Ben turned the column north until they reached old Interstate 40, then cut west. On the way north they passed through a dozen small towns, stopping briefly at each town. Ben had stopped searching for mass graves. The Rebels just didn't have the time. The towns were deserted, utterly devoid of human life. They bivouacked just across the Oklahoma state line in Texas.

In a small town in the panhandle of Texas, the Rebels found their first signs of life in weeks. The people were packing up and preparing to move south.

"It just isn't safe up here anymore, general," the spokesman told Ben. "We hid when the punks came through. Must have been five or six hundred of them all told. You seen what they did in Oklahoma?"

Ben nodded.

"We alerted the folks who were tryin' to make a new start of it all along the old interstate, and I believe most of them made it clear 'fore the punks reached their location. We've been out of radio contact and can't be sure about that. Problem is, general, we're so damn few and spread out high and wide."

"We're on our way to deal with the gangs," Ben told the man. "But until that is taken care of, I can't guarantee your safety."

"We understand." The local sighed. "Is this damn country ever going to settle down, general?"

"Someday," Ben assured the man. "That much I can promise you. But I can't give you any fixed date. I wish I could."

"Just kill the damn punks, general. If you can cut them down to size, we can manage the rest."

"Especially that damn Ray Brown," a woman added.

"That man is a monster. I've seen what he and his main bunch have left behind. That man is evil through and through."

Ben looked at the small group of about 50 or so men and women and a few small children. These were tough, hardy people, with no back-up in them. Given any kind of a fighting chance at all, they would willingly risk their lives to rebuild the country. But they had to have a fighting chance.

"I've seen it too, ma'am," Ben told the woman. "Ray Brown and his gangs came through our part of the SUSA, too."

"When you find him, general," another woman said, "kill him slow—make it last. Then burn the body and seal the ashes in concrete. I swear that man is a spawn of the devil."

Ben nodded, although he really didn't think Ray had any connection with the devil. Ray Brown was just a perfect example of a punk; walking proof that the bad seed theory was no unproven assumption. "We'll find him, ma'am. Rest assured of that. And when we find him, we'll kill him. That I can promise you. Someday this land will be free of thugs and punks, I'll promise you that, too."

"God bless you, Ben Raines," the woman said.

"Fuck Ben Raines," Ray Brown said. "He's been after me for years and hasn't been able to catch me. What makes him think this time will be any different?"

"Maybe the law of averages, Ray," Robbie 'Big Tits' Ford said. "I got to say we just got out of the ruins of New York by a hair."

"A cunt hair," her brother Hal said with a laugh.

"Shut up, Hal," his sister said.

Hal shut his mouth. His expression was that of a very petulant child.

"It was stupid killin' all them people," Tootsie Aleman said.

"You callin' me stupid, you dyke bitch?" Ray snarled at the gang leader.

"I'm callin' what you done stupid." The gang leader didn't back up. "What you done was toss gasoline on an open fire. You deliberately pissed off Ben Raines."

"Fuck him!" Ray repeated.

"Well, I'm game for that," Robbie said. "Then I'd have to kill him, I guess."

"You are a disgusting bitch," her brother said, whose own sexual tastes ran toward young boys.

"Shut up, Hal," his sister's reply was automatic.

Abdullah Camal, better known as the Camel, sighed and shook his head. "I agree with Tootsie. Me and Lumumba are pulling out and getting the hell away from you, Ray."

"So carry your black asses." Ray waved that off. "Who the hell cares what you and that equally ignorant Lumumba do? Personally, I'm tired of listening to the both of you run off at the mouth. Good riddance, I say."

The Camel's eyes narrowed with anger. He very much wanted to do or say something in rebuttal, but he knew too well that if he did, he would be dead within a heartbeat, for Ray had guards around him all the time. Abdullah stood up and stalked out the door. He was not gentle in closing it behind him.

"Stupid nigger," Ray said.

"Well, my God! I finally agree with you on something," Tootsie said.

"I'm thrilled beyond words," Ray replied. He turned his head and yelled, "Pete! What is Raines's latest position?"

"Our people just radioed in, Ray. Raines is in the panhandle of Texas."

"And Raines thinks he's so goddamn smart," Ray snorted. "He doesn't realize he's being tracked all the way. Big dumb bastard!"

"They're fairly intelligent, boss," Corrie told Ben. "But not nearly as smart as they think they are. We've had a good fix on them for several days now. We broke their code almost immediately."

"How many teams are tracking us?" Ben asked.

"Four, at least."

"Ray still in the mountains of Arizona?"

"Affirmative."

Ben smiled. "We'll cut south just west of Tucumcari. Have one platoon from each battalion except ours prepare to leave the convoy, starting tonight. Head them north. We'll do that for four nights. They're to link up just north of Flagstaff and sit tight until they get orders from me. Have the convoy stretch out and put more distance between battalions to compensate for the missing trucks. When we get closer, we'll shift more troops around, so when we're ready, we'll hit Mister Brown from all sides. I'm counting on the punks not having enough savvy to count the vehicles in the convoy."

"Someday we're gonna get a chance to kick some more punk ass," Jersey griped, adding, "I hope."

Ben cut his eyes and smiled. Jersey kidded a lot about kicking ass, but few knew the reasons behind that kidding. When Jersey had been but a child, while wandering helplessly and afraid just after the Great War, she had been seized by a gang and repeatedly raped . . . among other things. Jersey had absolutely no compassion in her for punks.

"We're going to get our chance to do just that, Jersey," Ben said. "I promise you."

"The sooner we can do that," Jersey responded, no humor in her eyes, "the better this world will be for decent people."

"Let's roll," Ben said. "Jersey's getting impatient."

"Damn right, boss. Kick-ass time!"

Twenty-Three

Those who had settled in and around Amarillo had been strong enough in numbers to beat back several attacks by Ray Brown and his gangs, but not without suffering some losses and almost depleting their supplies. Ben and his Rebels stayed around Amarillo long enough to see the settlers resupplied and then moved on, crossing into New Mexico without incident.

"The land of open sky," Beth said, reading from a dog-eared old tourist guide.

"What is?" Cooper asked.

"New Mexico, Cooper," Beth replied, exasperation in her voice. "Where do you think we are?"

"Looks deserted to me," Cooper came right back. "Hey, Jersey?"

"What, Coop?"

"Weren't you raised somewhere around here?"

Jersey was silent for a moment. "I spent some time with relatives down south of here, Coop. I don't remember a whole lot about it. I spent time between the Mescalero, Fort Apache, and San Carlos reservations.''

"I didn't think you were full Apache," Coop said softly.

"I'm not. I think I'm half Apache, half white. An apple.''

"An apple?"

"Red on the outside, white on the inside," Jersey said with a laugh.

"Want to take a side trip and visit any of those places, Little Bit?" Ben asked.

"No," Jersey said softly. "I really don't. I don't even remember my Christian last name, and I'm not sure about my Apache name, for that matter.''

"You think you still have family in any of those places?" Anna asked.

"Oh . . . I'm sure I do. But I wouldn't know them and they wouldn't know me. And they're probably having a hard enough time of it without some distant relation popping up.''

"Tucumcari in a few miles, boss," Corrie said. "Scouts report some survivors there.''

"The town was about 7,500 before the Great War," Beth informed them.

"How many live there now?" Ben asked.

"About 400, and they're all staunch supporters of Simon Border.''

"You've got to be kidding!"

"Nope. Simon Border's Temple of God and Faith.''

"Puke!" Jersey said.

"Shit!" Cooper said.

Beth made a horrible face at the thought of anyone worshipping anything Simon Border had to do with.

Anna lowered the window and spat outside.

"Ah, dear," Ben said. "That is not a very ladylike thing to do.''

"Who said I was a lady?"

Ben sighed and didn't pursue the subject. Being a father was something he was not all that good at.

"How are we going to handle the people up ahead, boss?" Cooper asked.

"They don't shoot at us, we don't shoot at them."

"Look there," Cooper said. "By the side of the road."

A crowd of people had gathered at the edge of town, many of them holding hand-painted signs—BEN RAINES IS THE GREAT SATAN.

"I don't think they like you very much," Corrie said with a smile.

"I sort of get that feeling," Ben admitted.

THE REBEL ARMY IS FILLED WITH FORNICATORS AND HARLOTS.

"I fornicate occasionally," Jersey said. "Helps take the edge off."

Cooper opened his mouth to say something.

"Shut up, Cooper," Jersey warned him. "Just don't say a word."

SIMON BORDER IS THE ONLY TRUE WAY.

"Only true way to what?" Anna asked.

Ben halted the column and stepped out of the wagon. He was instantly surrounded by Rebels in a diamond formation. He walked up to the group of people and they hissed and drew back as if Ben had some horrible contagious disease. The women were all dressed in drab shapeless dresses that covered them from neck to ankles and the men were dressed equally drably.

"You people need any help?" Ben asked in a friendly voice.

"Not from you," a woman replied.

"We have doctors with us." Ben kept his voice even. "Are your children all up to date with their shots?"

"With the help of His Holiness here on earth, Simon Border, the Lord will provide," a man told Ben.

"I see. Does everyone here in town feel the way you do?"

"Yes!" the crowd shouted in one voice.

"What a pack of screwballs," Jersey muttered.

"Well," Ben said, "if that's the case, we'll just move on and let you folks alone."

"Good riddance," a man said.

Ben waved his people back into their vehicles and they moved on without another word, but with plenty of very hard looks from the supporters of Simon Border.

"Good God!" Beth was the first to speak once the column was moving.

"I don't think God has anything to do with it," Ben said. "Those people have been had."

"But they were had willingly, General Ben," Anna said. "No one forced them."

As usual, the young Anna cut right through the fat and got to the meat of the problem.

"I feel nothing but contempt for the adults," Corrie said. "But what about the children?"

"The battle cry of the liberals back before the Great War," Ben told the group. "Whenever a social program was in danger of being cut, the liberals would start pissing and moaning about the children. They twisted facts, manipulated numbers, and sometimes just outright lied when it suited them. And Simon always professed to be a supporter of the liberal movement. I feel sorry for the kids back there, sure. But as it stands now, there is nothing we can do about it. Unless we want to start using force against the adults."

"Scouts report making contact with a guerrilla group about 25 miles ahead," Corrie said. "Little town at the junction of 129. They're on our side."

"Be nice to see a friendly face for a change."

The group they met a few miles down the road were

heavily armed and determined to live free, not under Simon Border's dictatorial regime.

"Simon's bit off a hell of a lot more than he's capable of chewing, general," one of the local resistance members who had been introduced as Tom said. "He's spread thin . . . way too thin for what he hopes to accomplish."

"But my intelligence people say he has a very strong army."

"Oh, he does. And it's an army filled with fanatics. Don't sell them short, for are all prepared to die for their beliefs. Come on, general. Let's get inside out of this damn wind and have something to drink. We'll talk better there."

In the man's very comfortable home, coffee was served by Tom's smiling wife. "It's Columbian," she explained. "Simon apparently worked out some sort of deal with the gangs of punks before they invaded our land, and some warlords down in Central and South America. Simon and the gang leaders trade them women to sell into whoring and men to use as slaves, and they sell or barter, or however they do it with the punks, the raw materials to manufacture dope up here. We hijacked a couple of loads of coffee on the way through here." She grinned. "And shot the shit out of their convoy."

"Now they fly it in," Tom said.

"My intelligence people sure dropped the ball on this one," Ben said. "We had no idea there were entire communities who were resisting Simon and his nutty ideas."

"Not their fault, general. We just couldn't be sure if they were the real article or if they were lying when they said they worked for you. We stay in touch by short wave, so we all agreed to hedge our bets to be on the safe side. I don't know whether you know this or not, but Simon has a secret police that would put the Gestapo to shame. They not only look like Hitler's Gestapo, they act like that bunch of thugs. They wear black uniforms with red armbands.

And a lot of people they pick up for questioning are never seen again.''

Ben toyed with his coffee cup for a moment. He shook his head. ''Conditions are a hell of a lot worse over here than I realized. But I've got a man in here; one of the best spooks in the world. I don't understand why he hasn't notified me of all this.''

''He's probably linked up with a resistance group and running for his life, general.''

''I have a very difficult time visualizing Mike doing that, Tom.''

''I hate to be the one to tell you this, general,'' Tom said, very hesitantly. ''But it's something you'd better give a lot of thought to.''

''What?''

''There is a very good chance you have some Simon Border people with you. He probably put people in your army a long time ago. He sometimes behaves as though he's about half nuts, and he may well be insane, but he's still a very smart man.''

''We went through a purge of the ranks months back,'' Ben told him. ''And we did turn up a few Simon Border supporters. But I thought we had them all. Damn!''

Tom was silent for a few heartbeats. ''I'd better warn you of this, general—everything north of I-40 and everything west of I-25 is Simon Border territory. You're going to have a fight on your hands when you get in those areas.''

Ben smiled, thinking of Jersey's comments about how boring it had been for so long.

''You looking forward to a fight, general?'' Tom asked, a puzzled note in his words.

''I've never shied away from one,'' Ben replied, as his grin faded and the thoughts of Simon Border having spies within his army took center stage in his mind. ''But no,

Tom. I'm not looking forward to a battle. But if Simon Border wants a fight, he can damn sure have one.''

''What about the possibility of your having turncoats in your army?''

''Oh . . . I'll deal with them. You can rest assured of that.'' Ben hadn't worked out just how he would deal with them, but he definitely would purge his ranks of Simon Border supporters.

Ben didn't have to ponder how he was going to do that for very long. That night the traitors within his ranks solved that problem for him.

Twenty-Four

As soon as Ben left the friendly home, he told Corrie to get his battalion commanders up for a meeting. One look at Ben's grim face and Corrie knew something was rotten.

"We've got Simon Border sympathizers all through our ranks," Ben told his commanders. "I should have guessed it."

"What are they waiting for?" Jackie asked. "Why don't they strike?"

"I think they've been waiting until we were inside Border's territory. So we can expect some sort of coup at any time."

"No idea who they are?" Dan asked.

"No. None at all. And I've got a hunch we're not going to have time to pull in polygraph and PSE operators to check everyone."

"You think it's coming down that soon?" Buddy asked.

"Yes, I do. I would say to pull in your most trusted people, but hell, who can we trust?"

"I think we can trust the old-timers," Jim Peters said. "I think we have to trust them."

"All right. Get back to your commands and quietly alert the old-timers. Captain Evans is in overall charge of the platoons that are leaving the column and linking up north of Flagstaff. He's a good man. I trust him. I'll personally give him a bump and alert him. I alerted President Jefferys first thing, so he's ready for whatever happens back home." Ben's face hardened and his eyes glinted. "I don't like people who shake hands with you with one hand and strike you with the other. So, when this coup attempt begins, I really don't want to have to deal with a lot of prisoners. Any questions?"

There were none. All present got Ben's drift, loud and clear. Treason carried the death sentence in the SUSA.

Ben watched the batt coms quietly leave the room. He sat alone for a time in the quiet room, his expression grim and his eyes holding a very dangerous light. Then he picked up his CAR and walked outside. "Heads up," he told his team. "The turncoats are sure to have noticed the batt coms coming and going and they might put it all together. I don't have any idea how many of our people are involved in this treachery. But it won't take many of them to cause a lot of damage. We're going to take some hits when it goes down. Let's see if we can't keep it at a minimum."

The night was closing in fast as Ben spoke and every one of his senses was working overtime. It might have been nerves responsible for his feeling jumpy, but he didn't think so. The column was inside Simon Border's territory, and the coup attempt could just as easily come this night as any other. Ben paced back and forth and up and down for over an hour, his thoughts dark and savage.

"Batt coms all back with their commands," Corrie broke into Ben's thoughts, and he was grateful for the intrusion.

"Everything quiet with their commands?"

"No problems. Yet," she added.

"How could any Rebel, who has lived free under the laws of the SUSA and the Tri-States philosophy, ever fall for Simon Border's bullshit?" Jersey asked.

"I think you just hit the nail on the head, Jersey," Ben said. "New people." He looked at Beth. "How many new people in our bunch, Beth?"

"Since returning from Europe . . . about 50. The same for the other battalions, since we enlarged battalion size."

"That's it. Corrie, bump the batt coms, advise them to—"

Shots shattered the quiet night before Ben could finish his sentence and Ben and team jumped for cover just as bullets pocked the side of his motor home.

Jersey leveled her CAR and gave the muzzle flashes a full magazine of .223 rounds. Screams of pain and shock ripped the night as Ben's outer circle of protection quickly formed up around him. They left one small perimeter open, for Ben and team to lay down a field of fire. His protection platoon knew if they didn't let the boss at least mix it up some, he would raise holy hell.

A tremendous flash and roar lit up the night sky as one of the turncoats tossed a grenade under the gas tanks of a truck and it went up with a bang.

"I'm intercepting their transmissions," Corrie said in a calm voice. "Their objective is to kill you, boss."

"What else is new?" Ben said.

Jersey grinned and Anna frowned.

More explosions and flashes of fiery light colored the sky as the turncoats blew up several more vehicles.

"All battalions reporting fighting," Corrie called over the din of approaching battle.

"We finish it tonight," Ben said.

M-16 fire cut the night all around Ben and his team.

None of them turned a head. They kept all eyes on their perimeter.

"Here they come," Cooper called. " 'Looks like about two dozen of them."

"Praise God and Brother Border!" came the shout from within the ranks of those turncoat Rebels rushing toward Ben and his team.

"Put them down," Ben ordered, lifting his CAR.

The team opened up, splitting the night with .223 rounds, all weapons set on full auto.

The line of rushing traitors went down in a sprawling heap as several hundred rounds impacted with flesh, followed by screams and howls of pain.

"They're not wearing body armor!" Beth called. "What the hell's the matter with those people?"

"That's how they can identify themselves from us," Ben called during a few seconds' lull in the fighting. He ejected the empty magazine and slipped home a full one. "But I think I would have picked a better method."

Several of Ben's protection platoon suddenly turned and leveled their M-16s at Ben. Ben caught the movement out of the corner of his eyes and hit the ground just as the men fired. Within seconds, the turncoats were riddled with bullet holes. But a large hole had been opened and the traitors poured through, breaching the inter circle.

One jumped inside the ruins where Ben and team had taken cover and slammed into Ben, knocking the CAR from Ben's hands and dropping his own as well. Ben recovered his balance and slugged the man on the jaw, addling him long enough for Ben to get set and pop him again.

"Death to all Satanists!" the turncoat screamed, charging at Ben.

Ben didn't waste the wind replying. What was the point? He kicked the traitor on the knee and when the man involuntarily reached down to grab his shattered knee,

Ben brought his fist down on the back of the man's neck, driving the man face-down on the ground.

Before he could put the finishing touches on the attacker, another jumped on Ben's back, riding him to the ground, screaming oaths and praising Simon Border.

Ben rolled and the man loosened his hold. Both men came up, knives flashing in the night. Ben had no time to see what his team might be doing, other than being locked in hand-to-hand combat with other turncoats.

The turncoat slashed at Ben and Ben sidestepped what would have been a lethal cut to his belly. He parried another thrust and brought the edge of his heavy knife down on the man's arm, nearly severing the arm from the elbow down. The traitor screamed and lost his blade. He staggered back, the blood gushing.

Ben stepped in close and swung the heavy blade, the razor-sharp edge striking the man on the side of his neck and almost decapitating the attacker. Ben whirled around in a crouch before the dying man hit the group.

A dark shape came out of the night and Ben just had time to duck before the M-16 the attacker was using like a club whistled over his head. The turncoat lost his balance and fell into Ben. Ben's knife went clattering off.

Ben kneed the man in the groin and heard the air whoosh out of him as the pain ripped through his body. Ben hammered at the man with a big right fist, striking the attacker several times in the face. Still the man hung on, flailing away at Ben with hard fists. The two of them rolled around on the ground, and ended up out of the ruins of the old house and about 50 feet away from Ben's team, both of them losing their helmets.

Ben recognized the man; he'd been with the Rebels for years. So much for trusting all the old-timers, he thought.

The men lunged to their boots and the turncoat clawed at his flap holster for his 9mm. Ben slugged him on the jaw with a right fist and followed that with a left, addling the man, but not knocking him down. Ben kicked out with a boot and the toe of his boot caught the man on the knee. That put him down.

Ben stepped back and delivered another kick to the man's face, his boot catching the man on the mouth. Teeth and blood flew. Ben recovered his balance, took aim, and kicked the man on the side of his head just as hard as he could. He heard the man's skull pop under the impact. The attacker lay still on the ground.

Ben turned, his eyes searching for his knife and his CAR. He saw the knife blade glinting in the faint light and scooped it up.

"Boss!" Cooper called.

"Here, Coop."

"We beat them back. You all right?"

"Only my dignity bruised. Where's my rifle?"

"Here!" Anna called, rushing up and looking up into his face. "Are you hurt, General Ben?"

"No, baby. I'm all right. You've got blood on your face."

"Not my blood, General Ben."

The camp was quickly settling down. The brief but brutal fight appeared to be over.

"Report!" Ben called.

"Radio took a round," Corrie said. "It's busted. I'll have to get another from the communications truck."

"Four down here, sir," the officer commanding the protection platoon called. "One dead and three wounded."

"Your radio still working?"

"Yes, sir."

"Get me a report."

"Right away, sir. Are you all right?"

"I'm fine, son."

Rebels began rushing up to check on Ben. Ben assured them all he was unhurt.

Corrie was handed another radio and quickly got on the horn. The portable satellite had not been damaged during the fight. "They had a brief fight back home," Corrie called. "President Jefferys and Secretary Blanton are all right. The home guard and the reserves put the coup attempt down hard. They're mopping up now."

"The battalions with us reporting only a few casualties, sir," the second radio operator said. "They have taken a number of turncoats prisoners."

"I'll want them questioned extensively," Ben said. "And then shoot them."

The bodies of the turncoat Rebels were buried the next morning without fanfare. Their attempted coup had accomplished nothing for them except death, and for Simon Border and his followers, it had served only to intensify the hatred the loyal Rebels felt toward anyone who would try to interfere with their way of life.

As the long column began pulling out the next morning, heading west, there was none of the usual banter among the Rebels. They wore grim expressions and, to a person, their thoughts were of Simon Border and his followers, and those reflections were not at all pleasant.

"We're going to deal with the punks first, and then go after this nitwit Border person, right, General Ben?" Anna asked.

"We're certainly going to deal with the punks," Ben replied.

"Then Simon Border?" Anna persisted.

"Maybe," Ben hedged that. "We have to consider what might happen to the entire country if I were to declare open war against Border and his followers."

"And also what might happen if we don't," Anna added.

Ben smiled. Anna spoke her mind, always. "That too, dear."

"We either deal with the problem now, or it will grow and grow. Never stop. Like a cancer."

"You might be right," Ben conceded.

"The man has shown himself to be untrustworthy," the young woman pressed on. "Right?"

"Right, dear."

"He wants to destroy our way of life, right?"

"Right, dear."

"Even though we agreed to live in peace with him, right?"

"Absolutely right, dear."

The other team members were all smiling, letting Anna run with the verbal ball.

"So what is the problem? Let's go kick his butt and then we can get on with our lives, right? In the old country, if another gang tried to move in on our territory, we fought. If they wanted to live in peace with us, we gave that a try. If it didn't work out, then we did away with them. It's just that simple in my mind. Nothing complicated about it."

Ben chuckled. How to explain to Anna that he didn't want the entire northern hemisphere to blow up in their faces? How to explain that Simon Border had millions of followers, all ready to die for their leader?

"I think we're already committed, boss," Cooper said.

Ben cut his eyes to the driver. "Could be, Coop. But this time let's walk on the side of caution."

"You mean, deal with the punks and then back off?"

"That's right."

"I'll bet Simon Border will never let us do that," Anna again stepped in.

"You never give up, do you, Anna?" Ben said with a laugh.

"Have you ever given up, General Ben?" she responded.

"Well, no, I guess not."

Anna tossed her head. "And I don't think you will give up with Simon Border, either."

"Oh, you don't?"

"No."

"I guess that settles that, then?"

"Sure does. So now we go kick Simon Border's ass, right?"

"Maybe. We'll see."

"We will," she said confidently. "He'll force us to do it."

"You're probably right, Anna."

She nodded her head. "A holy war. It won't be pleasant."

"Sure as hell won't," Ben muttered. "Judgement day."

Twenty-Five

The column rolled on across the state, encountering no further trouble from either punks nor Simon Border supporters ... until they hit the outskirts of what was left of Albuquerque.

"Scouts reporting Border's troops are waiting for us just east of the city," Corrie reported.

"Tell the scouts to find us a route south," Ben replied. "We'll avoid trouble with Border's people whenever possible."

Ben felt all the eyes of his team on him. He ignored the curious gazes. The last thing he wanted in the battered country that was once America was a religious war. So for all his big talk now, his troops knew he had been running a bluff against Simon all along—let them think what they would. Ben's primary objective was to deal with the punks. If Simon Border would let him in to do that, and then let him out, Simon could damn well have his wacko nation.

But Ben knew he was hoping against hope. Putting off

the inevitable. But be that as it may, he would, by God, put off any head-to-head confrontation with Simon as long as he could. Maybe in time, when Simon saw that the Rebels would keep their word . . .

"Taking any route south is going to throw us miles out of the way," Corrie broke into his thoughts.

"Take the southern route," Ben ordered.

"Won't work," Anna muttered, just loud enough for her adopted father to hear. "Nutso Border wants a fight. We might as well give it to him."

Ben pretended not to hear her comments, knowing that none of his team really knew what a religious war would do to the already torn-apart nation. North America could well turn into another Northern Ireland, with various factions fighting each other for centuries.

Ben shook his head. He couldn't allow that. He just couldn't.

He sighed. But damned if he could figure out how to prevent it.

He certainly couldn't allow Ray Brown and his dope-producing crowd to continue making their poison and spreading it all over the nation. Ben was firm about that. Back in the '80s he was one of many citizens who openly and often supported the death penalty for drug dealers. *For all the good it did,* he remembered sourly.

Miles later, Corrie said, "Scouts have found an ideal place to bivouac."

"Go a few miles further," Ben ordered. "Let's put as much distance as we can between us and Border's people."

"And if they follow?" Anna asked the question Ben had suspected was surely coming.

"We'll deal with that should it happen. I can't believe Simon's commanders would be that stupid."

A few miles further: "Scouts report that Border's troops

have left the outskirts of the city and are following us," Corrie told him.

Ben twisted in the front seat and looked at Anna. She was smiling at him. The rest of his team managed to keep straight faces.

"You find this amusing, I suppose?" Ben asked.

Anna shrugged her shoulders noncommittally.

"Yeah, right," Ben grumbled. To Corrie: "I thought Tom told us everything south of I-40 was out of Border's territory?"

"That's the way I understood it. But he also said that the resistance forces scattered throughout the area weren't strong enough to tangle with Border's people head-on, remember?"

Ben nodded. "Yeah, I remember. Any word from Mike Richards?"

"Nothing."

"All right," Ben said with a sigh. "Have the scouts find us a defensive position and prepare to make a stand."

Anna laughed. Ben ignored her.

"Do you people have a death wish?" Ben radioed the long column of Border's people.

"We are the Reverend Simon Border's Guards of God," came the reply.

"Oh, my word!" Beth sighed.

"Guards of God?" Ben blurted over the air.

"That is correct."

"Why are you following us?"

"To engage you and destroy you."

"Confident son-of-a-bitch, isn't he?" Ben muttered. He keyed the mic. "On whose orders?"

"We are acting under the orders of our Supreme Commander here on earth, the Reverend Simon Border. You have unlawfully invaded our territory."

"Supreme Commander Reverend Simon Border," Cooper muttered. "I guess we'll have to salute the nut before we shoot him."

Ben broke up with laughter at the serious expression on Cooper's face. "Let's try not to go that far, Coop."

"I will give it all my attention," Anna said.

"I'll sure you will, dear," Ben said, very drily. He lifted the mic. "We are not here to make trouble for you people. We are after dope manufacturers. Once we deal with them, we'll leave your territory."

"You will never leave our territory, Ben Raines. You will be buried here."

"Enemy convoy steadily closing," Corrie said. "Range, ten miles."

"Get the tanks in position." He keyed the mic. "Don't be a fool, mister. Don't tangle with us. There is no need for it."

"Prepare to meet God, Ben Raines, and answer for your sins."

"He's broken off, boss," Corrie said.

"They are really, by God, going to meet us head-to-head," Ben said, astonishment in his voice.

"Range, nine miles."

"Let them get close," Ben ordered. "Tank commander take over now."

Corrie looked at him. "You want our tanks to mix it up with theirs?"

"If that is what the tank commanders choose to do."

"Their tanks are pieces of shit, boss," Corrie pointed out. "Nothing but death traps."

"I am fully aware of that."

Simon's tanks looked to be restored Korean War vintage, probably taken from various military museums . . . although Ben found it hard to believe that any commander would put such dilapidated equipment out in the field for men to die in. He also wondered where in the world Simon found so many of the old—and Ben meant really *old*— Patton tanks. The approaching tanks appeared to be gasoline powered, and that made them nothing more than rolling bombs up against Ben's ultra-modern tanks.

"Fools," Ben muttered moments later, when the first of the enemy tanks came into view through binoculars.

The Rebels waited.

"This is going to be a shooting gallery," Coop said.

"They picked the midway, Coop," Ben replied.

"That they did, boss," Coop agreed. "I hope they enjoy the show, 'cause it's gonna be the last one most of them will ever see."

"Range, three miles," Corrie said.

Ben's tanks waited, diesel engines softly grumbling.

"Range, two miles."

Ben's tank commanders opened up with their main 120mm guns, using armor-piercing ammunition. The terrain below where Ben and his team waited and watched blossomed in puffs of fire. The infantry coming up behind the tanks were left wide open to Ben's mortar crews, who were busy dropping the lethal surprises down the tubes.

It was bloody carnage before the Rebel eyes and Ben did not call a halt to it until there was nothing moving on the bloody battleground before him.

"Let's see what we have left," Ben said.

"Damn little," Beth muttered under her breath.

"Enemy soldiers are retreating," Corrie said. "Those few that can still walk, that is," she added.

"Let them go," Ben told her. "Simon's army is not as well-trained and certainly not as well-equipped as we were led to believe. This defeat just might convince him to leave us alone. But I doubt it."

The wind shifted, bringing with it the odor of charred human flesh.

"Do we bury the enemy dead?" Corrie asked.

"No," Ben said softly. "We do not. But let's go see what kind of equipment they have."

When Simon Border received the news of the defeat of his Guards of God, he sat for a moment, too stunned to speak. Border was not a military man. He knew very little about tactics or equipment. He had millions of followers, and they were well-armed with modern rifles and machine guns and mortars, but nothing to even remotely compare with Raines's Rebels. Contrary to what had deliberately been put out, Border's people had few tanks (a hell of a lot fewer now).

Border's police had subdued and whipped into submission those who at first resisted and refused to follow his wacky doctrine by sheer force of numbers, not because of superior equipment and armament.

Simon never dreamed that Ben Raines would actually fight him. He always felt that Ben would back off when push came to shove.

Simon really didn't want to fight Ben Raines and the Rebels. He was fully aware that no one had ever waged a successful war against the Rebels, and that was something Simon just could not understand.

What did the Rebels have that made them so seemingly invincible? Simon knew they were a godless bunch; their society was very nearly wide-open, and so permissive he was surprised God had not destroyed it just as He had done with Sodom and Gomorrah. Simon had prayed fervently for God to destroy Ben Raines and all his followers, but then he realized that God was leaving that task up to him. He and his followers must destroy Ben Raines.

Simon sighed heavily. Oh, how he wished he could speak to his idols: Harry Falcreek and Raldo Reeves and Clute Gingsing and Flush Bambaugh. They would know what to do. But they were long gone, probably gone during the first few days of the Great War.

Simon rose from his desk chair to pace the huge study of his mountain home. He didn't care how he got rid of Ben Raines and the Rebels, just as long as it got done. In his mind, the end certainly justified the means.

If he had to use punks to accomplish that, so be it. He'd use the criminal element and then dispose of them when the job was finished.

"Oh, me!" he sighed. Doing God's work sure was tiring.

"Stupid," Ben said, looking over the slaughter. "Most of these tanks were pulled out of service years before the Great War. Death traps. Look at these rounds that were blown clear from that hulk. Poorly made. Hell, they might have blown up in the barrel when they tried to fire them."

Cooper was inspecting a cache of rifles taken from the dead. "Their M-16s are in good shape, though," he said. "Plus a mixture of AKs."

"I wonder if the Guards of God are the elite of Border's Army of the Democratic Front?" Jersey asked.

Ben shrugged. "If they are, and this is the way he's equipped his army, they're in deep trouble."

"Cecil on the horn," Corrie said, walking up. There was a faint smile on her lips. "He has some bad news for you."

"In addition to the attempted coup?"

"You might say that."

Ben took the mic. "Go, Cec."

"Emil Hite should be approaching your position shortly, Ben."

Ben sighed. "I thought I assigned him to . . . where did I assign him?"

"He's been bouncing around from battalion to battalion, Ben. The proverbial bad penny, so to speak. Everybody likes him, but no one wants him."

"What happened?"

"He asked Thermopolis for permission to take his, ah, company of followers and visit friends up in Arkansas. Therm didn't think anything was amiss, so he gave permission. That was two weeks ago. Emil just reported in. He's approximately a hundred miles east of you as we speak."

Ben shook his head and tried to hide his smile. Whatever else Emil Hite might be, he was a resourceful little bastard . . . that was probably why he'd been a reasonably successful con artist before the war. "All right, Cec. Thanks for the info. We'll wait for him."

"Everything else is calm here, Ben. We've ferreted out the traitors and dealt with them."

Nice way of saying Cec had ordered the turncoats either shot or hanged. "Have you had any word from Mike Richards?"

"Not a peep, Ben."

"Ok, Cec. We'll be on the lookout for Emil and his people. Thanks for the warning."

"Oh, there is one more little item, Ben . . ."

A tiny warning bell went off in Ben's head. "What might that be, ol' buddy?"

"Emil has a group of reporters with him. Just thought you should be warned. Take care, Ben. Ol' Black Joe out."

Cecil was chuckling as he broke the transmission.

"Ol' Black Joe," Ben muttered. "And people say I have a strange sense of humor."

"One thing about it," Beth remarked. "With Emil along, we can be entertained."

"That's one way of putting it," Ben replied. "But who

are these damn reporters with him? The only ones I've given permission to travel with any battalion are with Tina's 9 Batt."

"Emil obviously monitored the last transmission," Corrie said. "He's on the horn."

With a very audible sigh, Ben took the mic. "Go, Emil."

"My general!" Emil shouted and Ben winced. "Commander of the army whose mission it is to save the world and bring peace and prosperity to every law-abiding citizen . . . plus a chicken in every pot."

"Emil, cut the shit."

"Oh. Very well. I found a group of press types stranded along the way, general. I couldn't leave them to the hostile elements, so I brought them along."

"Who are they?"

"A group of very fine and highly principled men and women from the NUSA, my general."

"A bunch of goddamn liberals, you mean."

"Well, I suppose that is one way of putting it."

Ben shook his head. "All right, Emil. We'll wait for you. Corrie will give you our coordinates."

Ben handed her the mic. "You might tell him we're in the Okefenokee Swamp."

"You think he'd believe it?"

"No. But it was a nice thought."

Corrie spoke with Emil for a moment, then broke it off. "He'll be here about noon tomorrow."

"Now it really gets interesting," Ben said.

Twenty-Six

"My God, General Raines!" Clyde Mayfield blurted. "Aren't you going to give them a chance to surrender?"

Ben lowered his binoculars and gave the reporter a disgusted look. "No."

"But they're human beings, with guaranteed rights!" Ms. Cynthia Braithwaithe-Honnicker squalled.

"They're murdering, raping, torturing, dope-dealing, child-killing, mind-destroying scum," Ben bluntly informed the reporter. "Do not speak to me of the rights of criminals. I heard enough of that shit back before the Great War. When people such as yourself were trying your damnedest to destroy the nation. Now shut up, Ms. Bra-Burner-Homewrecker, or whatever the hell your name is."

"Well!" Cynthia stamped her foot—her left one. "I will not permit you to speak to me in such a manner."

"I believe I just did," Ben replied. He turned to Corrie. "Fire!"

Rebel 155mm self-propelled Howitzers, M-60A3 tank

main guns, and 105mm Howitzers, all of them positioned several miles to the rear, opened up on the little town in the valley. The Howitzers were firing a mixed bag of rounds: HE-M1, M413 (which contained 18 M35 grenades), and WP. The town in the valley, which scouts had slipped in and out of two nights in a row, held the gangs of Craig "Frankie" Franklin, Foster "Fos" Payne, and Thad "Killer" Keel.

The old buildings in the town below the hill where Ben stood with his team and the knot of reporters that had accompanied Emil Hite westward, exploded in a shower of brick and wood and shingles and pieces of commodes and sinks and various body parts.

The scouts had reported that one of the buildings contained a large lab that was capable of producing huge quantities of methamphetamines and other illicit drugs. Ben knew that some of the materials used in the manufacture of those drugs were highly flammable. They sure were. The large building located in the center of the town went up like a billion Roman candles all mixed in with dynamite.

Body parts went soaring high into the sky along with several flaming motorcycles. About 50 feet off the ground, the tanks on the motorcycles exploded.

"My, my," Ben said. "This is quite a show. Are you reporters getting good pictures of this event?"

"Barbaric!" Clyde Mayfield said.

"Grotesque!" Ms. Braithewaithe-Honniker said.

"Inhuman!" Lance Nightengale sniffed.

"Right," Ben said. "Corrie, tell the gunners to keep pouring it on until I give the order to stop."

"But those left alive may want to surrender!" another reporter protested.

Ben had been introduced to her and he thought her name was Noel Honeypucker, or something like that. He ignored them all.

Rebel snipers were laying back outside the town, waiting. They did not have long to wait. Several dozen gang members lived through the artillery barrage and tried to make a run for it. The Rebel snipers cut them down.

Noel Honeybun, or whatever her name was, and Cynthia Double-last-name, were openly weeping at the sight of those poor, poor rapists, murderers and child molesters and so forth going down under the snipers' rifles. The men were being manly, keeping a stiff upper lip and all that. But Ben could tell they were outraged at this travesty of justice.

"Cease firing," Ben finally gave the orders.

At first the quiet was unnerving to those not accustomed to it.

"We'll go in and take a look around when the fires die down," Ben said. "For now, everybody take five."

"I'm hungry," Anna said.

Honeyjugs and Braithewaithe-Honniker looked at the young woman, undisguised horror in their eyes.

The men with them both wore an expression of astonishment at her announcement.

"Me, too, Anna," Ben said. "Let's break out the rations." He glanced at the reporters. "Care to join us for a mid-morning repast?"

"You . . . you . . . monster!" Honeybutt raged at him.

"There will be a full report of this outrage submitted to President Altman," reporter Lance Nightengale blathered.

"Give him my best when you see him," Ben said.

"You are the most arrogant, unfeeling man I have ever encountered!" Clyde Mayfield opined.

"My mother didn't think so." Ben did his best to look hurt. He couldn't quite manage to bring it off.

"Why don't you ladies and gentlemen come with me?" Emil Hite stuck his mouth into it. "I've found some shade and you can rest for a time."

"Thank you, General Hite," Honeybags said. "I'm glad to see there is at least one civilized human being with this unit."

"General Hite?" Ben questioned.

Emil drew himself up to his full height, which wasn't much over five feet. "President Jefferys himself bestowed that rank upon me," he announced. "For all the good work I've done with the Rebels."

Ben nodded. "Wonderful, Emil. Now take the reporters and go away."

As Emil, his gaggle of followers, and the reporters ambled off, Beth whispered, "Do you suppose Cecil really gave Emil the rank of general?"

"You can bet I'm going to find out," Ben told her. "Although I don't know what I'm going to do about it if it's true." He paused, and then smiled. "Oh, yes, I do. Yes, indeed. I hope it is official. If that's the case, Emil is now directly under my command." Ben laughed.

"You have a very wicked look in your eyes, General Ben," Anna said.

"Yeah, I've seen that look before," Cooper said.

"I'm thinking how Emil would like to be attached to the kitchen for the duration."

"I wouldn't do that," Beth warned.

"Why?"

"Then we'd all run the risk of being poisoned."

"I never thought of that," Ben admitted.

"Besides," Corrie said, "you can't put a general on KP."

"It was a good thought, though, boss," Jersey told him. "We'll all think about what to do with Emil."

Ben looked at her. "Jersey, I *know* what you'd like to do."

The diminutive bodyguard smiled. "Naw, I wouldn't really shoot him. But Emil sure as hell *thinks* I would."

* * *

Emil stayed out of Ben's way and did his best not to draw Ben's attention as the convoy traveled west. None of the reporters traveling with the Rebels would speak to Ben after the carnage (their words) at the little town, and that was fine with Ben. Emil, his entourage and the reporters were at the rear of the column, and Ben hoped they all stayed there.

Ben spent a day and a night at Socorro before turning west on old Route 60. The town, which once boasted a population of about 15,000 was now reduced to less than 500 people. But they were solid Tri-Staters and determined to remain that way.

Ben had supplies flown in and made sure the residents had everything they needed to continue growing. Then the column moved on.

The spokesperson for the group in Socorro warned Ben that the punks were going to be in force from that point on, if the Rebels stayed on their present route.

"I plan to stay on it all the way," Ben said, not giving the man the slightest clue where "all the way" might end. "You wouldn't happen to know what gangs we might run into next down the line, would you?"

"I sure do, general. My people have scouted them out pretty well. Some punk by the name of Les Justice, and two more gangs run by a punk calls himself Jack Brittain, and the other gang is headed up by a road whore named Karen Carr. And that slut is one mean person. She is bad to the bone, believe it."

"Oh, I believe you," Ben replied. "I've seen some of her work." He smiled. "But Ms. Carr is about to run up against the baddest dog on the block."

"And that's you, general?"

"That's me."

*   *   *

It wasn't much of a fight. The baddest dog on the block didn't even have to growl all that much. The Rebels hit the punk-occupied town at dawn with artillery and blew it apart. Ben ordered the reporters kept in the rear, so, as he put it, "The sight of vicious career criminals being killed wouldn't traumatize them for the rest of their lives and probably render them incapable of earning an honest living."

The reporters did not see the humor in Ben's remarks.

Ben and his team walked through the ruins of the still-smoking town. This time, despite Ben's request that they stay in the rear, the reporters came along.

"Be sure and bring along a box of tissues," Ben told Beth. "So these left-wing assholes can have something to wipe their weepy eyes with."

"Or have a snit on," Jersey added.

"That, too," Ben said with a smile.

The press was grim-faced as they toured the shattered town, doing their best to avoid looking at the torn-apart bodies. To their credit, none of them lost their breakfast, but Ben could tell that was accomplished only with a great effort on their part. None of them were about to give Ben the satisfaction of seeing them barf.

Dozens of punks had escaped the barrage, but they didn't get far. There were snipers placed in a wide circle around the town. A few punks did manage to get clear of the killing field, scattering in all directions. Those few might return to a life of crime, but more importantly, the backs of the gangs involved had been broken and the heads cut off.

When Ben ordered his people to mount up and move out, leaving the bodies unburied, the reporters went into a towering snit.

"That is inhuman!" Ms. Braithwaithe-Honnicker howled. "They deserve a decent burial."

"Why?" Ben asked, as he rolled a cigarette. "They weren't decent people."

"Besides," Anna said, "the carrion birds have a right to eat."

"You are a very callous young lady," Ms. Honeysuckle said.

"Big deal," Anna replied, and walked away.

"Is that attitude typical of the Rebels, general?" Mayfield asked.

Ben knew a loaded question when it was fired at him. He smiled and said, "We all have different personalities and outlooks on life."

The shattered body of Karen Carr was pointed out to Ben. He compared the ripped and explosives-mutilated body with a picture his intelligence people had found and grunted.

"That's her," he said. "Or what's left of her. We can close another chapter in the book."

"The poor girl," Ms. Honeyducker moaned. "I'm sure her life was filled with abuse and poverty."

Ben gave the woman a very dirty look. "Lady, half the people in the Rebel army grew up in abject poverty in the aftermath of the Great War." His voice was harsher than he intended it to be. "Many of the other half grew up in families that were staggering and struggling for years under an unfair tax burden brought on by liberal Democrats. Don't talk to me about the poor, poor criminal. We all control, to a very large degree, our own destinies. So just knock off the whiny liberal bullshit when you're around me. It's making me nauseous."

The reporter matched the general look for look, but she kept her mouth closed, which was what Ben wanted.

"Have the bodies of Brittian and Justice been found?" Ben asked.

"No," Corrie replied. "But when we talked with a few of those left alive they said they were together in the lab when it blew. Nobody got out of that place in one piece."

"Dreadful!" Ms. Braithwaithe-Honnicker said, holding a handkerchief to her dainty nose, then marched off with the other reporters. To have a snit, Ben figured. Having snits was such a private thing.

Ben spread a map on the hood of a HumVee and traced a line with a fingertip. "We'll cut south, staying with this road. There is a useable airport here—or at least there used to be. Have the scouts check it out and if possible, we'll resupply there. Then we'll cut north and come up behind Ray Brown. Have those designated troops begin a slow drift off from the convoy. Any word at all from Mike Richards?"

"Not a peep, boss."

"Let's roll."

At a small town some miles south, the Rebels cleaned up the old regional airport and waited for the cargo planes to come in. Mike Richards picked that day to show up. He was haggard and dirty, and had lost weight, but he was alive. He came wandering in with a group of resistance fighters who looked to be in just as bad shape as Mike.

"It's been hell, I can tell you that," the chief of Rebel intelligence told Ben, after wolfing down two sandwiches and a couple cups of coffee.

"What happened, Mike?" Ben asked.

"I hooked up with a guerrilla unit and we got cut off deep in Border's territory. Radio took a hit and was useless. We've been running and dodging and hiding ever since. Simon's gone on a rip-roaring rampage against any who don't fully support him and his movement. He's blocked all roads—and I mean all roads leading into his territory.

Too many people were trying to get out and get clear of that so-called religious leader. He's a fanatic, Ben. There is no other word to describe him.''

"He's killing those opposed to him?''

Mike nodded his head. "Yes. Some of them. Imprisoning others. Making slaves out of some. Simon has really gone off the deep end.''

"His army?''

"Not much in the way of tanks or artillery, old stuff mostly, but he's got several million men and women under arms.'' Mike took a deep pull from his refilled coffee mug. "It sure as hell won't be an easy nut to crack, I can tell you that.''

Ben frowned. It was not what he wanted to hear, but it really came as no surprise. "So you figure we'll be tied up fighting Simon for some time?''

"A long time, Ben. Surely months, maybe years.''

"I was afraid you'd say something like that.''

"It's the truth. As hard as it is to have to say, it's the truth.''

Ben sighed and leaned back in his chair. "We'll deal with the punks, then turn our attention toward Simon Border. I damn sure can't have the punks behind me and Simon in front of me.''

"I can tell you that you've got about eight more gangs to go through before you get to Ray Brown.''

"You know his exact location?''

"I do. I can pinpoint it for you on a map.''

"Later. Right now, get some rest. We'll be moving out as soon as we're resupplied.''

"If you don't mind, I'd rather head back out with the group I came in with.''

"No problem. They look tough enough.''

"There are about 10,000 just like them scattered all over Simon's territory. They been fighting Simon ever since he arrived out here. They might not share our political philosophy, but they share one thing in common."

"And that is?"

"They despise Simon Border with an intensity that would be difficult to put into words."

"That's good enough for me. I'll tell supply to give you anything you want. Including," Ben said with a smile, "a spare radio."

"Make it a small one. Traversing those mountain trails are hard on an old man."

"I hope I don't have to find out just how hard they are."

"Ben?"

"Yes?"

"Gear yourself up mentally for a long campaign against Simon and his followers. It's going to be one of the most difficult wars we've ever fought."

"What are the odds of any mass surrender?"

"Slim to none."

"You're just filled with good cheer, aren't you?"

Mike grinned. "Simon says he has God on his side."

"I doubt that, Mike. I really doubt that."

"Do we, Ben?"

"I think God is neutral in this, Mike. I think He's been waiting for thousands of years for humankind to strike a happy balance."

"Think we'll ever make it?"

"I know this much—Simon Border won't. His time is running out."

Twenty-Seven

"We didn't get the sister of the brother-and-sister team," Ben was informed. "She's out of town. Her brother told us that just before he died."

"Did he say where out of town?"

"No, sir. But we did find the body of Dale Jones. Or rather, what was left of it. A few gang members got away, but not many. No more than a dozen, tops."

Ben glanced at Beth and she said, "That leaves eight major gang leaders still out there. And intel reports that Ray Brown has three of them—Sandy Allen, Dave Holton, and one more whose name is unknown to us."

"How many surrendered?"

"Eighteen. Nine men and nine women."

"And never any kids," Ben mused.

"We haven't seen any yet on this push. Not that belong to the punks, anyway."

"Odd."

"I have some good news and some bad news, boss,' Corrie said, walking up.

"Give me the good news first, please."

"Cecil just got word that the governments south of the border are cracking down on drug traffickers, coming down hard on them. The heads of those government are asking for our patience and understanding. They're working as hard as they can to stem the flow of raw materials."

"I recall that same line before the Great War," Ben replied. He waggled a big hand from side to side. "But that's President Jefferys's and Secretary Blanton's area of expertise. We'll let them worry about that and wish them good luck. Now give me the bad news."

"When we finish with Simon Border, the Secretary General of the UN wants us to go to Africa."

Ben took that bit of news calmly, for it came as no surprise. Although he had voiced his objections about going to Africa many times, to many people, he'd been expecting the request to go. He shook his head and sighed. "Well, we certainly have the time to think about that. And we will give it a lot of thought. Mount up, people. Let's finish the job at hand and then see if I can talk some sense into Simon Border."

"It'll never happen," Anna said.

"What?" Ben asked. "Going to Africa?"

"No. Talking some sense into Simon Border."

"Stranger things have happened, Anna."

"Name one."

"I was afraid you were going to ask that. Come on. Let's roll."

The column was significantly smaller now, and there was nothing Ben could do about that. Three battalions that had been held in reserve had joined the battalions that had split away from the main column. One had linked up with Buddy's column, one had joined Jackie Malone, and the third with Jim Peters. Ben's 1 Batt and Dan's 3 Batt were moving up from the south. Ray Brown and those gangs with him were now in a box.

The Rebels had passed through several towns where the punks were reported to be holding out. They found only the signs of a very hasty retreat, and all indications showed that the punks moved north, to link up with Ray Brown.

"Got you," Ben said with a smile, just moments before he turned his own short column north for the final assault against the punks.

In his stronghold in the mountains and forests of Arizona, Ray Brown took the news philosophically, for this time the career criminal knew he was boxed in tight with no place to run.

"I thought Simon Border was supposed to help us when Raines started his push against us?" Sandy Allen asked.

"Don't be stupid," Ray responded. "Border was using us, man, that's all."

"Why?"

"To get Raines deep inside his claimed territory, that's why."

"Raines will kick his ass, Ray."

"He might," Ray said with a smile. "But it won't be easy. Simon's got a couple of million men and women under arms. They'll kill a lot of Rebels before it's all said and done."

"Ray, aren't you scared a bit?"

The gang leader thought about that for a moment, then shook his head. "Naw. Me and Raines had to meet sometime. This is as good a time as any. Just like I said before, Raines has got to be 50 years old at least. Hell, he's past his prime. I'll take him out with one hand."

"But all our plans . . . ?"

"It's over, Sandy," Ray said. "Done. We had a good thing going for six months or so, now it's done."

"So now we start over, right?"

Ray smiled and again shook his head. "Maybe a few of us will, Sandy. But for most of us, it's over. We're in a box. By the time those dumbasses tracking Raines figured it out, it was too late. Raines has moved in about three of his beefed-up battalions in addition to what swung off from the column along the way. We're trapped."

"How about slippin' out a few at a time?" another gang leader suggested.

"You can try it. Fine with me. Some of you might make it. But I'm stayin' here and facin' hot-shot Raines. We're gonna settle this thing once and for all."

"OK, Ray," the gang leader said. He stood in front of Ray for a moment, shuffling his feet. "Ah . . ."

"Oh, hell, Buzz!" Ray told him, no anger in his words. "You can cut out anytime you like. I'm not gonna feel hard toward you. But I will tell you that the odds of you making it clear are real poor. Look here, man." Ray stood up and moved to a map of the state. "We're here, Buzz." He put a finger on the map. "Right here in this little town. There's a main road goin' east and west and a main road goin' north and south. Raines has all them blocked. There's all kinds of dirt and gravel roads runnin' in all directions. Raines has them blocked, too. Raines has put an entire battalion of special operation troops all around this town. They're layin' 'bout ten miles out in a huge circle, just waitin' for someone to try to make a break for it. He's got snipers out there with long-range .50-caliber rifles just waitin' to kill somebody. You ever seen a .50-caliber rifle, Buzz? No? You'll never hear the round that drills you, man. You're dead before the sound reaches you. You've heard the sounds of helicopters and planes for the last two, three days, haven't you, Buzz? Sure you have.

Those are part of Raines' army. Those are helicopter gunships and those damn souped-up and reworked P-51Es. They're in the air during the day, weather permitting, looking for somebody to kill . . . and that's *us*, Buzz. At night, Raines doubles up the patrols." Ray smiled. "He's a thorough bastard, give him that."

"You . . . knew all along that Raines was gonna do this?"

"Sure. It's Raines's style. I been studyin' the bastard for years. But," Ray sighed, "I was figurin' on a little more time to get clear. The son-of-a-bitch outfoxed me. That's life, Buzz. Take the good with the bad, man. But there just might be a way out. One way. Now listen, you people—when the artillery bombardment starts, we cut out, on foot. I mean, we get clear of this town just as fast as shank's mare can carry us. We go in all directions. We take two, three days' supply of food and water, a blanket, a poncho, and a weapon. That's all. We got to travel light. Some of us will make it. Not many, 'cause the goin' is gonna be tough as hell. But a few of us will make it. If we can get four or five miles clear of this town, we hole up. We find us a spot to hide and we make like gophers and we don't move. The Rebels will look over what's left of the town, and then pull out. It's the way they been doing it ever since he began this push, weeks ago. We can't try to run before the artillery barrage begins. Raines is anticipating us doin' that. We got to time this just right. Now get on back and talk to your people. Get some supplies together. Keep two canteens filled up to the brim. Be ready to go. Go on, get out of here."

When the room had cleared of all but a few of Ray's most trusted people, one asked, "You really think we can make it out of here, Ray?"

"Some of us. If we don't panic. That's the trick. We've got to keep our wits about us. Once in the timber, we move very cautiously—alert all the time. Raines won't be expecting us to be ready for him. So we've got to be ready.''

When Ray was finally alone, he sat very still for a time. Everybody else could run, but not him. He'd pretend like he was running toward the timber, then double back. This time, he silently swore, he'd kill Ben Raines. If he could think of some sort of edge, that is. If not, he'd run like a rabbit and forget all about the rest of these damn losers.

Ben got the artillery in place, but it was only with a supreme effort on the part of his people, for the terrain was rugged and the county roads in very bad shape.

Ben, however, had no intention of using artillery to finish off the last of the punks. He just couldn't be sure they'd gotten all of Simon Border's infiltrators and he couldn't take a chance on divulging his real plans until the very last minute.

The country was totally unsuitable for tanks, and they would be confined to the four main roads, when Ben decided to call them up.

He had briefed his batt coms on his plans, and what Ben had in mind came as no surprise to any of them. They knew how much Ben hated Ray Brown.

Ben pulled in another battalion and added them to those ringing the town and patrolling the mountains and forests. Ben was determined to put an end to the punks, once and for all.

Mike Richards showed up with his band of guerrillas and they looked much better than the last time Ben had seen his intelligence chief.

''You eating regular now, Mike?'' Ben asked with a smile.

''You bet. Ben, I wanted to come back to see you close the book on the punks.''

''Oh, they'll always be punks, Mike. But probably never

in as large a concentration as those we've been hammering for the past months. Now tell me the real reason you returned so quickly."

Mike chuckled. He rose and refilled his coffee mug, then turned and faced Ben, a serious expression on his face. "Simon is preaching a holy war, Ben. He's telling his faithful that this war will be the war to bring God back to the nation. I remind you again, the man has millions of followers, and not just confined to his territory."

Ben spread his hands. "I know, Mike. I know only too well. I've told the man repeatedly that once we deal with the punks, we're out of his territory. But if he wants a war, there is not a damn thing I can do to prevent that from happening. I spoke with the fool not an hour ago. Told him that I'd forget all about his Guards of God attacking us back up the road. Told him again that once Ray Brown is dealt with, if he'll let us, we're out of his territory. He said he would bury us all here and then broke the transmission. I've back-pedaled all I'm going to. I just can't do anymore."

"What's happening back home to meet this challenge, Ben?"

"Factories working around the clock. All planes and helicopters and tanks ready to roll. All battalions on the move toward the eastern edge of Simon's territory."

"Nineteen battalions against twenty million of the faithful, all of them religious fanatics, ready to die for God and Simon Border?"

"I don't see that I have any choice, Mike."

"Oh, I understand that, Ben. I wasn't criticizing you. Just, well, appalled at the odds, that's all."

"Join the club."

"Well, when you decide to move, I've got teams of people scattered all over Border's little kingdom, sitting on ready to launch a guerrilla action. We'll be able to help some."

"We?"

"Oh, I'm going back into Border's territory. I, ah, well, I feel I can be more use in there, that's all."

"Found you a woman, huh, Mike?"

The chief of intelligence at first looked disgusted, then the man actually blushed. "Damn, Ben. How do you do that? I'm going to have to put some credence in the long-standing rumor that you possess a third eye."

Ben laughed at the man. "I'm just a good guesser, Mike. That's all."

"Well, yeah, I did sort of take up with a lady. And she is a real lady, Ben. She got taken in by Simon's line years ago and moved west with a group of people. Didn't take her long to see through the bastard, though. She's been part of a guerrilla unit for several years."

"You want to pull her out and move her to Base Camp One?"

Mike shook his head. "I've already suggested that. She won't hear of it."

"Then I'll tell you what to do, Mike—you head on back and stay with her. Give us a good fix on your location, and I'll arrange to have to you resupplied by airdrop. Hell, there is nothing for you to do here. Go on back up north and get set up for the push."

"That's firm then, Ben? We're really looking at a religious war?"

"I don't see any way out of it." Ben didn't say anything about the request that when the Rebels finished in North America, they make plans to head for Africa. Ben knew how opposed Mike was to that.

Mike was of the opinion that if the Rebels went to Africa, they could be bogged down there forever.

And Ben wasn't too sure the man was that far off base in his thinking.

After Mike had left, Ben sat for a time alone in his motor

home. His people were almost ready to strike at, as Mike put it, "the last bastion of punks."

And then . . . the fight that Ben knew would possibly, no, *probably* tear the country apart. But he didn't see any way out of a fight with Simon Border. Border was the type of so-called Christian that drove Ben away from organized religion when he was just out of his teens, and Ben had never gone back.

Ben had been baptized as a youth, had read the Bible all his life for inspiration and comfort, and still did, often, believing strongly in God and in some type of life after death. But he worshipped God in his own way and was a strong Old Testament man. Ben was a strong law and order man, but one's personal life was their own business. Ben believed in maximum freedom with a minimum of laws, and no interference in one's personal life as long as that person obeyed the laws of the SUSA. Ben didn't give a damn if a person sat nude in their bathtub worshipping a bucket filled with kumquats . . . just as long as that person did not try to convince a person under the age of consent that their way was the best way and the only way.

That's where Ben drew the line.

Ben walked outside to stand for a moment, breathing deeply of the cold late fall air. He looked around him. Beautiful country. He cut his eyes as Corrie walked up to stand beside him.

"Those goofy reporters are in the rear with Emil," she said.

"Good. Everything set?"

"Sitting on ready."

"No unusual activity in the town?"

"No, sir."

"Ray's got something up his sleeve, because he sure knows we're here."

"No way he could have found out what we have planned."

Ben nodded his agreement with that. "Well, we'll see in the morning. We hit him at first light."

Twenty-Eight

The Rebels, Ben and his team with them, had moved into position during the early morning hours. This was their type of assault and to a person they excelled at it. The first assault team had moved to within a few yards of the old town limits and waited for Ben's signal. Not one of the first to go in had made a sound during their advance. They waited like silent death for the first gray shards of lights to lighten the eastern skies.

"Now!" Ben whispered to Corrie; she radioed the command, and the Rebels surged forward.

All around the town's outer limits, the Rebels started chucking grenades into buildings, giving those inside a very rude, if brief, awakening.

Ray Brown had been awake for several hours, tension making him unable to sleep. When the first muffled explosion reached him, the gang leader knew Ben Raines had outfoxed him—again. He grabbed his rucksack and rifle and headed for the back door.

"That miserable bastard!" Ray muttered, running for the timber. There were screams of fright and shock and pain ripping the cold air, drifting to him.

Suddenly, all the air whooshed out of him and he went to the ground hard, losing his rifle as he hit the earth. He looked up and cussed as he fought for breath.

Ben was standing over him, smiling.

"You asshole!" Ray gasped, holding his stomach where Ben had popped him with the butt of his CAR.

"My scouts pinpointed your location days ago, punk," Ben said. "I've been waiting for you to make a run for it."

"Then go ahead and shoot me, you bastard!"

Ben shook his head. "Oh, no, punk. That would be too easy. Get up."

Ray had caught his breath, now breathing easier. He laughed at Ben. "Are you nuts, old man? You really want to tangle with me, one-on-one?"

"That's right, Brown. Mano-a-mano. Are you intelligent enough to know what that means?"

Ray crawled to his knees. "I know what it means, Raines."

"Unbuckle that pistol belt," Ben ordered. "And do it very carefully."

"With pleasure, Raines." Ray tossed the belt, with its holstered pistol and knife, to one side. "Do I get up now?"

"By all means, punk." Ben had laid his CAR aside and removed his battle harness, tossing it on the ground.

Ray looked around as he rose to his feet. Ben's team was standing off to one side. A dozen other Rebels were standing silently, watching. "What happens when I win, Raines?"

"No chance of that happening, punk."

"This is no-holds-barred, Raines? Anything goes?"

"Just the way I like it, shithead."

Ray cursed and charged Ben. Ben sidestepped and

tripped the gang leader, sending him sprawling on the ground. Nothing hurt except his pride.

"Get up, hot-shot," Ben taunted the gang leader. "Damn, there isn't much to you."

Ray jumped to his boots, cussing Ben. He swung at Ben, missed, then connected with a glancing left to the face.

Ben stepped back, shook his head, and popped Ray twice, a left and right combination, belly and jaw.

The twin blows drove the younger man back. Raines might be middle-aged, the thought jumped into Ray's brain, but the bastard could still punch. Ray stepped back and spat out blood, then stepped in close and both men stood toe-to-toe for half a minute, exchanging blows, most of the blows falling on arms and shoulders, doing little damage to either combatant.

Ray was 20 years younger, but he was badly out of shape. Ben, on the other hand, had been living in the field for years, and maintained a daily schedule of calisthenics, which he followed religiously.

Both men stepped back to catch their breath.

Ray noticed then that the gunfire had all but stopped. Raines's sneak dawn attack had destroyed what was left of the gangs. The son-of-a-bitch had sworn he would do it, and he did it.

Rage filled Ray and he stepped in close and took a swing. Ben ducked the punch and hit him hard on the mouth, pulping his lips. Ray just then noticed Raines had slipped on a pair of thin leather gloves seconds before the fight. Ray knew that the gloves would not only help protect the hands, but enable the man to hit harder.

Just to prove the point, Ben popped him again, this time on the nose, and the blood flew. Ben followed that punch with a right cross. Ray backed up, involuntary tears flooding his eyes.

Ben took that time to bore in and really hammer at Ray

with hard hitting and hurting lefts and rights, forcing the younger man back.

Ray lucked out with a wild swing that connected against Ben's jaw and forced Ben to stop his advance and clear his head. Ray wiped the blood away and stepped in close. Bad mistake on his part. Ben lashed out with a boot that caught the gang leader on the knee and brought a howl of pain. Ray dropped his guard and Ben hit him four times in the face, swelling one eye and further pulping Ray's lips.

Both men stood facing each other, and as if on cue, dropped their hands to their sides to rest for a moment.

"Pretty good for an old man, Raines," Ray gasped.

"Oh, you haven't seen anything yet, punk," Ben panted.

Ray got it then. Raines was going to beat him to death. "You're crazy, man!"

"Just a man who likes dogs, you piece of shit!"

"Dogs," Ray whispered. "You're doing this because of dogs?"

"Among other reasons."

"I hate dogs. I got bitten by a dog when I was a boy."

"That's wonderful, Ray. Makes a lot of sense. I've been shot several times, but I don't hate guns. I've been divorced a couple of times, but I don't hate women. Assholes like you who lack character can always find some excuse for your cruelty." Ben lifted his hands and balled them into big fists. "Come on, Ray. Have you turned chickenshit on me?"

Ray stepped forward and ran right into a left and right to the face that staggered him and further bloodied his face. Ben smiled at him.

Ray got scared. For the first time in a very long time, the gang leader realized he was going to lose a fight—to a man 20 years his senior. Ray turned and tried to break through the circle of Rebels. He was very rudely shoved back.

"Fight, you punk bastard!" a burly Rebel taunted him.

"I've had it, Raines!" Ray yelled. "I surrender! I give up!"

"When you're dead I'll consider your request," Ben told him, then knocked Ray down.

Through a blur of pain, the gang leader scrambled to his feet. His nose was leaking blood, his lips were bloody, there were several cuts on his face, one eye was rapidly swelling shut. He turned in all directions, seeking a way out of the circle of uniformed men and women. He was trapped. Screaming his fear and rage, Ray charged Ben. Ben buried one big fist in Ray's stomach, the blow doubling him over and putting him to his knees, coughing and puking and gasping for air. Ray held up a hand. "Enough," he gasped.

"How many of your victims said the same thing, you punk bastard?" Ben snarled at him.

"My God!" Ben heard Ms. Braithewaithe-Honniker cry. "Give the man a chance. He wants to be rehabilitated."

"Oh, he's going to be completely rehabilitated," Ben told the reporter, not taking his eyes from Ray Brown. "You can believe that."

Ray scurried toward Ben, on his hands and knees, looking like a very large and very ugly bug. Ben kicked him in the face, the boot knocking Ray back and landing him on his back. Ben stepped back, his hands at his side.

"Get up, punk. You either get up and fight me, or by God, I swear I'll kick you to death."

"You brute!" Ms. Honeyducker yelled. "You savage monster!"

"Yeah, yeah, yeah," Ben muttered.

Ray slowly got to his feet. A Rebel wetted a towel from

his canteen and tossed it to Ray. Ray caught it with his face.

"Don't say we're not fair, punk," the Rebel called, then laughed.

Ray wiped his face with the wet towel and hurled it back toward the Rebels. Then he stepped forward, raising his fists. "All right, Raines," he panted. "I got my second wind now. Now I'm gonna stomp you."

"Very doubtful," Ben said, then leaped at Ray, both boots slamming into the gang leader. One boot striking the man in the chest, the other boot catching him full in the face, Ray hit the ground.

"Oh, good move, boss!" Beth called.

Ray slowly rose to his hands and knees, blood pouring from his smashed face. He painfully turned his head at the sounds of gunfire. "What's that?" he managed to mumble the question.

"Firing squads," Ben told him.

Ray suddenly lunged at Ben, trying to grab him by the knees. Ben stepped out of the way and all Ray managed to grab was air. He landed on his belly, stretched out on the ground.

"That's kind of pitiful, Ray," Ben's words reached him through a mist of pain. "I thought you were a big tough boy. You sure had a lot of people fooled."

"Finish it, you son-of-a-bitch!" Ray gasped.

"All right," Ben told him. "If you insist." He stepped forward and grabbed Ray's head with his big hands. One sudden twist and all present heard Ray's neck break. Ben stepped back and looked at the knot of utterly horrified reporters. "Now he's rehabilitated," Ben said.

Ms. Honeymucker fainted.

Twenty-Nine

The backbone of the gangs had been broken, the head cut off the snake. Ben knew that several hundred gang members had escaped the assaults that had stretched from very nearly coast to coast, but those few hundred were disorganized, demoralized, and leaderless. Ben had no intention of pursuing them.

Now Ben knew he had to deal, in some manner, with Simon Border. He would make one final attempt at talking some sense into the man. If that failed, then there would be war.

Ben now had eight battalions with him, the remainder of his battalions set to roll, being held at the ready on the edge of Border's territory.

Ben moved his people out of the mountains south to a larger town that had an airport. Once there, he ordered the reporters to board planes and get the hell out of his sight and keep it that way.

"You are a very rude person, General Raines," Ms. Braithewaithe-Honniker told him.

"Yeah, yeah, yeah," Ben muttered. Once the planes were airborne, Ben turned his attentions toward Emil Hite.

"I'm not going to send you back, Emil."

"Thank you, my general," Emil said humbly. "You won't regret it."

"That remains to be seen, Emil. But I'm going to give you the benefit of the doubt. You stay with the column, and stay out of trouble. You hear me?"

"Yes, sir!"

"Fine. Now gather up your followers and get ready to pull out."

"Yes, sir!" Emil saluted, French-style, palm out, and spun around, almost falling down before recovering his balance and hustling off.

Ben smiled. Emil was now and had been for years a colossal pain in the ass, but a likeable one. His smile faded as a darker thought entered his brain. Ben and his Rebels were hundreds of miles from home base, deep in the territory of a man who, in Ben's opinion, was mentally unstable and who had sworn to destroy them all.

Ben decided to try Simon one more time, even though he knew it was a useless gesture. But Ben wanted it clear at least in his mind that he had done everything within his power to avert a war with Simon Border.

After several unsuccessful tries to contact Simon, Corrie shook her head. "No go, boss. They're not responding. I'm sure they hear us. They're just not going to answer."

"See if you can contact Mike."

She had the man on the horn within seconds and handed Ben the mic. "What's going on up in the holy land, Mike?"

"Preparing for war, Ben. Against the 'Great Satan.' That's you, in case you've forgotten."

"How could I forget being equated with the devil? Does Simon have a timetable for this war?"

"As soon as you try to leave. I was going to contact you later on and advise you of this, Ben. I'm getting ready to pull out with my people. It's about to get real scary here in Colorado."

"I won't ask you where you're going. Just keep in touch."

"Ben, we don't know where we're going. Simon's put everyone on high alert. It's dangerous for a non-believer just to glance out the window."

"Can we get out, Mike? Back to our own borders?"

"Not without a hell of a fight, Ben. Simon's had his factories working around the clock for months, cranking out war materials. Billions of rounds of ammo. And he has advised his people that this will be a fight to the death."

"Shit!"

"That's what it's turning into."

"They believe him, Mike? Simon's followers, I mean?"

"Oh, yes, Ben. Simon is the father, if you get what I mean."

"I get it, all right. Anything else, Mike?"

"That's about it."

"I guess all I can say is good luck."

"Same to you, Ben. I'll be in touch."

Corrie had switched to another radio and when Ben turned around, he noticed she was listening intently. He waited and when she signed off, she wore a very worried expression. "What's up, Corrie?"

"Simon's people are on the move, heading this way by convoy. They're about 75 miles to the north of us. Scouts are staying a few miles ahead of them."

"How many?"

"Thousands," she said softly.

"Thousands?"

"Yes, sir. Loudspeakers on the trucks blaring religious music. To use one of the scout's words, it's awesome."

"Tanks?"

"Only a few. But plenty of towed artillery. And they've got a lot of 81mm mortars."

"Those old 81s have a good range on them," Ben mused. "About 5,200 yards. They could deal us some misery. All right, Corrie. Give the orders to pack up and mount up. We're heading south."

"We don't stand and give them a fight, boss?" Jersey asked, disappointment clear behind her words.

Ben sighed. "I don't want to kill these people, Little Bit. I thought after we kicked ass with Simon's Guards of God he'd get the message. But he didn't. He wants a fight. Well, I'm not going to be the one who starts it. If his army catches up with us and forces a fight, we'll fight. But they're going to be the aggressors, not us. Let's go."

By the afternoon of the second day of their roll south, it became clear that Simon's people were closing the gap. Ben had thousands of tons of heavy artillery and tanks to move, and they could not travel at any rate of speed which would enable them to get clear of Simon's people, who were traveling mostly in trucks and able to roll faster.

"Forty miles and closing," Corrie reported.

"Shit!" Ben swore. He kicked a rusted can across the highway and cussed and stomped some more. Then he settled down and opened his map case, spreading the map out on the hood of a HumVee. "Okay, people. God-dammit!" He thumped the map. "Tell the scouts to find us a place between Casa Grande and Tucson. I want as much high ground as possible. Bump Buddy and tell him to take his special ops people and roll on ahead, link up with scouts. Find him a good ambush spot and get set.

We'll be a few hours behind him. Now, then. I'm going to make one more attempt to talk some sense into Simon Border. And Corrie, after you've bumped Buddy, see if you can raise that . . . so-called man of God."

"For all the good it will do," she added.

"Right."

Buddy's battalion on the move, both Ben and Corrie were surprised when Simon came on the horn. "What do you want, Raines?"

"To try to convince you that I just want to clear your territory without a fight, Simon."

"You made your bed, Raines. Now lie in it."

"Not too original," Ben muttered. He keyed the mic. "We don't have to fight each other, Simon. It isn't going to accomplish anything."

"I shall be rid of you, Raines. One less plague upon God's earth."

"Simon, your stubbornness is going to get a lot of people killed."

"My people do not fear death, Raines. They know a better life awaits them beyond the veil."

"I believe that, too, Simon."

There was a few seconds pause before Simon again spoke. "You believe in life after death, Raines?"

"Certainly I do. I've been washed in the blood."

"I find that hard to believe. Why did you turn your back on God and embrace the devil?"

"I didn't, Simon. There are churches all over the SUSA."

"Which one do you attend?"

"I don't, Simon," Ben answered truthfully. "I worship God in my own way."

"I knew you were a heathen, Raines."

"Oh, me," Ben sighed. He opened the mic. "Simon, call off your troops before it's too late. Once they engage us, we'll have no choice but to fight."

"A state of war now exists between us, Raines. If you want to avoid bloodshed, I will, of course, accept your unconditional surrender."

"The man is a fool," Cooper said.

"His yoyo definitely has a short string," Ben agreed, and his team laughed at his expression. "Simon, surrender is out of the question. Why not just let us leave your, ah, country?"

"You started this, Raines. Now I shall finish it."

"I'd have more luck talking to a fence post," Ben muttered. "You won't even discuss our leaving peacefully, Simon?"

There was no response. Ben tried again. Nothing. Simon had broken off.

"All right," Ben said, resignation in his voice. "Simon wants a fight, we'll give him one. Let's roll, people. We've got to get set up."

Several hours later, Corrie called, "Twenty miles and closing."

Ben glanced at his watch. "It'll be about two o'clock when Simon's troops come into range."

"They're within range now, sir!" Jackie Malone said.

"Our range, Jackie," Ben corrected. "I want them in close and for them to open this dance. I will not be the aggressor."

"Yes, sir."

Ben looked around. "Where is Emil?"

"With Jim Peters's 14 Batt," Corrie answered. "Jim told Emil if he tried to slip off or pull anything stupid, he'd shoot him on the spot."

"That should keep Emil quiet for awhile. He's about half scared of Jim. Corrie, give the orders—body armor on. I want everybody in full protective gear. Absolutely no exceptions."

"You think this is going to end up eyeball-to-eyeball?" Jersey asked.

"It's possible. If Simon's people are as fanatical as we've been led to believe, they might try a human wave attack."

"If they do," Beth said softly, "this is going to be a damn slaughter."

"Yes, it will, Beth. They've got to come across several miles of flats out there." He shook his head. "It's all so stupid and pointless."

"Are those people about to attack us really Christians, boss?" Cooper asked.

"Well, I guess so, Coop," Ben replied after a few seconds' pause. "What am I saying? Sure they're Christians. But they've taken their faith to the extreme. They've been suckered by a charlatan named Simon Border. And now they're going to die for Simon Border," he added softly.

"Fifteen miles and closing," Corrie reported.

"Is Buddy's battalion in position?"

"Ready to close the pinchers."

"Can you contact the commander of the . . ." he sighed. "Enemy column?"

"Negative. I've been trying. They refuse to respond."

"Scouts say they have 105s?"

"Affirmative. Both 155s and 105s, towed."

"The 155s have a range of approximately 20,000 yards," Beth said. "The 105s have a maximum range of 16,000 yards. That is using conventional rounds."

"I would be very surprised if Simon's people have rocket-assisted artillery rounds," Ben said.

"We have no intel indicating they do," Beth replied.

Ben rolled a cigarette and waited. Someone handed him a mug of coffee and he was so deep in thought he thanked them without even looking around to see who it was.

"Range ten miles," Corrie said.

"Five more miles and they'll start throwing the big boys

at us," Ben said. "When the first enemy rounds land, we open up with everything we can throw at them. Give that order, Corrie."

"Yes, sir."

The minutes and the miles rolled by, the column drew closer.

"Five miles and closing," Corrie said.

"No sign of their artillery breaking off and setting up?"

"No, sir."

"What the hell's wrong with that commander? We're going to be looking down each other's throats in a few minutes."

Several more minutes ticked by before Corrie announced, "Range, approximately three miles. The column is stopping and setting up."

"They wanted close enough in to use their mortars," Ben said. "They're going to throw everything they have at us. Tell the scouts to pull back out of incoming and act as forward observers."

"They're using 155s and 105s and they're worried about mortars?" Cooper asked. "Doesn't make sense to me."

"I don't believe Simon has many combat-experienced people, Coop. I think he's depending on sheer numbers to defeat us."

"Crazy," Cooper said. "This is a crazy, stupid war. It's so . . . unnecessary."

"It's necessary for Simon, Coop," Ben replied. "He has to show his people his way is the only way, and the best way to do that is to defeat us."

"But he can't defeat us, boss."

"Not in the long run, Coop. But we're going to take some heavy losses before we begin to turn the tide. This is not going to be some easy win for us. As accustomed as we are to that."

The first incoming round exploded far short of the first line of Rebels.

"Fire!" Ben said. "And may God be looking the other way during the course of this war."

Thirty

At first the battle appeared to be another wholesale slaughter. Ben's gunners were dropping in rounds with almost pinpoint accuracy and Buddy's people had opened up with machine gun fire from the ridges on either side of the enemy column, raking Simon's troops with deadly fire.

Finally the commanders of Simon's troops got the message and ordered a retreat from that pretty little deadly valley. Ben let them go.

"All units cease firing," he ordered. "Let's get out of here while we can."

But if it took an hour and a half to set up, it took an hour and a half to break down and get back on the move.

"Scouts report that Simon's troops are circling around and preparing for a counterattack," Corrie said.

"You have got to be kidding!"

"No, sir."

"Can Buddy's people hold them back?"

"No, sir."

"No?"

"The enemy appears to be preparing a human wave charge."

"They're crazy, boss!" Cooper said.

"Are we ready to go?" Ben asked.

"Ready to mount up."

"Tell Buddy to get the hell out of there. Everybody mount up and roll."

"We're bugging out?" Beth asked.

"You're damn right we are."

"Batt coms are requesting orders," Corrie pressed him.

"Bug out, Corrie. Head south for I-10."

"Too late, sir. Here they come. It's a human wave charge."

"What the hell is that sound?" Cooper asked. "Sounds like music."

Ben listened for a moment, then shook his head. "It's 'Onward Christian Soldiers.' That used to be my very favorite song. They're pushing it through loudspeakers."

"Fifteen hundred yards and closing," Corrie said. "Hundreds and hundreds of them, boss."

"Stand and fight," Ben ordered. "Open up with everything. Cut them down."

This time it was a slaughter. The Rebels threw up a defensive line and opened up with every weapon at their disposal. The plain below them became a killing field as Simon's troops went down in bloody mangled heaps. After what seemed an eternity, but was only a few minutes, someone in command on the other side got smart and began calling for a retreat. Simon's troops began slowly pulling back, leaving hundreds of dead and wounded behind them.

Overhead, the carrion birds had already begun their slow circling.

"Now let's get out of here," Ben ordered.

* * *

"There are uprisings by Simon Border's followers all over the nation, Ben," Cecil said. "It looks as though it's a full-blown religious war."

"And we, *I*, caused it by invading Border's territory." It was not put as a question.

"No. I don't believe that at all. Put that out of your mind. I think Simon was looking for any excuse to kick up trouble. I think those so-called Guards of God were sent in as cannon fodder."

"I never thought of that, Cec. But you may well be right about it."

"Don't try to make it back to Base Camp One, Ben. You'll probably just have to turn right around and head back. I would suggest you try for Texas, set up a base, and wait and see what happens."

"Providing we can get out this state, you mean."

"It's that bad?"

"It's very bleak, Cec. Besides, I don't want to fight a damn religious war on our territory."

"You have a plan?"

"A piece of one. I'm going to try for Tucson and the old air force base there. Either there at Davis-Monthan or at the old international airport. We can clean up the runways and be resupplied there. I hate to go on the defensive, but I just don't think I have much choice left. We'll check it out and let you know."

"I've never heard you sound so down, Ben."

"Well, hell, Cec. Things start looking up for the nation, then it falls apart. We prop everything up, then it all comes tumbling down once more. It's like a yoyo. It gets damned depressing as the years go by."

"What alternative do we have, Ben?"

"That's what's got me in such a funk, Cec. We don't

have any alternative. We've talked about bunkering in— we both know that won't work, not in the long run. But a religious war, Cec?"

"We didn't start it, Ben."

"But can we finish it? I mean, really finish it?"

"I can't answer that, Ben. Only time will tell."

"Are you going to be all right?"

"Oh, sure. I've put the entire SUSA under high alert. Our borders are sealed. I've opened our chemical warfare bunkers and readied the delivery systems. I've told Simon in as blunt of terms as possible I will use the most lethal gas in our arsenal against his people if they try anything."

"Getting tough in your old age, aren't you, Cec?" Ben said with a smile.

There was no humor in Cecil's reply. "I like our way of life, Ben. I think it's a fine and noble experiment that worked, and I mean to see that it continues. So Simon Border and his religious freaks can go fuck themselves."

That brought a chuckle from Ben. "I'm happy to know I won't have to worry about the future of the SUSA, Cec. What does Secretary Blanton have to say about your decision?"

"He supports it, Ben. And so does his wife . . . well, let's just say more so than not."

"That is interesting. Okay, Cec, anything else?"

"I guess that's it, Ben."

"Okay. We're on the move."

"Good luck to you."

"Good luck to us all, Cec. And give my best to President Altman when you talk to him."

"Will do. Take care."

Ben hooked the mic and stood silent for a moment. Then he smiled at Corrie. "Let's get this circus on the road, Corrie. Looks like we're going to be in Arizona for awhile."

"Everything is coming unglued, isn't it, boss?"

"It sure seems that way."

"I hate to bring this up," Jersey said. "But I will—has anybody considered a K-Team going in and killing Simon Border?"

"Yes," Ben replied. "He's virtually untouchable. He has a dozen homes deep in the Rockies. Most of his own people don't even know where he is at any given time. Yes, Jersey, we've considered it several times."

"So . . . ?"

Ben sighed, almost painfully. "We watch the country tear itself apart in a religious war, I suppose."

"And then?"

"Those of us who survive start all over."